Deception Past

Katmoran Publications
www.katmoranpublications.com
katmoranpublications@verizon.net

Deception Past

A Novel

ISBN: 978-1-939484-04-8

First edition 2010
Second edition 2013
Copyright © 2010 by Franki deMerle

This is a work of fiction. All characters are fictional.

Other books by Franki deMerle

Ripples on the Surface, first collection of poetry

Child of the Universe, second collection of poetry

Dragonfly Dreams, a novel about dreams that connect us, dreams that come true, and dreams that reveal the past. "There are places we can only reach in our dreams while our bodies sleep."

Five Flowers, a novel of five historical Tudor queens who reincarnate in Victorian London's Whitechapel district and again in the US in the 1960s; a work of historical reincarnation (all characters are historical).

Please visit the author's website at www.reincarnationbooks.com

Please visit the author's page at www.IndependentAuthorNetwork.com

Please visit Katmoran Publications www.katmoranpublications.com

Reviews

Reviews for Deception Past

"…masterpieces you have developed are easy for any Reader to Enjoy." – Heidi Priestman.

"…While it is summarized as 'a story of betrayal and forgiveness', I felt there was so much more…. There are awareness lessons that can be learned and applied by the reader in daily life if they so choose to see them…. A very great story that sweeps you along the way." - Ann M Hauer

"…There is so much to like about it. Some of my favorite parts are your narrative philosophical entries about the need for peace; just allowing time to take you on the journey of life. Your writing is beautiful."- Vicki Lindstrom

"Franki deMerle is a compelling writer, a bewitching voice, and has an enchanted 'take' on reality."-Billy Kravitz

"…One of the most thought provoking books I have read in a long time. Deception Past made one think about society, history, and the tendency we as humans have of deceiving ourselves throughout our life…."-Marta Moran Bishop

Deception Past

Franki deMerle

Major Tarot Cards

I.	The Magician
II.	The High Priestess
III.	The Empress
IV.	The Emperor
V.	The Hierophant
VI.	The Lovers
VII.	The Chariot
VIII.	Justice
IX.	The Hermit
X.	The Wheel of Fortune
XI.	Strength
XII.	The Hanged Man
XIII.	Death
XIV.	Temperance
XV.	The Devil
XVI.	The Lightning Struck Tower
XVII.	The Star
XVIII.	The Moon
XIX.	The Sun
XX.	Judgment
0.	The Fool
XXI.	The Universe

Contents

Prologue

May 1886
Amherst, Massachusetts

Emily Dickinson burned with the desire to be loved. She felt somehow her feverishness was merely a manifestation of her yearning to be freely accepted for who she was.

To be free …

She craved acceptance after so much rejection, indifference, and isolation. Everywhere there were judgments. Always other people had their judgments. Emily was too unconventional. She didn't follow social protocol. She longed to be accepted in the same way she had opened her heart and warmly accepted Nature just as she found it. No manmade conception of "perfection" was required. No judgments or changes were necessary when you truly loved. But she hadn't found that love from any male human being. Her one true love had rejected her for someone more appropriate for his status in life. Yes, she had loved deeply in this life, but only Nature reciprocated that love.

Judgments were a way of life for "civilized" humans. How could a person be judged by the relative shade of their skin pigments? Yet masses of humanity had spilled rivers of blood over just such a concept—as if it actually made any sense. Emily had seen it split her country in half and still, two decades later, she could make no sense of it.

Humanity was delirious with judgments and burning with rage to fight over any difference. Yet all of physical creation and all of life were made of the same stuff, and each creature was uniquely different from all the rest. How could life be property? And yet, even after the slaves had been freed, women were still the property of men.

She had lost her stomach for the insanity long ago. She had tried to share her perceptions, insights, and sense of wonder at the true innate perfection of all creatures just as they are, but most people thought she was daft.

She could no longer keep food in her stomach. The bedclothes were soaked with her sweat. Emily didn't fear death. Death was the lover who would finally accept her just as she was. In death she was free to be herself, knowing that death wouldn't judge her. She laughed to herself, maybe even laughed out loud, remembering how the good Christians, who had tried to so hard to save her from her natural self, had feared the judgment of death.

But death is natural, she thought to herself, *and Nature does not judge. If anything, death is the great liberator who frees us from the shackles and prisons we let others talk us into.* She had tried many times to express the thought poetically. No need to try again.

She smiled quietly with closed eyes knowing she had not been talked into being anyone else's idea of who she should be. She had paid a price in heartaches for her liberty as she found how many would not love her if she would not be someone else. She would not belong to any man, because any man who claimed to love her, but wanted to own her instead, did not know the real meaning of love. The man, who in recent years had finally accepted her as herself, had already been liberated by death. The wounds were deep and invisible, but she had found a far greater truth. All those Bible stories other people taught as "the word of God" were written by men wanting to play at being God. The burning bush may well have had some divine insight to impart, but some mere human male wrote down the interpretive story with prejudice.

Next time around, I'll try again to get more involved with people, she thought to herself as she reveled in her delirium, *but I won't conform to their judgments. They can burn me at the stake if they want, but I'll be free. I'll do things my own natural way. I'll make music, and I'll write, and they will judge me. I don't care about their judgments. I'll be myself. I'll be free. They'll reject me, and I'll die fighting for liberty from stupid judgments. There is a rage in me to fight against that insanity of man that judges people for the color of their skin and their gender. They can burn me alive for that if they choose, and they probably will. I know death will come and liberate me. I will play my music and publish my stories even though I'm a woman or have dark skin or refuse to be controlled or dominated by Christians or any other religion. This river of sweat has freed my soul. Death is here to liberate me.*

The black carriage arrived in her upstairs bedroom and parked parallel to her sleigh bed. "You have come for me," she said to Death, "and I will not reject you, judge you, or keep you waiting."

The door to the carriage stood wide open, beckoning to her with fully open and accepting arms. She accepted the embrace and felt neither weight nor pain as she floated into its total acceptance. She would live again, fight freely for her liberty, and never accept the judgments of

Prologue

others until at least some of them had accepted her thoughts and writings just as she presented them.
This would be her liberation.

Chapter 1

Magic Mirrors
(The Magician)

Illumination of reflections
In the light we see
But only through interpretation
Delusions misperceive

How easily we fool ourselves
Convinced by misbelief
Limitations hide the will
Disguising our true strength

*

2007
Huntsville, Alabama

Brenda:

My name is Brenda Campbell, and I'd like to tell you a story. I can't help but share my feelings and thoughts with you as well. A camera only presents a picture through the eye of its own lens, and so I include my own ideas, so you may understand the camera through which the picture of this story was taken. I was born in Alabama in the late twentieth century. My parents were Delusion and Chaos. I lost them both to themselves.

My father was Chaos, and I adored him. Everyone did. He was, after all, a rising rock star. He craved the attention. He reveled in it. He was my

1

mother's true love, as well as her way out of poverty. She grew up in a trailer court and saw herself as a nobody. She saw him as somebody who would change that. But she was somebody. She was my mother. I loved them both. I lost them both.

Our lives were lived through the mirrors of perception and choice. By acting on our choices, we created the magic of bringing our dreams and desires to life. Mostly that wasn't so good. Many dreams were nightmares. Many desires caused nightmares for those who loved us. This happened to both my parents. My mother, Delusion, reacted to my father, Chaos, by burrowing deeper and deeper into her delusions. My father created nightmares for everyone who loved him.

Each individual writes his or her own story, which is then witnessed through other people's mirrors. I was very confused for many, many years, because my own mirror reflected the delusions I inherited from my mother. My mother spiraled downward out of control, because she was only reacting to the events and people around her. She never saw that she had other options. I had to work through the delusions to see that I had options. I had to see my options first before I even knew I had choices to choose from. My father allowed his own craving for attention to offer him options that most people would never have dared choose. As I said, he caused chaos in all of our lives.

He left my mother overwhelmed. Being overwhelmed can be perceived as painful if approached with fear or resistance—but it's a mind-opening expansion of awareness otherwise. One simply has to let go of preconceived limitations. For me, it's easier to take one moment at a time and not buy into other people's beliefs. That way I'm open to whatever is happening as it happens without getting confused about what's "supposed" to happen.

Stories are not real in the sense that we see them through the delusion of our memories. It doesn't matter whether it's the mirror, the brain, or our choice of perception that inverts the image. The image is only a reflection. Unrealistic expectations are disappointment, but they only occur when you have expectations. I know this sounds cynical, but there is no such thing as perfection. I suppose I am cynical after what I've been through, but I've learned a lot about expectations. Expectation of perfection is disappointment, and disappointment is a type of pain. The desire for the finished product is the delusion we use to keep ourselves from being happy—like a carrot on a stick. That means the solution to pain is somehow getting in between the neurons—being in the synapse or being the energy instead of the particle. Maybe the right thought can somehow evaporate the impulse before it reaches the other side of the synapse. Maybe pain is the karma of impulses. Maybe we misperceive our own pulse or that of our society or of our universe. Maybe the magic of life is all about perceiving and choosing perspective.

The story I'm about to tell is viewed through the mirrors of many eyes, but it passes through mine to you. So first you should know some things about me. My ideas are the threads of light, and they are often dark, reflecting throughout the story. They are the threads that weave the story together. I don't want to challenge your personal beliefs, but rather I challenge you to suspend judgment of other perceptions and remain open to the perceptions of the characters that follow.

My mother was the eldest daughter in her family. She had one older brother, my Uncle Mitch, and five younger sisters. They all grew up together with their parents in a trailer. Maybe it was her delusions that kept her sane in her childhood. Uncle Mitch, the only son, was considered to be the odd one. From my perspective, he was the only sane one. He saved me and my cousin Jamie. We all appear later in the story when Sand, the main character, meets my Aunt Sylvia.

It is inevitable that I have colored this story with my own prejudice and beliefs. Because of what happened to each of my parents, I have no faith in established institutions or organizations. I have no faith in society as a whole, just the few people in my life I've come to trust. Unlike Sand's father, my father was a social outcast. He lived by his own rules, and it caused him and everyone else a lot of trouble. My mother believed in social conventions like family and marriage. Those were her delusions. It made her fragile. In the end, she shattered like a glass mirror.

The twenty-two Major Arcana of the Tarot Cards my Uncle Mitch gave me are the mirrors I use to see past my own delusions. The symbolism in each card is a guide for a certain stage of life, or type of event in life, or chapter in a story. It's a story that can be superimposed on all human lives in that it involves love, joy, tragedy, death, betrayal, and ultimately the forgiveness that liberates us from our burdens. That's why I've used my cards here to tell this story. The cards work best for me as mirrors when I suspend judgment and just see what is.

The first card is traditionally called The Magician. Magic, like life, is all done with mirrors. We see the world through our own reflection. We project ourselves and our feelings onto everyone we meet. It's like the reflection of our dreams. In dreams we interact with other characters, but all of those characters are part of ourselves. Think about it long enough and you'll get confused about which is the reflection and which is being reflected.

Deception, like the magician, always works through distraction. Our stream of consciousness is in constant motion. We are energy more than we are particles. If this were not so, the death of our bodies' energy would not be the greater loss. But energy is never lost. Our movement in the cosmic dance is our eternal essence. What we perceive as our stage must always change. What we perceive as ourselves must always die, but our movement in the cosmic dance survives.

Sand, the lady this story is really about, was a very special friend of ours. She opened Pandora's Box and revealed Chaos to us, though it took me years to accept the truth. She also never gave up on my mother when my mother was lost. Sand taught me by example to forgive rather than to judge, and because of her, I learned to forgive even my father.

There seems to be a lot of speculation among those who don't remember what happens to us when our bodies die. A lot of people buy into religious dogma that gets pretty descriptive in physical terms, and a lot of it's not pretty at all. The problem with that is the dogma forgot it's supposed to be describing non-physical stuff, but then the people who wrote the dogma forgot altogether what they wanted to describe in the first place. If you remember, there's nothing to worry about. If you don't remember, isn't it enough just to trust that whatever is supposed to happen will happen? For me, yes; for most, apparently not, but when my time

comes, the last thing I want is another shock I didn't
see coming just because I believed in a delusion.
I'm inclined to consider those with memories and
disavow those who rely only on what others without
memories tell them to believe.

People who don't remember are like people
who dream in black and white; or maybe they're
more like children and everything is a fresh, new,
and exciting experience. In a lot of ways, those who
remember living before have forgotten how to be
children, because they remember being adults, and
they have to learn to be children again. Once they
do, they never forget, even when they're grown up.
Sand was like that. She remembered having lived
before this life.

*

Memphis, Tennessee

Her name was Sandra Strasberg. Most
people early on called her Sandy, but her closest
friends just called her Sand. Eventually that's all
anyone called her. She liked to visualize the eternal
sands of the infinite beaches of the planet's endless
oceans being ground down and broken by time and
pressure into ever more infinitesimal pieces of sheer
existence. She liked to think of herself as part of the
sands of time, constantly flowing in one direction
while some external hand kept turning the invisible
outer walls of the universe upside down.

Sand was born an hour and twenty minutes
after midnight on the Saturday right after
Thanksgiving Day, 1953, at the original St. Joseph's
Hospital in Memphis, Tennessee, before a second
St. Joseph's Hospital was built. Sand's family,

which was her mother Louise, father William, and older brother Jody, lived in a two-bedroom house. They were proud to own it. It was on the east side of Memphis—3059 Harris Avenue to be exact. It was a green clapboard house, and it had a separate garage and a redwood fence that enclosed the backyard with two mimosa trees. Sand enjoyed climbing the mimosa trees. There were a lot of German immigrants in Memphis, which included her paternal grandparents. There was even a place called Germantown on the east side of the city.

They were a nice-looking family. William had been considered a lady's man in his youth. He was tall and slender with bright, twinkling blue eyes and straight brown hair. Louise was simply beautiful. She had naturally curly dark hair, blue eyes with naturally dark lashes and brows, and the prettiest dimples when she smiled. She even had the figure to match. Both children inherited their parents' good looks. Jody got his mother's curly dark hair and his father's face. Sand had her father's straight brown hair and mother's face and dimples.

"Ours was not a kind family," Sand's older brother, Jody, would explain later in life when they were both adults, and then leave it at that. Their father always laughed when he told the story of how he had left Jody with the priest at the Catholic school swimming pool for a swimming lesson when Jody was five or six years old, and then came back later to find his only son alone and in tears because the priest had wanted Jody to take off his brand new swimming trunks. Jody had so looked forward to wearing those new swimming trunks for his first lesson. The priest told him he had to swim naked, but Jody had refused. So the priest went off and left the child all alone. Jody hid in the shower room, where his father later found him when he came to pick him up after the swimming lesson that had never taken place.

Sand never understood what part of the story it was that their father found so amusing. They say each sibling in a dysfunctional family has a unique experience. The same is probably also true of dysfunctional religions. Being Roman Catholic was Sand's mother's idea, even though Louise didn't actually believe very much of what the Catholic Church preached. She just liked the drama of all the rituals and sacraments; maybe it unconsciously reminded her of another time and place.

Sand's parents told her she was born with a round blue mark on her upper back; it had quickly faded and disappeared. She carried a puffy scar on her left middle finger where a tumor was removed with dry ice just after her birth. Her surviving birthmark, a brown teardrop on her right forearm, stayed with her the first fifty years of her life, and then faded away. Even with birthmarks and birth defects, people are marked by their experiences, physically as well as emotionally. Sand's fear followed her past her death to her birth. What had been the destruction of her physical body became the marks of her birth.

For Sand it was all about fear—the remembering, the premonitions, and the family she came to be part of. Sand's fear was fire. She had nightmares of fire as a young child. She had parents who yelled and argued so much that Sand was terrified of them. Sparks flew daily in the Strasberg house. Sand learned early on that her parents couldn't be trusted with her memories, because they didn't believe her. She could trust her father with her premonitions though. Sand's father told her that his mother had premonitions all the time. His mother was clairvoyant, a spiritualist. Sand never got to meet her paternal grandparents, because they died before she was born.

Her father told her to pay attention to her dreams because they were important. There were very few and precious things Sand's father ever told her when he wasn't angry or yelling or finding fault. So this one she paid attention to, and from early childhood on, Sand always remembered to pay attention to her dreams. Her father had learned it from his mother, and he and his mother were right.

As a very young child, Sand dreamed there was a horrible smell in the house, and a smoky black cloud hung in the air over everything. It was hot and hard to breathe, but she never saw the fire. The smell made her want to vomit. She knew something was burning. She knew there was a life-threatening danger in the house, even though she was too young to understand fire, had never been burned, and had never heard about anyone who had burned to death. She just knew it was a danger that couldn't be escaped. That was a dream she kept having.

Other than that dream, as far back as Sand could remember, she remembered being inside an oven. The men in black uniforms put her there, and the burn she remembered most vividly was as her right forearm pushed against the hot oven wall, removing the tattooed number that had been put there. The word in Sand's mind, which had separated from her body in shock from the pain, was liberté. One of her left fingers had been broken by those men in black uniforms earlier, after she'd been stripped naked and forced to endure hours of their verbal and physical abuse. She had been shot in the upper part of her back and couldn't fight back or resist being shoved in to broil. She was terrified, and again there was the sickening smell, which combined with the heat and smoke, made it almost impossible to breathe. Pain shocks the nervous system and the mind disassociates, but she felt the terror of seeing what was to be as they put her into the open, hot oven. It's not something easily forgotten. The really scary thing is that fear can become a habit.

Growing up, Sand was confused by the two recurring nightmares. The dream about the house with the black cloud was vague and what preceded and followed it changed each time, but the other nightmare was a vivid memory that repeated itself exactly the same way each time. She was in an adult body, naked and being dragged by men in black uniforms toward a brick building. To the right of the building next to the wall was where they let go of her, and she sank to her knees onto the ground with her head tucked under her body. There was a loud bang. She felt even more pain searing through her upper back and neck, and she knew she'd been shot from behind, but she was still conscious. Then the uniformed men picked her up and carried her into the brick building toward the left side of the room. It was the room with the ovens. The ovens were in a row across one wall. She could feel the heat emanating from them, and the smell coming from them was ghastly and overpowering. She saw they were putting her into one of the ovens. She felt sheer horror and wanted to retch as she saw bones and ashes in the glowing embers of those who had died and burned before her. They were still glowing eerily as their heat reached out and enveloped her. The uniformed men were going to burn her alive.

They put her into the oven and closed it. She felt the finality of the door closing on her life, and she felt the hatefulness of their actions. Their total lack of compassion reminded her of why she had fought them. She realized defiantly that the tattoo they had put on her forearm was burning off. She remembered one word, liberté.

Sand woke up with the word liberté on her tongue and ringing in her head. She knew the word, and she knew what it meant, but she didn't know it was French until she yelled it at Jody one day when, still very young, they were wrestling on the floor. She had broken free of his grasp and shouted, "Liberté!"

"Where did you learn French?" he asked her. Sand didn't even know it was French until Jody said that.

*

Sand was born with flat feet that couldn't support her a year later when she first tried to stand up, except when she stood heels together and toes pointing in opposite directions like a penguin. Penguins don't actually stand that way, but Sand was told over and over, once she learned to walk, that she walked like a penguin. Penguins don't do a lot of running. It's hard to know which way you're going when your feet are pointing in opposite directions. After that, Jody always teased her whenever she ran.

When Sand was four years old, her mother took her to a big building full of people and left her there. Her mother never told Sand why or if she was ever coming back. Sand was lost in a sea of lots of other little girls of various ages and sizes, and some very bossy women who were pushing the little girls into lines and yelling at the children to make strange positions with their feet. Sand tried to do what they said, but it hurt, and none of it made any sense. She was in ballet class, but she didn't know what ballet was or why she was being yelled at to arch her flat feet. Eventually her mother came and took her home. Sand told her mother, "I don't like that place."

But her mother told Sand, "Shut up." They didn't talk about it any more, but then her mother took her back again a couple of days later. Sand thought by the way the women at the ballet class yelled at her that they didn't want her there anymore than she wanted to be there. It was strange going from the waking life of a frightened, confused four-year-old to dreams of black smoke and death and then back again. Sand really didn't know what was happening. She was overwhelmed.

After several times of being left at that frightening ballet place, Sand finally figured out when her mother was planning to take her there again. She refused to go. Her mother locked her out of the house in retaliation. Sand was so confused and upset that she pounded on the door until the glass in the window above her shattered. If someone had only taken the time to show her and explain to her what ballet was, she probably would have loved it, although she'd already had enough yelling at home. Still, the broken glass didn't exactly help to smooth things over between Sand and her mother. Sand had earned the reputation of being a difficult and unhappy child.

Sand's mother, Louise, told her over and over from as early as Sand could remember that her feet muscles didn't finish developing because she was born prematurely. Even though her mother was very impatient and always in a hurry, she always took the time to explain that Sand was born prematurely because her mother had tried to get rid of her, but Sand had survived. Sand's father told her she was born very suddenly and ahead of schedule in the middle of the night. She wasn't supposed to be born until Christmas. Sand didn't think her mother ever told her father what she'd told Sand, but even though her mother very rarely told the truth about anything, Sand didn't see that the two stories necessarily conflicted. Maybe her mother didn't think Sand understood what she was saying, but the way she carefully and patiently—very much out of character for Louise—explained it every time, she seemed to mean for Sand to understand. She also told Sand that before Sand was born, she and Sand's father already had the child they wanted. They had their son to carry on the Strasberg name, which wasn't even Louise's name, and Sand wasn't even an afterthought. Louise said the pope wouldn't let them use birth control, and abortions weren't allowed, and that's why she got stuck with a daughter. In later years, Sand discovered her mother had lied yet again about the birth control when she found a pack of condoms by her parents' bed. The lack of admiration between mother and non-afterthought was mutual. They never bonded. Sand could never decide if her parents really didn't like her, or if they were just unhappy people. Children see themselves as the cause of other people's unhappiness, especially when it's directed at them; and overly critical, verbally abusive parents, like William and Louise Strasberg, didn't hesitate to blame everybody else, including Sand.

They said very cruel things to her and to Jody that should never be said to a child.

Chapter 2

Early Reflections
(The High Priestess)

Thought creates activity
And leads us to discovery
Encountering society
That brings no kind relief

A culture built of outer shell
Not knowing what's inside
Requires reflection of oneself
To bring the truth to light

*

Brenda:

The second card in my Tarot deck is The High Priestess. She's depicted as gazing at the reflection of the moon, which reflects the sun, in a pool of water. Reflection is all perception. I see people as animals, and humans, like all other animals, fear pain. Humans are blessed or cursed with frontal lobes to anticipate the pain and devise scheming and deceptions to avoid the pain. I like to think it's those scheming and deceptive frontal lobes that give us imagination as well as the ability to foresee and avoid consequences. I enjoy using my imagination to envision a world where every event has meaning, at least to me, and since I'm the center of my world, my thoughts take on multiple

15

dimensions of meaning. And yet with all the life that surrounds me, mine is a singular perception.

I know I perceive at the expense of what I ignore. We are all ignorant of what we don't choose to perceive. Sand's mother chose to ignore the memories her daughter tried to tell her about. My mother couldn't see what was coming either, no matter which event was coming at her. The clues were always there that something was wrong with the picture, but she never saw them. I know I'm a lot like my mother, so I overcompensate by being cynical and skeptical in my own defense. I want to see it coming, whatever is about to happen, even though I can't. So I'm careful not to buy into other people's delusions, because my family had enough to go around. I suppose every family has their own.

As the flawed people we are, we would never be able to see our whole selves unless we were conscious and unconscious at the same time— unless we used mirrors that could somehow transcend time and space. Do the parts of ourselves that appear to change over time die, fade away, become dormant, or merely go underground, unconscious? As the bits that make up the cosmos move in their eternal dance, stars become visible or disappear from our limited view. The stage sets and characters continue to change.

I can only perceive what I sense. Sensitivity is a prerequisite for feeling pain. For all the show of confidence and declarations of faith, those who don't remember living before are more afraid than those who do. That's why they need blind faith, because this world is a very scary place when you don't know where people go when they leave it. Maybe it's better to admit being a coward than to forget that we all are. It all comes down to labels and judging to fill in the missing memories. But when you have memories, you have to rely on them, because they are all you really have.

Our only means of deceiving ourselves is with our thoughts. Our only means of perceiving our deception is with reflection. I've worked hard to be able to see myself clearly in the mirror to avoid my parents' mistakes. Sand was different in that she had her own memories, premonitions, and dreams to guide her.

*

Memphis, Tennessee

Louise Strasberg, Sand's mother, was born Louise Carolina Nelson two years after her older sister, Clarabelle Georgia Nelson, and five years before her younger sister, Virginia Lynette Nelson. The sisters also had two brothers. Rudy, short for Rudolph, was Clarabelle's twin brother, and Roger, who was three years younger than Louise, who died of diphtheria when he was just eight years old. The Nelson family converted to the Roman Catholic Church after young Roger died.

All three Nelson girls had good looks and figures to match. Clarabelle and Louise had dark hair, but Virginia was a redhead. Roger had also been a redhead and a nice looking boy, but Rudy hadn't been quite as fortunate. He had the same dark, curly hair as Clarabelle and Louise, but he couldn't pass for handsome, and he wasn't very tall. However, Rudy was the hero of the family, having served in England in the US Army Air Corps during World War II. He worked as a mechanic on the planes that flew across the English Channel on bombing raids over Germany. He didn't see action himself, but he survived the war. When he came home, he worked as an automobile mechanic and TV repairman.

By the time Sand was born, Aunt Clarabelle was a Catholic pariah for being a divorcee. After high school, Clarabelle had trained as an x-ray technician. It wasn't long before she met a handsome, young doctor. He went into private practice, they married, and Clarabelle switched from being an x-ray technician to being her husband's office manager. The divorce came after years of arguing about who was really in charge of the office and about Clarabelle drinking too much and helping herself to Valium.

Aunt Clarabelle was nice to Sand, but they didn't see each other very often. Sand's parents had nothing nice to say about Clarabelle or Virginia. Clarabelle was divorced and Virginia never married. Sand's parents believed women were either supposed to be married or become nuns. Virginia lived with her parents, took care of them, and helped support them by working as a bank teller. Their father was an alcoholic and worked part-time as a security guard at a liquor store. According to Sand's mother, a woman's only value was in being a wife to either God or a man. Louise chose to ignore the fact that Virginia kept their parents in a nice but modest home with food on the table. Louise never discussed Clarabelle's alcoholism or drug addiction, but Sand's father never hesitated to mention both, as well as his father-in-law's drinking, whenever the opportunity presented itself.

After the divorce, Clarabelle went to work as an accountant. When Sand was four years old,

Clarabelle accepted a job offer from a man she met at a party. He ran an accounting firm in the little town of Arab, Alabama. Clarabelle moved to Arab (with the accent on the long vowel of the first syllable). Several years later, she moved north from there to Huntsville, also in Alabama. Aunt Virginia stayed in Memphis with her parents.

*

1958
Memphis, Tennessee

When Sand was four years old, her mother always chose what clothes Sand wore each day. One day she had laid out the clothes Sand was to wear on Sand's bed, but Sand knew they weren't right. Sand wanted to wear the clothes she remembered wearing when she was an adult—the black wool V-neck sweater, the black trousers and boots, and the black beret, even though she didn't remember the word "beret" and didn't know what to call it. Sand's mother believed that girls under the age of sixteen should never wear black, so there was nothing black in Sand's wardrobe, but Sand didn't understand that. She remembered wearing those clothes. She proceeded to pull all of the clothes out of her dresser drawers looking for the clothes she remembered were hers. They weren't there.

Her mother was horrified when she came into the room and saw the mess. "What have you done?" she exclaimed.

"I want MY clothes," little Sand demanded, "the black ones."

"You've never had any black clothes," her mother insisted, but Sand remembered wearing them—the feel of the wool and boots and the look of them. There was a lot of yelling in the Strasberg house, and Sand wondered what her mother had done with her things.

One day Sand was playing by herself on the kitchen floor when her mother suddenly jumped up from the table where she had been sitting quietly and yelled, "You don't treat me right. I'm leaving and never coming back!"

Louise went straight to the closet by the front door, pulled out her coat, put it on, and left the house, slamming the front door behind her. Having no sense of time at her young age, Sand had no idea how much time passed before her mother eventually came home. But Sand had believed Louise meant she was never returning until she actually did. Sand never did find out what that was really about. Sand couldn't possibly understand that her mother's behavior couldn't be explained or understood within Louise's limited belief system, or how frustrated and unhappy Louise was. All Sand understood was that her mother hated her.

What Louise managed to teach Sand was that Sand didn't have any talents and that no one could possibly love her. Parents making fun of their own child is terribly cruel. Teaching one's child that the child is responsible for things going wrong of which the child has no understanding is terribly cruel. The cruelty doesn't have to be intentional to be real. Where others might have seen Sand as a beautiful flower, Louise seemed to try to destroy her so no one else would notice her instead of enjoying the beauty she had created and sharing it with others. Or maybe she saw her daughter as a poisonous plant, but whatever the reason, that was the parenting choice Louise Strasberg had chosen, consciously or unconsciously.

*

The Brown family that lived next door to the Strasbergs on Harris Avenue also had a son and a daughter. Their son was Jody's age, but Cathy, the little girl with long blond braids, was two years older than Sand. They still played together anyway. Cathy Brown was a sweet child, and Sand loved her.

Cathy was sweet and kind but also small and skinny. She was not a strong child. Before Cathy was allowed to start the first grade of school, she was required to take shots to keep her from getting polio. There were three shots altogether. After Cathy had her first shot, she didn't want to play so much. She just wasn't quite herself. Then after the second shot she complained of a sore throat, and her mother wouldn't let her leave the house. Sand wasn't allowed to visit her the next day or after that. A week later, Cathy Brown died of polio.

Sand's mother came to her and said quietly, "Cathy has gone to heaven." Sand said nothing in return, so Louise left her alone.

Sand knew that "heaven" meant somewhere up in the sky. She also knew heaven wasn't a real place. People didn't just go off into the sky anymore than they lived inside a box in a hole in the ground. At least that's not what had happened to Sand when she died in the oven. She wondered where Cathy really went and if she'd ever see her again. Sand missed her playmate.

When Sand's parents were getting ready to go to Cathy's funeral, Sand expected to go with them. She didn't know what a funeral was, but after all, Cathy Brown was Sand's friend. Sand's parents never played with Cathy, but instead, Sand was left at home with Jody. She asked, "Why?" as her parents were leaving.

Her mother said, "Funerals are no place for children."

*

Brenda:

When a person lives a "normal" or average lifespan, childhood comprises a very small percentage of that life in linear time. That's deceptive. Whatever is experienced in those first years of early childhood sets the stage for what we believe we can expect throughout our lives. So much of what happened as a young child is forgotten over the passing of time, and we have to be aware of it consciously before we can choose how we perceive those early events.

Sand Strasberg's inner child chose to reveal more of her past early on than most people's do in adulthood. That awareness gave her the benefit of making some choices at much younger ages than was considered "normal." It also kept her from focusing consciously on the less pleasant aspects of her external environment.

Sand grew up conscious of more of what could be considered as belonging to the spiritual rather than physical realm and less conscious than most of her peers of her immediate, everyday, physical environment. As a result, she was less developed emotionally and socially when it came to making conscious choices in those areas. But the need for love is stronger than the desire to hate. Hate is a sense of betrayal or rejection. If followed all the way back to its roots, it's really a sense of guilt that can only be resolved by self-forgiveness.

My own family had trouble with forgiveness, but the way I see it, if we didn't make mistakes, we wouldn't gain deeper understanding. We all make mistakes, and we all need and want to understand, so why does it take so long for us to learn to forgive? Neither Sand nor I could ever have survived emotionally without that basic skill. Once we take that step, it feels so much better that it's just too hard to go back. So then how could Sand's parents be so cold and unforgiving as to teach their child to feel worthless and unlovable? They didn't understand, and Sand didn't understand, but none of them had learned how to forgive.

As with most human stories, this one involves pain. I know a lot about pain from personal experience. Pain is lessened by being acknowledged by others as much as it is intensified by denial.

People are made of layers. Painting is done in layers. Writing is also layered. Music has layers of harmony, counterpoint, and rhythm. Dreams are in layers. Communication and perception are often layered. Reflection is done in layers.

People are interwoven in my life in layers, just as my relatives were woven throughout Sand's life. I think the universe has its own timetable for everything, but then the universe is busy constantly balancing itself. The human race is just one layer of the universe. Time is multiple layers like everything else. Time is just communication and perception, interaction and reflection. It's important to let things happen in their own time without trying to force them. It's important to let the story unfold in its own space.

Somewhere along the way, God became human, and humans made God into their own image. This did not bode well for the rest of the animal kingdom. Somewhere along the way, God became male, and males made God into their own image. This did not bode well for the opposite gender. Somewhere along the way, God took up residence off world. This did not bode well for the planet. Whatever choices were made in the past, we're all stuck in the present moment with the consequences of those past choices. I cannot avoid the consequences of the choices my parents made. I can only try to make my own choices more carefully. Sand was also affected by the choices of everyone around her.

Stories usually have heroes, but you'll have to sort this one out for yourself. I used to think my father was a hero just because he was my father. And he got a lot of applause and publicity along the way, but just being a rock star didn't make him a hero. I've learned the hard way that society never praises the true heroes. I once met an HIV/AIDS researcher who published her research results at her own expense, even though she was unemployed. There was no applause. There was a man in Buffalo, New York, who dug his way through five plus feet of snow to check on his elderly neighbor's well-being. He made the evening news one time, but not the immigrant working at McDonald's, struggling with the English language, who took the time to find a plastic lid that actually fit securely on my large diet Coke so it wouldn't spill in my car. And he smiled sincerely while he did it. He was a hero to me, and I have to tell this story through my own set of mirrors.

I know I'm sharing my nightmares, but I want to add a word of caution. One can internalize these dark parts of oneself by dwelling too much on the morbid details. Instead, I recommend looking for the bigger picture, the compositional elements that weave the story together, and the symbolism of those elements. I try to remember we're in a house of mirrors and reflections.

Chapter 13

Tides
(The Empress)

Nature versus society
The natural versus technology
The men must always fight
Or compete to find what's right

Diversity is Nature's way
Tolerance brings harmony
The women must cooperate
For survival of their babies

*

Brenda:

Children are naturally more in tune with
their own natures than adults. Layers are added
gradually as we grow up. Then we seem to spend a
lot of our years trying to peel them back again to
find our inner selves—at least that's how it
happened for me. Then in old age, some rediscover
their natural, childlike natures.

For me, Mother Nature symbolizes being in
harmony with oneself and doing whatever is
natural, and that's what The Empress card in the
Tarot represents. Maybe she's really a child. Maybe
she represents the ideal mother, Mother Nature
herself.

Deception Past

*

September 1959
Memphis, Tennessee

On Sand's first day of school, she found out from the other kids that there was something called kindergarten, which she had missed. She didn't know what it was, but it made her feel like an outsider from the start.

She attended a Catholic school where all students were required to wear uniforms and attend Mass before school started every day. The church and the school were adjoining big, red brick buildings. Sand wasn't quite sure how she'd come to know all this or how she'd managed to find her way into the pew right in front of the altar after her mother had left her at the big, double front doors of the church, but Sand had never had a front row seat before. Her mother always sat in the back near the doors so they could make a quick getaway when Mass was over. Once Sand had asked her mother, "Why do we always leave in such a hurry?"

Louise explained, "When the priest leaves the altar, Mass is over, and we don't have to stay and talk to anybody."

Sand had fun in the front pew giggling and playing with the other first graders during the Mass, but as soon as the priest turned and walked out through the door behind the altar, Sand took off at a trot down the aisle with her new friends following close behind, only to be met midway down the aisle by a nun playing goalie. The children were shooed back into their pew and told to wait until everyone else had left. The nuns had their own orderly system. First graders sat in front, second graders behind them, and so on. When Mass was over, the oldest students in the back left in single file. Each pew emptied in order from back to front. Once it was the first graders' turn, they were made to walk silently in a single line through the labyrinth of the school to their new classroom.

Sand had always been told at home that she would have a nun for a teacher. There was something about the big, cover-up, penguin costume that Sand had pictured in her mind. She had absolutely no doubt that the penguin teacher would be her best friend and refuge from the chaos that was home life. But when she got to her classroom, there was no nun, only Mrs. Heiser, an elderly lady who wore glasses and her grey hair in a bun behind her head.

After a week or two in first grade, the class was divided into three reading groups by level. The red group was the accelerated learning group; the blue group was the average reading group; and the white group was for slow readers. The red and blue groups were assigned seats on opposite sides of the classroom with the white group in the middle. The red group got the row of desks next to the windows. The children were required to sit in their assigned seats all day, every day, even when they weren't reading.

Sand's favorite color was blue, but she was assigned to the red reading group. Sand didn't like being on the far side of the room from the group of her favorite color, even though it meant she could look out the window. She tried several times to just move to the blue group, but Mrs. Heiser was too observant and insisted Sand stay in the red group. From Sand's point of view, school was sliding downhill fast.

Deception Past

*

October 1959

One day Mrs. Heiser left the room for a while. While the teacher was out of the room, things reverted to the normal state of unattended six-year-olds, and the room filled with laughter. Sand hadn't made friends with the other kids in the red reading group because she knew blue was her color, so when the kids got to playing loudly as children do, Sand was sitting alone in her desk contemplating another escape attempt to the blue side of the room. That's when Mrs. Heiser walked back in, and all the students who weren't in their seats were sent into the coat closet behind Mrs. Heiser's desk at the front of the classroom. At first Sand thought she'd missed out. If she'd only been out of her chair, she wouldn't have to be in her chair now. Mrs. Heiser started to teach again, at least until the coat closet started laughing and talking. That was when Sand saw Mrs. Heiser take a big wooden board out of her desk drawer and go into the coat closet. Sand was wide-eyed and glad she was in her chair. The only thing she heard after all the sounds of hitting was the crying that came from the now feared coat closet. Sand wondered why children weren't supposed to laugh in school. Come to think of it, there wasn't a whole lot of laughing at home either, but it had sounded nice while it had lasted.

Sand never knew what to expect at school from one day to the next. In that sense, school resembled home. There was some sort of structure in both places, but Sand couldn't make sense of what it was in either place. The adults never explained it to the children.

29

One day at lunchtime, Sand was busy playing bumper car lunch boxes with two boys in her class. By the time they realized there was no one else in the cafeteria that they recognized, they giggled uncontrollably at the realization. The cafeteria was now filled with bigger and older children, and they were the only three left from their class. They didn't know how it was they had been left behind, but there were no longer any familiar faces in sight.

The trio left the cafeteria laughing. Always before there had been someone, some adult teacher, telling them what to do. There was a freedom in being forgotten. The cafeteria was in a separate building from the classrooms. The two structures were joined by a covered walkway that ran alongside the paved playground. The playground was full of children, so Sand and the two boys joined the other children on the playground running and laughing. Not knowing how to tell time, and not understanding the concept of the school's schedules, the first graders enjoyed themselves freely.

Sand didn't understand why the nun they didn't know yelled at them as they were herded off the playground, up the steps, inside, down the big hallway, and into their classroom. Sand didn't even know how it was the nun knew where their classroom was—Sand didn't even know how to find it by herself. Her fellow classmates were all sitting in their desks in their neat rows. Mrs. Heiser was not amused. She spoke sternly to the three truants, explaining how important it was to stay with the class. She explained that when they were finished eating their lunches, they were supposed to play on the playground, and then they should come back to

the classroom as a group. That was when Sand
realized there was supposed to be a pattern, and that
the pattern was supposed to be repeated every
school day. She wondered why no one had bothered
to explain that from the start and why Mrs. Heiser
yelled at her and her two friends for not knowing.

*

December 1959

When it was getting close to Christmas and
the children were easily excited with anticipation of
the holiday, Mrs. Heiser gave the class a Christmas
party. There were cupcakes with chocolate frosting,
and every student got a toy—well, actually a small
Christmas tree ornament. Sand's was a Santa Claus.

That evening, Sand went to hang her new
Santa Claus on the Christmas tree at home. Her
father and Jody had brought home the fresh tree, put
it up in the dining room, and strung lots of big, fat,
colorful lights all over it. Sand was standing in front
of it trying to decide where was the best place to
hang her Santa Claus when Jody came in from the
kitchen carrying a big pitcher of water.

"What's that for?" Sand asked.

"I'm watering the tree," Jody answered.

"Why?"

"Because if you don't water the tree, it gets
dry; and if the tree dries out, the lights will set it on
fire, and the house will burn down."

Sand agreed that watering the Christmas tree
was a very good thing to do. She looked at the
strings of big, fat, colored lights. They were very
pretty for something so dangerous. She hung her
Santa Claus next to a pretty blue light.

That night, Sand dreamed she was standing on the ocean shore at night looking out to sea through the darkness. She could hear the waves lapping at her boots and smell the salt of the sea. She was chilled even though she was wearing a black coat over her wool sweater and wool slacks. She never heard the oars, but a small boat rowed by two men appeared out of the darkness. It sat low in the water, and as they approached the beach, the men jumped into the cold water and struggled to pull the boat carrying two wooden crates up onto the beach. Once the boat was emptied, as the men carried the crates to a nearby house, she and another woman stashed the boat and oars out of sight in some brush nearby before following the men into the house. Once inside, one of the men opened one of the boxes, and Sand saw it was filled with Christmas tree lights. None of the lights were colored; they were all clear, and they didn't have exactly the same shape of Sand's Christmas tree lights, but they were close enough, and that had to be what they were. When Sand woke up the next morning, she knew that's what they had been.

*

1960

The school year, which seemed to go on forever, was broken in half by the Christmas break. One day shortly after Sand went back to school, a smiling young nun dressed in full penguin regalia came into their classroom. Mrs. Heiser announced that Sister Mary Bernadette would be teaching arithmetic from then on. Then Mrs. Heiser left the classroom. Sister Mary Bernadette seemed so nice and friendly that Sand sat up and paid close attention. This turned out to be a daily occurrence and became routine.

One day during Sister's math class, Sand realized she needed to pee, so she raised her hand to ask permission to go to the lavatory just like she'd been taught. Sand didn't raise her hand very often in class, so she hadn't really noticed until now that Sister Mary Bernadette had never called on her for anything. Ever. She kept her arm up in the air until it got tired and then switched arms, but Sister never seemed to notice. Sand knew she couldn't just get up and leave the classroom—Mrs. Heiser always noticed when she had tried to just move to the other side of the room, and she had never succeeded in getting past the goalie penguin when she'd tried to leave the church. Finally, as the matter became more urgent, Sand began to wave her hand frantically and then desperately in the air, but Sister just went on teaching and smiling as if Sand wasn't even in the room. And then it was too late. Sand put her hand down.

Nobody noticed until after Sister had finished her class and left the room and Mrs. Heiser returned. Then the boy across from Sand in the next row of desks raised his hand, and Mrs. Heiser immediately called on him.

"There's water under Sandra's desk," he said and pointed.

"There shouldn't be," Mrs. Heiser responded, and proceeded to start the next lesson. Sand didn't know if she should be mortified or relieved, even though she was already both.

After school, her mother was upset when she saw that Sand had wet her school uniform. "Why didn't you raise your hand and ask to be excused?" she demanded. Sand didn't bother to answer.

Then one day toward the end of the school year, the whole class was given a special test. Mrs. Heiser explained in her usual everyday serious tone how important this test was, how to mark the answers on the answer sheet, and that no one was to begin the test until told to begin. As soon as they were told to begin, Sand discovered she had no clue how to answer any of the questions. She looked all around to see if any of the other students seemed to be marking the answer sheet, but before she could deduce if they were all as perplexed as she was, the chair in which she was sitting with its attached desk suddenly jerked out of the row it had neatly been in all school year. As it slid toward the back of the room, she turned around to see Mrs. Heiser pushing her, desk and all. Sand was left parked against the back wall with no explanation of what was happening. Thinking she had just failed out of first grade and that the whole ordeal of school had been all for nothing, she blacked out.

When Sand finally learned that it was the last day of school and that she would, in fact, be promoted to second grade, she was glad it was all over. It had been exhausting and a great disappointment. After that, grades and the attention or approval of teachers and authority figures just never seemed to be a high priority for her.

*

June 1960

Sand had already learned to follow what was natural for her rather than other people's rules and

34

preferences. She had already learned not to trust what the adults told her because they didn't trust her. It was simple child's logic.

When Sand and her mother were in the kitchen one day, she asked Louise, "When can we go and visit the other people I remember from when I was grown up?"

"What?"

"Like my friend. I can't remember her name. You know, the young woman with blonde hair in the house with the room with the round wall? I really miss her."

"Who are you talking about? What are you talking about?" her mother responded.

"My blonde-haired friend. There was a single bed with a wooden cross on the wall above it, and she had a white toy poodle stuffed with Christmas tree lights."

"You're dreaming things up again," her mother scolded.

"Am not! I miss her." Sand stomped her foot for emphasis.

"Quit making things up," her mother admonished.

"I carried the poodle and bear and elephant in my bicycle basket, and they had Christmas tree lights in them," Sand insisted.

"I have no idea what you're talking about," her mother argued. "That never happened, and we don't know anybody or any house like that."

"Do so!" Sand ran out of the kitchen in tears.

Her mother insisted Sand had dreamed it all up, like her dreams about black smoke in the house, her dreams about wearing black clothes and boots and a beret, and her dreams about dying. Her mother said none of these things existed. But Sand remembered. She couldn't remember her friend's name, but she remembered her. She didn't remember where the house was, but she knew it had been real. She knew she used to go out at night dressed in black with her friends to get the crates of Christmas tree lights. The boxes would come from somewhere out at sea; one or two men, her friends, would bring the crates ashore in a small boat. Then she and her blonde lady friend would sew the clear Christmas tree lights into toy stuffed animals. She remembered carrying some of the animals past men in black uniforms. She remembered a bear and an elephant. She remembered being burned alive in an oven by the men in black uniforms. She would never forget that memory or those black uniforms.

Sand knew deep down inside that it was natural to laugh and be happy. When one was in harmony with one's true inner being, one would always choose what was harmonious and brought contentment and peace to that inner being. But all around her, Sand was encountering adults that somehow didn't understand. Yelling, arguing, denial, and unpleasantness surrounded her. She didn't understand why that was. She just knew nobody believed her when she told them things she knew to be true and something was very wrong.

Even though Sand's mother was Catholic, her father wasn't. He had agreed when they got married to let Sand's mother raise their children in the Catholic Church. He promised not to interfere, and he didn't.

One evening after dinner, when Sand and her father were sitting alone in the in living room, Sand asked, "Why don't you go to Mass on Sundays with Jody, Mom, and me?"

He answered, "Religions are made by people, and going to church is a social thing."

That made sense to Sand. It also left her with more questions like, "If it's supposed to be a social thing, why do we only sit at the back of the church so we can rush out as soon as Mass is over and not have to talk to anyone?"

But she didn't ask.

Chapter 4

Man-Made Dreams
(The Emperor)

Is technology the master or the slave?
What price is put on life
When people are told it must be done
Don't they have the right to decide?

The paradox of power
Is what cannot be controlled
Leaders will only be followed
If chosen by the fold

*

Brenda:

Huntsville, Alabama, was a small town in the northern part of the state on the Tennessee River. It was originally settled around a fresh spring some miles north of the river that came to be known as Big Spring. The town relied on the cotton industry before World War II, but during the war, work for most women and men ineligible for the draft and left behind on the home front was found at the military installation known as Redstone Arsenal. Jobs for the United States Army offered better working conditions and were a way to contribute to the war effort. The town boomed over the next decade and didn't know when or where to stop. When Dr. Wernher Von Braun moved his rocket science team to Huntsville in the 1950s, the Arsenal began to grow in population as the US Army hired personnel to support the birth of the US space program.

It was all about man conquering Nature, overcoming gravity, and controlling the very environment to be escaped. It was very much like The Emperor of the Tarot ruling his domain. Humanity's millennia-old dream of flying to the moon was to be realized by animals and men confined in tiny compartments and fired like live ammunition at the target of desire. The original American astronauts were pilots, men of military backgrounds, who liked to be in control of their circumstances. Inside their cramped space capsules, they were totally at the mercy of the forces that propelled them. But they were also disciplined and willing to sacrifice themselves for the advancement of their civilization in pursuit of humanity's dream.

*

August 1960

William Strasberg saw the economic advantage of the new space program and moved the family to Madison County, Alabama. He wasn't particularly happy with his new job, but it paid well. He was responsible for being a good provider for his family.

Louise appreciated the increase in family income and lower cost of living in what was then a rural area. She had mixed feelings about being away from her family in Memphis, but now she was closer to her sister Clarabelle. Still, she missed the big city shopping. The way she saw it, they had traded the shopping opportunities for the money they needed to shop.

Jody didn't like moving away from the friends he had in the city to some nowhere place. He felt like an outsider. City kids were very different from rural kids. Even though they had only moved two hundred miles, peoples' accents were different and difficult for him to understand. He came to see himself as a misfit.

*

Sand saw moving as an adventure. She hadn't liked much of anything about her first year of school and was glad she'd be going to a new one. This time she didn't harbor any expectations and pretty much ignored anything anyone tried to tell her about her new school. She'd just wait and find out for herself.

Sand's family bought another two-bedroom house in Madison County outside the Huntsville city limits west of town just off Highway 20. In a few years, it would be the western edge of the city. As in Memphis, Sand's older brother, Jody, slept in what was intended to be a den. The house at the corner of Sheri Drive and Deramus Avenue was brand new. Sheri Drive was a dead-end street in a small, brand new subdivision called Sherwood Park, which was surrounded by farmland. At the end of the street was a cow pasture. A creek ran behind the pasture on the north side and fed the woods that grew there. Jody and Sand's childhood explorations revealed cotton fields on the far side of the woods as well as the shack of a black family that sharecropped the fields. The shack had no electricity or plumbing.

Deception Past

The dirt was red Alabama clay and the trees were a mixture of mostly pine, oak, and sweet gum with blackberries, wild plums, poke berries, and sumac scattered throughout. Continuing north of the cotton fields were more woods that gave way to Highway 72, which ran east-west and later came to be known as University Drive. To the east of the woods and fields, the University of Alabama in Huntsville, or UAH, and Cummings Research Park would take root and grow.

Sand attended another Catholic school, but this one was much smaller and the church wasn't attached. Where the school in Memphis had been red brick, this one was green stucco. The school was just north of downtown Huntsville. All the classrooms were downstairs, and the convent where the nuns lived was upstairs. The church was several blocks away, so the students only attended Mass before class on special religious days. On those days, they walked to the church from the school and back afterward. Because they weren't allowed to eat breakfast before Mass in those days, when they got back to class, there were donuts and milk for purchase in the classroom.

The church itself had its own demons. In the physical structure, Civil War soldiers used to tie their horses to the communion rail, or so the students were told. Sand figured that's why they took out the communion rail when she was a child and didn't replace it. Actually, it was because the life-size statue of St. Joseph had come crashing down through the communion rail one day during the service, but the congregation was small and didn't have the money to replace it. No one ever said if St. Joseph had jumped or was pushed.

41

Spiritually, pedophiliac and alcoholic priests were considered superior to women who were only allowed to be wives or nuns. As her father had told her, religion was all invented and run by people. As Sand got older, she noticed women were allowed to be teachers, secretaries, and nurses too. Big deal. As she later learned, all of it was decided by the white male dictator of the foreign country that governed the Church.

Nobody at church or school believed Sand either when she talked about her previous life wearing her black clothes and smuggling Christmas tree lights in stuffed animals past the men in black uniforms, so Sand didn't believe them when they talked about Heaven, Hell, and Purgatory. It wasn't long before she stopped talking about her memories to anyone. She got tired of being told that only the Pope could decide what to believe. How did the Pope know anything about what Sand remembered anyway? After her brief experiences with adults in this life, she just couldn't believe that any one of them could be infallible as they claimed the Pope was. She didn't buy into the whole Catholic thing.

*

1961

North Alabama was different from the rest of the state. Ever since the former Nazi rocket scientists took over Huntsville in the 1950s, that part of the state was never the same. Along with the German scientists and their families came people from all over the country, and eventually all over the world, for the great space race with the Soviet Union. The US Army on Redstone Arsenal, and later the Marshall Space Flight Center, provided jobs for the local people as well. Working people commuted from all over north Alabama and southern Tennessee. Sand's father worked for the army. The Germans also started a symphony orchestra in Huntsville, which helped to further elevate the growing city from its former status as a small cotton town. The University of Alabama located a branch there specializing in engineering and astral physics and eventually grew in size and branches of academics. The former Nazis put Huntsville on the map. Their integration into local society was much easier than that of the black families who had been working hard for the South's economic benefit for generations.

Sand and the other neighborhood kids were used to the ground shaking whenever a rocket engine was tested on the Arsenal. The Redstone rocket engines were heard and felt, but only seen on television when they were launched down in Florida. The Saturn Is were big and powerful, but the Saturn Vs that were to carry the Apollo capsules into orbit and on to the moon would shake the windows of the houses in Sherwood Park. When they were tested at Christmas, the vibration could shake down a Christmas tree, and so could a tornado. Huntsville lay directly in a path the locals referred to as Tornado Alley. So it became a custom for the Strasbergs to tie up the Christmas tree every year so it was anchored to bookcases or the piano Jody played or to other pieces of furniture depending on which part of the living room they put the tree in that particular year.

Astronauts were favorite heroes of the children at that time. Sometimes the training astronauts visited Huntsville's Marshall Space

Flight Center, and sometimes the local families would turn out to see them drive by in a convertible. Sand's favorite was Virgil "Gus" Grissom. She especially liked it when he named his Mercury capsule Liberty Bell. She listened to the reports of his flight and splashdown on the radio, and when the Liberty Bell sank, she was relieved and grateful Gus Grissom had made it out alive and didn't drown. Sand tended to root for underdogs anyway, but when everyone started saying Grissom had panicked and blown the hatch prematurely, she just knew deep inside that wasn't true. Sand believed in Grissom.

*

1962

One morning in February before class started, while Sand was in third grade, there was an announcement. The principal, a nun, went from class to class and told the students, "Last night, Sister Mary Leo, the fifth-grade teacher, was taken by God during the night. She passed on peacefully in her sleep. This morning we found her with her hands folded in prayer. She's now in Heaven with the saints."

Sand didn't buy it. Obviously the woman had died, but "with her hands folded in prayer?" *Who sleeps like that?* she thought.

There was a funeral Mass for Sister Mary Leo and attendance was mandatory for the whole school. Every student was required to file past the open coffin in front of the altar and look at her. Sister Mary Leo was laid out in full penguin costume with a rosary in her hands, which were together as if praying. Her skin was gray, and she looked as dead as she was. All the breath, life, and spirit had gone out of her body.

Sand wondered what had really happened. She understood the purpose of making everybody look at the body was so they would contemplate their own eventual corporeal demise. It was at that moment Sand finally realized none of these people except her actually remembered having lived and died before; or if they remembered, they knew better than to say so. Nobody talked about where Sister Mary Leo may have actually gone. They just said she was in Heaven.

*

1963

In Sand's fourth-grade year, the nuns moved out of the upstairs and into a new convent that had been built for them in the south part of town next to a new Catholic elementary school. (Huntsville at that time had no Catholic high school.) Of course the story that circulated among the students was that the ghost of Sister Mary Leo had run the other nuns off, and that now she haunted the empty rooms upstairs. So much for heaven, hell, or purgatory for Sister Mary Leo.

Then one afternoon in late November, when Sand was in fifth grade, class was interrupted. The principal came to the door and whispered something to Sand's teacher. Then the teacher turned to the students and said, "President John Kennedy has been shot in the head and has died." He was the only Catholic president the United States ever had.

45

The class was required to stand and pray for the late president. As Sand joined in the prayers and cried because she liked the president for no particular reason, she thought of his young children left fatherless. His daughter, Caroline, wasn't much younger than Sand, and both Caroline and her brother, John, Jr., had birthdays at the end of November like Sand. She was really praying for them. She understood it must be awful to lose a father and wondered what would happen to the family.

Louise Strasberg was devastated by the news. President Kennedy and his wife were close in age to her and her husband. It felt very personal to her. She couldn't wait to tell Jody and Sand the awful news when they got home from school. She had to tell someone. She didn't even wait for them to enter the house. As soon as she saw them coming toward the door, she opened it and said soberly, "You know your president has been shot."

"We know," Jody answered.

Sand wondered how everybody had found out about this scary event that had happened two whole states away in Texas. She was learning about the effect of the new mass media linked together by satellites, as well as the shock of a presidential assassination.

William Strasberg had learned about it at work soon after it happened. He came home very serious and stressed. "The country is under attack," he told his family.

Sand could tell by her parents' reactions that the event was unprecedented for them. They seemed to think at first that there was more to the shooting than just one lone gunman. When he was killed, Sand gathered from her parents' conversations that they thought something dreadful was happening in the country, but she didn't really understand what it all meant. The fear in the air was palpable.

That evening and through the rest of the week, the Strasberg family watched on their black and white television set as Lyndon Johnson was sworn in as the new president. They saw the gunman, Lee Harvey Oswald, shot and killed. Later they watched former President Kennedy's widow and children pay their respects at his casket. Sand noticed that at least the casket was closed. She liked that better than when she had to view Sister Mary Leo's body. The family watched the funeral procession replayed over and over on TV until the images were impossible to forget. But as the weeks passed, the Christmas holiday season arrived, nothing else had befallen the United States, and things gradually returned to normal.

*

1964

By January, Sand seized the opportunity to sneak out of class, and she went exploring in what used to be the nuns' living quarters. All the walls were painted green, just like the outside of the building. It was an old building built before the days of air conditioning, so there were air vents and passageways in the walls between the rooms big enough for a child to crawl around in with room to spare. The openings to the big air ducts looked like trap doors, only they opened out vertically from the walls instead of horizontally from the floor or ceiling.

Sand was in one of the former bedrooms—
two single cots, small tables and desks were still
there—when she heard a woman's voice scolding a
child as they came up the stairs. Not knowing where
they were going, and not wanting to get caught
skipping class, Sand stood on a table and climbed
into the nearest ventilation tunnel. All the air vents
were up high, a few feet below the high ceiling. The
tunnel Sand climbed into just happened to lead to
the bathroom. The woman's voice also went into
the bathroom. The vent door was partly ajar, as
were they all; it wouldn't have made much sense to
have air ducts and have them closed. Through the
partial opening, Sand could see a fully costumed
nun, the third-grade teacher, undressing a third-
grade boy until he was naked, and scolding him the
entire time. He was crying. The teacher ran water in
the tub, made him get in it, and then proceeded to
bathe him, concentrating in particular on his private
parts. The whole time she was doing this, she
scolded him for getting so dirty on the playground,
but she never washed his face, hands, or clothes.

Sand didn't tell anyone what she had seen.
She didn't want to be caught skipping class, and she
didn't want anyone to know about her new hiding
place. She already knew the clergy didn't think very
highly of her anyway. It was pointless to try to talk
to her mother, since that would just bring on another
hysterical outburst. She was afraid Jody would
laugh at her, or worse, tell someone else. She knew
what she'd witnessed was wrong, and she felt like
she was bad for having seen it, but her curiosity was
aroused about what those nuns were really up to.

Sand continued to sneak out of the class the
same time each day and explore upstairs. Some of
the teachers still used the dining room to eat lunch

that they brought upstairs from the school cafeteria. Sand poked around the kitchen and found a broom in the corner and cabinets filled with chocolate covered cherries and pecans, assorted other chocolates, and cookies of all kinds. One day one of the older nuns came upstairs while Sand was in the kitchen, so she grabbed the broom and pretended to be sweeping up. The nun thanked her for her diligence and offered to make her a cup of tea, but Sand was worried that she'd pushed her luck too far, so she said, "No, thank you, Sister. I need to get back to class now." Then she left.

In March, the Strasbergs moved into the new home Sand's parents had built. The land where the cow pasture had been, and the area just beyond the creek in the woods, had all been developed, expanding the neighborhood and more than doubling its size. All the new roads on the north side of the neighborhood dead-ended at the fields and woods right before the cotton fields started. All the roads in Sherwood Park dead-ended somewhere. Only the four roads that ended on the south side of the subdivision connected to a road that led somewhere outside the neighborhood. That road was Madison Pike, which ran east and west. The Strasbergs moved north less than a mile to Delaney Road. The field at the end of Delaney was where the now abandoned sharecrop family's shack was. The old shack where the black family had lived was still there, although it was now falling apart. That was where Sand found the book of hand drawn Uncle Remus cartoons that were so well done. The drawings of Br'er Rabbit, Br'er Bear, and Tar Baby looked exactly like the cartoons Sand had seen on TV. It was a treasure that she hid in her underwear drawer.

It was the book of Uncle Remus cartoon figures that inspired Sand to start writing. At first she just scribbled little observations about the drawings on scraps of paper. That evolved into little stories about them. Before long, Sand was writing short poems. She didn't show them to anyone. She just stuck them in her clothing drawers, pillowcases, pockets, and books. They always seemed to just disappear but, unlike the Uncle Remus drawings, she wasn't very attached to her poems.

One Sunday at the end of that school year, Sand's mother told her how the particular young nun that taught third grade—the one that Sand had seen bathing the little boy—was leaving the convent to get married, and that she wouldn't be teaching any more. "Isn't it wonderful?" Sand's mother said on the way home from church in the car. "Now she'll be able to have children of her own."

*

July 1964

That summer, Sand was walking to the convenience store with the gas station at the entrance to the neighborhood on Robin Hood Lane with Jonathan Moreau, a friend who also lived in Sherwood Park. Jonathan was a couple of years older than Sand. He had an older brother Jody's age, and that was how they had met. Unlike Sand's family, Jonathan and his brother, Nathan, who were both very athletic, had a very stable, loving family. They were kind people, and they were Southern Baptist. Jonathan and his brother and sister attended public schools like Jody. Jody went to public school because the Catholic elementary schools only went through eighth grade, and he was already starting high school.

Suddenly, there was a loud squeal of tires followed by a loud thud and shattering of glass. Less than a block away, a car had plowed headlong into a telephone pole. Sand and Jonathan didn't see how it had happened because they'd been talking, but they saw the results. Maybe the driver was avoiding a cat, dog, or squirrel in the street. Maybe something was happening inside the car that distracted the driver and caused her to lose control. Whatever caused the crash, a little boy about three or four years of age was lying on the ground in front of the car with his head split open and his blood pouring out onto the grass of somebody's front yard. The green grass was soaking up the red blood and turning almost black. A woman came running out of the house with a pale blue blanket that she put over the motionless boy to try to keep him warm.

He bled out. He was dead before the ambulance arrived. It had been a woman driving, but Sand wasn't sure if she was dead or just badly hurt. There was blood all over her face, so Sand couldn't really tell what the woman looked like. She was limp and unconscious when Jonathan tried to talk to her, as well as when she was later removed by the paramedics. Sand didn't know, but she assumed that the woman was the boy's mother.

After the unconscious woman was taken away in the ambulance, one of the adults said, "It would've been better if the woman died and went to Heaven with her son instead of having to wake up later and learn that he'd been killed while she was driving."

Sand didn't understand this. Why would anyone want the woman to die?

Jonathan told Sand, "We should pray." He closed his eyes and bowed his head.

Sand respected his silence with her own while she wondered if the little boy would remember the crash when he was someone else.

Later that summer, when Sand discovered her little book of Uncle Remus drawings was missing from her underwear drawer, she emptied all her dresser drawers onto the floor searching for it. When her mother found her on the floor in the mess of clothes, she just sighed loudly in exasperation.

Sand told her desperately, "My little book of Uncle Remus drawings is missing. I can't find it anywhere!"

"That thing?" Her mother responded in disgust. "What business did you have with that anyway? It was trash. I threw it away."

Sand proceeded to empty all the trash cans in the house and then headed outside to look in the garbage cans, but her mother followed her and smiled with satisfaction as she said, "The garbage was picked up yesterday afternoon."

Sand felt that something very precious had been lost. She continued to write poems, but she began to keep track of them. She was very careful after that to hide them from her mother.

*

September 1964

Just after school started, Sand's maternal grandfather died in Memphis. Everyone said he'd passed away. Nobody used any version of the word death. Sand understood it was an acknowledgment that his true essence had passed onto somewhere else when his body died.

The doctors never figured out why he "passed" even though they did an autopsy, so they just called it natural causes. The family made the four hour drive to Memphis to be with the rest of the family.

In the funeral parlor at the wake, Aunt Clarabelle told Sand, "Everyone in the family is required to view the body."

"I don't want to," Sand said quietly.

"You have to," Clarabelle explained. "It's tradition."

"I've already seen dead bodies," Sand protested. *They looked lifeless*, she thought. *They were dead. Why would anybody want to look at a dead body?*

"But he was your grandfather. Everyone else has already viewed him. Now you go." Clarabelle gave Sand a gentle push toward the casket, so she went. He was just as grey and eerie and dead as Sister Mary Leo had been, and he was also dressed in black and white—a black suit and tie and a crisp, clean white shirt.

At the funeral, Mrs. Nelson, Sand's grandmother and Louise's mother, who was less than five feet tall and not at all a large woman, was led up to the casket by the priest to say good-bye to her husband of over sixty years before the funeral home personnel closed the lid forever. Sobbing, she leaned over him, grabbed hold of his lifeless body with both her arms around him, and started to drag him out of the coffin. She had him halfway out before five grown men, including the priest, Uncle Rudy, and Sand's father, were able to stop her and put the deceased back into his casket. Sand was mortified. Her grandmother just wasn't ready to let go, but he was already gone.

Later Mrs. Nelson made a scene at the graveside too, begging to have the coffin opened up again while it was sitting in its grave. Fortunately for Sand, that request was denied.

After the burial was over and Mr. Nelson had finally been laid to rest, the whole stressed-out family went back to Sand's grandparents' house, where Sand's mother, Louise, and her sister Clarabelle got into a yelling match. They were arguing in front of their widowed mother over which one of them would get which possessions. Sand's grandmother and Aunt Virginia were still very much alive and living in the same house, and many of the possessions in dispute belonged to them, but Louise and Clarabelle didn't seem to notice. Sand tried to rationalize that maybe her mother and aunt weren't ready to let go either and just needed something of his to hold onto.

That night, because there were so many people staying in the small house, Sand had to share her grandmother's bed. Sand had no clue how to deal with her grandmother's grief. She lay awake the whole night listening to her grandmother cry, but she just didn't know what to say or do. She hardly knew her grandmother, since they had been living in different states, and the way her grandmother had behaved at the funeral and graveside had seemed pretty creepy to Sand. But Sand just didn't know what to do, so she turned her back and listened to the poor old lady cry the entire night.

Probably no one in the crowded little house got much sleep, and the next day tempers continued to flare. Sand had nowhere to hide from the yelling. She just wanted it to stop.

After more arguing about who was going to take what stuff, Sand's father, William, had had enough. He grabbed a sewing table made by the late Mr. Nelson for his wife, who was still very much alive, and threw it into the trunk of his car. Then he stormed back inside, informed Clarabelle, "You can have whatever's left," and turned to his family. "We're leaving NOW."

Sand was crying and confused. She couldn't understand why the adults were doing this to her grandmother. She could see both her parents were out of control, but she was relieved to be getting away from the situation. Aunt Clarabelle was always out of control anyway but seemed to want to be in control of the family on this occasion, and Sand didn't understand it was because Clarabelle was older than her siblings. Sand also wondered about Uncle Rudy, who had already disappeared.

The widowed Mrs. Nelson was left lost and alone in her grief. She had become invisible to her own family.

The Strasbergs got home pretty late that night after driving back to Huntsville. The drive back was in silence, except for Louise and Sand crying. When they got home, they all went to bed without speaking.

The next morning, Sand saw Jonathan Moreau at the school bus stop. "Where were you yesterday during all the excitement?" he asked, but before Sand had a chance to respond, he continued, "There were police cars and ambulances on your street all afternoon yesterday. They were there on into the evening. They were all parked at the house across the street and two doors down from yours."

"But that's where the family nobody knows lives," Sand interjected.

"Right," Jonathan continued. "They were a family of four. The father worked, and his wife was a stay-at-home mom who didn't socialize with anybody. It turns out they had a retarded school-age son who didn't go to school and a baby girl."

"They've only lived there for a few months," Sand explained. "What happened?"

"They died."

"All of them?" Sand asked in disbelief.

"Yesterday afternoon the father called the operator on his phone," Jonathan told her. "He told the operator, 'I've shot my wife and two children, and now I'm going to shoot myself.' The operator heard the gun go off and the phone drop. None of the neighbors heard the shots or noticed anything until the police showed up."

There had been no police cars or ambulances on the street when Sand's family had come home. The bodies had already been removed by then.

Jonathan reminded Sand, "We should pray for the family."

"They're gone, Jonathan," Sand replied. "Pray all you want if it makes you feel better, but it won't change anything except to make you feel better."

"You need faith," Jonathan told her. "I don't need to believe what other people tell me when I already know what I know," she answered and left it at that. She knew he didn't understand what she meant, but that was OK.

Chapter 5

Traditions
(The Hierophant)

Is the glass half full or empty?
Regardless there's room for change
Traditions evolve or are broken
Nothing stays the same

When power becomes aggressive
The passive march in spite
Of vain attempts to control
What they know in their hearts is right

*

Brenda:

     Sand grew up in Alabama during the Cold War, the Cuban Missile Crisis, the early days of manned space flight, and the Civil Rights Movement led by the Reverend Dr. Martin Luther King Jr. The textbooks used in the Catholic elementary school Sand attended were different from the ones used in Alabama's public schools. The Catholic school books were integrated. Wherever there were pictures of children or groups of people, they included racial variety. It made a big difference. It was clear to anyone looking at those pictures, anyone not disabled by denial that is, that all the people in the pictures were people. It was so obvious. Sand couldn't understand why her parents and her parents' friends couldn't see the obvious.

Tradition can be good or bad, but it's always dangerous to challenge. Just like The Hierophant of the Tarot, society expects its traditions, right or wrong, to be followed. These were times of social change, times when many traditions were challenged. These were dangerous times.

*

1966

The white adults talked a lot about how dangerous Dr. King was. Sand heard the fear in the adults' voices when they made comments like, "That damned nigger is gonna get the colored people all stirred up and start a revolution," and "Those coloreds are going to take over, and then no place will be safe for us," and "That upstart King is going to put coloreds into our schools and take all our jobs," and "White people just aren't safe anymore."

But Sand liked Dr. King. She listened to him on the radio in her bedroom. He taught peace, not violence. He just wanted people to obey the law—the Civil Rights Act of 1964. It wasn't the white people being chased down by police dogs and hit over the head by white police clubs, so why did her parents and neighbors think they were the ones who weren't safe? What did the white people really have to be afraid of, or was their fear really an expression of their guilt at how they had treated their fellow human beings? Sand liked what Dr. King was saying and doing. In Sand's world, the difference between generations was like the difference between the new color televisions and the old black and white TVs.

58

Deception Past

Huntsville, Alabama, was the location of the Marshall Space Flight Center, where white, male engineers designed rockets for the US space program. They were well paid. "Manned space flight" meant exactly that in the United States—men only. And they were all white men in those days, just like the president. The United States was in a cold war and a space race with the alleged enemy, the Soviet Union, which first put a woman in space. The United States, the land of the free white men, was in a cold civil war to keep fellow Americans from voting, receiving equal pay, and sharing public toilets and drinking fountains. American citizens were the sun and the moon, casting light at different slants, with only some of them realizing they could actually share the same sky. Awakening realization, referred to more commonly as consciousness-raising, was a stressful, difficult, and dangerous process.

Most white kids in Sand's age group grew up with segregated textbooks and the idea that the South would rise again. It was the white South's way of denying and avoiding facing that it had been responsible for misery, slavery, and incredible bloodshed, not to mention the superficial, but more important reason—the humiliation of defeat and having been proven wrong. Sand always hated everything the dead Confederacy stood for. The American Civil War was about slavery, but Sand grew up being taught that it was really about states' rights. She didn't buy that either. All it meant was that it was no longer politically correct to be publicly racist, and so the Civil War was about the states' right to allow slavery.

Sand couldn't figure out why poor, young white men had voluntarily fought for what she liked to call "The Confederate States of Stupidity." If the Confederacy had won, those poor, young white men would have had nothing but poverty and indebtedness to the rich landowners as a reward. Only the rich elite of the Confederacy would have been entitled to any rights.

Jonathan Moreau's Southern Baptist church was all white. People of color were simply not allowed. Sand questioned him on this when she finally came to realize it was the case. "Don't you think Jesus would have prayed with black people too?" she asked him.

"They have their own churches," he answered. "They have their own neighborhoods, and they have their own churches. They don't need to come to ours. That's just the way it is. It's always been this way. It's our heritage."

"Jesus prayed with criminals and probably had dark skin himself," Sand insisted. Jonathan refused to continue the conversation with a nonbeliever.

Sand had read the New Testament, and what she saw in practice around her didn't fit with what she had read. Sand had become aware of how people could get stuck in the past when they believed they'd found a scapegoat on which to blame all their woes in the present. For the Nazis it was the Jews, even though Germany was a predominantly Christian country and Jesus had been Jewish.

People in the South insisted that flying the Confederate flag was honoring their heritage. They referred to the class structure defined by skin color as their culture. Everything was fine by the whites as long as the blacks knew their place. George Wallace was the governor of Alabama, and as governor he had stood in a school doorway to block the entry of black children trying to attend school. He was a hero in the white South for intimidating those threatening elementary school children.

Jonathan told Sand he respected Governor Wallace, but to Sand, Governor Wallace was nothing more than a bully. The Southern white culture was a culture of bullying and hatred. It was Dr. King who was preaching peace and justice.

Jonathan attended public school and read segregated books. Sand tried to avoid talking to him about racism, because she couldn't relate to his interest in the Civil War and his obvious admiration for General Robert E. Lee. Sand was pro-Union, and Jonathan was pro-Confederacy. When he would bring up the subject, Sand would listen to him rant for a while and then comment, "If Lee was such a great General, he wouldn't have lost the war."

Still Sand and Jonathan were friends. They would visit each others' houses. Sand had learned that her mother was always nice and friendly whenever someone from outside the family was in the house. She had noticed the difference ever since she was little. Whenever Louise Strasberg was around anyone from outside the family, she was peaches and cream; but when it was family only, she was more like grapefruit and vinegar or buttermilk and chili peppers.

Sand found it difficult to express her feelings physically. She tended to save her feelings for her poetry, which she still kept to herself. Her parents were never overtly affectionate. They only got physical when they were angry. Jody and Sand were the same way. Come to think of it, none of Sand's mother's family was any different. It seemed to Sand that when only family was present, someone was always angry. But Sand had been observing over the years that other families were different. At first she thought it was just because they too, like her mother, were putting on an act when an outsider was there. Then she began noticing one discriminating factor. Other people touched when they weren't angry.

Sand felt self-conscious and uncomfortable around people who touched each other. Sand was only used to touching in the form of hitting, and she definitely didn't like that. The Moreau home was the first place she noticed the disturbing custom of physical contact. It wasn't practiced at Sand's school or church. The Moreaus often greeted each other with hugs and kisses. They often put their hands on each other's forearms, shoulders, and necks and put their arms around each other. Sand thought it was refreshingly sweet to see other people demonstrating their affection. The problem was that whenever any one of them touched her, she cringed. She would feel her body go ice cold and shrink away. She didn't know how she was expected to react. She didn't know what she was supposed to do and had no clue how to return the gesture. So instead of continuing to enjoy their company, Sand avoided visiting Jonathan's family. With their differences in religion and politics, the two friends saw less and less of each other.

*

January 27, 1967

One night Sand was home alone with Jody. Louise and William were out somewhere playing cards with their friends—something they did on a regular basis. They belonged to a bridge club made up of adults who had moved to Huntsville from Memphis, and the couples in the club took turns hosting the games in their homes. This particular January night, the bridge club was playing at someone else's home. Sand and Jody were watching Captain Kirk and Mr. Spock in *Star Trek* on TV when a ticker ran across the bottom of the screen announcing that there had been a fire on the launch pad at Cape Canaveral in Florida.

Gus Grissom, Ed White, and Roger Chaffee had died in the fire in their Apollo I capsule. They were the first Apollo team, the heroes of the future that would lead the United States to the Moon. Nobody explained at the time exactly how the astronauts had died, just that there had been a fire in their capsule caused by an electrical spark igniting the pure oxygen atmosphere that filled it. The astronauts couldn't get out, and nobody on the outside opened the hatch for them. The Apollo capsule was bigger than the Gemini and Mercury capsules had been but, as Sand well knew, was still smaller than the interior of a Volkswagen Beetle. Even men as short as Gus Grissom and the other astronauts in their big bulky space suits and helmets just didn't have much room to maneuver inside the capsule with the weight of gravity working against them.

Sand tried not to go to sleep that night for fear of dreaming of the oven again. She spent most of the night crying for her lost hero until finally she fell into a dead sleep.

She was on vacation in a different country. While she was visiting a market place, like an open mall, Sand ran into a friend—a tall slender woman with long, straight brown hair. Her friend had her three children with her, and she introduced Sand to her husband, a nice looking businessman with straight, dark brown hair. The family invited her to come home with them and stay the night in their living room. Sand slept on the floor. The husband had bought a new pair of light brown socks. Sand's feet got cold during the night so she put his new socks on. The next day, her friend was doing laundry, lots and lots of laundry, because they had children and because her husband had to make a short trip; so she had to wash the socks because he needed them. He was traveling with a friend of his who was a police detective. Sand was outside in back of the house with the children when the detective friend arrived.

The detective's name was Michael Brown. He was tall with wavy blond hair and wore a white shirt and dark brown pants. Sand liked him a lot. She felt it was mutual.

The house was in a city where the streets were made of water, and there were no bridges, so you couldn't cross the street except by boat. There was no private transportation, so the only way to go anywhere was to walk connected sidewalks, take the public ferries that ran up and down the street-canals, or cut through the alleys between the buildings. The house where Sand's friends lived was three stories, and the front of it was covered by a huge, ancient rhododendron tree made of very thick, very dark brown branches and trunk.

The husband and Detective Michael Brown left on their trip. They were supposed to be back by evening. They were traveling by ferry. By nighttime they hadn't returned, so Sand stayed over with her friend and the children. When the men still hadn't returned by the next morning, it was obvious to

Sand and her friend that something was very wrong. Her friend stayed with her children while Sand walked to the police station and found Michael's partner. She told him what had happened and what had not happened, and together they left the police station to investigate. She and the detective both suspected his partner had been on police business.

The detective learned that Michael and Sand's friend's husband had been returning by ferry when the ferry driver, a big, bald, ugly, angry man, had learned Michael was a police detective. The ferry driver apparently had some reason to dislike police detectives. He had pushed Michael and his friend off the ferry and then run them down with the boat and killed them.

The city decided to drain all the water from the streets, fill them in and pave them. After that, Sand was able to cross the street and actually stand on the spot in the middle of the street where the two men had been murdered.

When she awoke, dressed, and went into the kitchen, her parents were already talking about the Apollo tragedy and the setback to the American space program. Sand wasn't interested in how it affected the space race. She was grieving for the three astronauts.

*

April 4, 1968

Sand had finished eighth grade, which was as far as the Catholic school went, and moved on to ninth grade in a public middle school. Her mother questioned her frequently about how many coloreds were in her classes, but Sand's answer was always,

"I have no idea. The other students all look like people to me."

One morning after getting off the school bus and while walking up the steps to the door of the school, a white classmate named Angela, who also lived in Sherwood Park, asked her excitedly, "Did you hear the news? They shot him dead!"

"Shot who?" Sand asked, stopped cold at the thought of yet another death. "Who's dead?"

"Martin Luther King," Angela informed her, and then turned and went into the school.

Sand stood there stunned. Her other childhood hero, Reverend Dr. Martin Luther King Jr. had been murdered. He was a man of peace and forgiveness. Who would do such a thing? Why? But she knew the answer already. The ignorance of blind hate had murdered a man of peace. Had anything changed? Had the George Wallace regime and the Confederacy lovers won? Dr. King was Christian minister, and now he carried on the Christian legacy of martyrdom. Would the white bigots ever understand? Sand sat down on the concrete steps. She heard the final school bell ring as if in the far distance. She refused to go inside that day.

That evening she learned that Dr. King had been gunned down in Memphis. Sand was devastated that the murder had happened in the same city of her birth.

Sand's mother and Aunt Virginia engaged in a long and hateful phone conversation about how he'd gotten what he deserved. Louise repeated Virginia's comment, "It was all the fault of the coloreds for rising up the way they'd done."

Sand went to hide in her room and covered her ears as best she could to block out the venom.

She was afraid the whites were rising up to shoot down people of color. She didn't understand why they didn't just obey the Civil Rights laws and learn to get along with each other. Isn't that what Jesus taught? Weren't they all supposed to be Christians? Didn't the Sermon on the Mount mean anything to these people? Sand knew Dr. King was a great man and that her parents and the other adults were wrong. None of her white friends who pretended to have faith ever mentioned the need to pray for Dr. King.

*

July 1968

Jody's friend, Jonathan Moreau's older brother, Nathan, was willing to serve his country without question. The Moreaus were proud of being a family of faith with pride in their nation. When drafted, Nathan answered the call enthusiastically, and after basic training at Fort Jackson, South Carolina, and further training at Fort Polk, Louisiana, Nathan was shipped off to the jungles of Viet Nam. He was there for four months, two weeks, and three days before the Moreau family was notified that Nathan had been killed in action.

Nathan Moreau came home in his sealed casket and was buried in peaceful, scenic Maple Hill Cemetery among the grand old oak, maple, and sweet gum trees. He was given a military escort from the plane to the chapel on Redstone Arsenal and then from there to Maple Hill.

Sand attended the funeral with her parents and Jody. Sand and Louise cried when *Taps* was played, and both nearly jumped out of their skins when the guns fired in salute.

Mr. and Mrs. Moreau were left with their second son, Jonathan, and their only daughter, Jill, who was the youngest. They had each other and their faith.

Chapter 6

Karmic Attraction
(The Lovers)

We choose our path to illness
We choose our peace to health
We only choose each other
With roles we play ourselves

The heart speaks through its passion
It follows to the end
It must express compassion
Or plant new seeds to tend

*

Brenda:

In a way, we're like magnets. The laws of karma follow us like an invisible magnetic field, attracting and repelling events and other people. Like magnets, and like the Tarot Lovers, opposites attract. Love, or attraction, works in mysterious ways. It's hard to see through the layers of distractions all around and within us to decipher what's really happening at any given moment, but there's always an unseen force at work.

*

1913

In the second decade of the twentieth century, the Narim family left south central Asia a few months before Nadia, their first child, was born, and settled in London, England. Nadia's feet never recovered from having been bound by a nurse as was the Asian custom. It was a custom because it was important to keep women in their place and not let them go anywhere without the male family members' consent. The western world at that time had different customs but the same values where women were concerned.

Their second child, Salim, grew up in a world of privilege. As the older son, he would inherit his father's property, possessions, and the grand title of head of the family. He would get to keep his father's name. Salim was to be a man of entitlement who would make decisions for all the members of his family flock.

His older sister, Nadia had already inherited the privilege of taking care of her younger siblings and the housework. She was expected to marry and take her husband's name because women never had a name of their own. It was considered shameful if she never married, as daughters were only considered temporarily part of the father's family until marriage.

After Salim was born, Mr. Narim, an energetic, distinguished, self-made man, moved his family to France. There, their youngest son, Abdel, was born. The 1920s had begun to roar, and as a philosopher, Mr. Narim found the culture of Paris liberating as opposed to the stifling class structure and racism of England. The Narim family became the center of their own ever-expanding circle of patrons and admirers. The father published several volumes of his own thoughts, teachings, and analyses. The family prospered. Nadia, Salim, and Abdel were privileged, protected, and well educated.

Nadia's mother was an American by birth, slender, attractive, fair-skinned, and blonde. She had met Mr. Narim while traveling abroad as part of her upper-class education. He was charming and persuasive, and she fell under his spell. They married in spite of her family's explicit objections to his South Asian ancestry. He was not only dark skinned, but Moslem instead of Christian. He wore his hair long and wrapped in a turban and never shaved. She converted to Islam, and once married, she was disowned by her family. She never saw or communicated with them again.

Nadia inherited her father's dark skin, eyes, and hair but her mother's attractive face. She grew up entertaining a world of her own dreams and imagination in the well-tended flower gardens of her family's estate. Her parents were peaceful, kind, and loving people unaccustomed to raising their voices.

When as a very young child she first mentioned remembering a previous life in a different place where she had tended her own herb and flower gardens, both parents quickly discouraged her from mentioning it ever again. Mr. Narim was not at all interested in reincarnation. It was only the present that mattered to him. Mrs. Narim was frightened by young Nadia's comments and didn't want to hear any more. Nadia was eager to please her parents at that age, and from then on kept her comments to herself. At one point she tried confiding in younger brother Salim, but he ran straight to their parents and told them what Nadia had said. After that, she kept her mouth shut about her memories.

Music and studies were the priorities of her life then, and Nadia learned piano, harp, and the Indian vina, an exotic Indian instrument as sensual and vivid as her fantasies and the flowers on the estate. She loved children's stories from a variety of cultures and loved to find symbolism and similarities of belief systems in them. She loved her parents but, unlike them, believed that children should be encouraged to explore ideas for themselves and speak openly about memories and dreams of memories. Children, as well as adults, should be free to be themselves.

Nadia wanted to be a writer and reporter. She started writing poetry at a young age. She imagined she could use her memories to write her own novel someday. She studied hard in school with her goal in mind. She dreamed of the day she would be on her own, making her own living, and answering to no one but herself while earning her way in the world. She would do that by covering and explaining the events of the day accurately, clearly, and concisely to the reading public. She would keep her readers well informed. On her own time, she would write stories using symbolism from all the cultures and belief systems she would continue to learn about. Her future held wonderful possibilities, all expressed through writing. But her parents had more traditional goals in mind for her, and so her studies were limited to music and child psychology.

She was especially close to her father. He died suddenly before Adolph Hitler came to power next door in Germany. Nadia inherited all the household and maternal duties as their mother couldn't cope without her husband facing the world for her and telling her what to do. And someone had to look after Salim and Abdel. It all fell to Nadia. When her father died, Nadia lost both parents, and as their eldest child, became the substitute parent for both her siblings and her own mother.

Young Salim inherited position, property, and family authority. He was still a child, but it was his inheritance. His was a striking face with piercing, deep-set eyes. Abdel, by contrast, was a quiet, thoughtful child with a unique combination of facial traits that came from both of his parents' families.

Nadia's mother retreated from everything. She renounced living. Had there been a funeral pyre, she would have thrown herself onto it in despair by immolation. Nadia wrote poems and stories inspired by her romantic view of her parents' love for each other.

She found all of her time consumed by her mother's duties, but she adapted. Nadia was water in a family of fire. She didn't mind taking care of her family while pursuing her studies. She loved them, and she had big dreams for herself, even though she tended to keep those dreams to herself.

Then the Nazis invaded France. The Narim family suddenly found themselves leaving the world they had known. They left it all behind—home, routine, comforts, country, culture, friends, and neighbors, for mere survival free of racist oppression—as the Germans marched toward Paris. Ironically, this time they went back to England.

They found friends in London and just enough work to survive, but Nadia couldn't be at peace with herself as long as Paris was in the hands of conquering barbarians. She wanted to do something. She wanted to go back to France. She wanted to go home and live among friends in her own country. She was a young adult with memories of a past life. The thought of her own mortality in this life did not seem as relevant as freeing France.

She enlisted in service with the British military. Her English was good, but becoming familiar with certain idioms and comfortable with the culture was a big adjustment. She did her best. Being young, she was motivated to fit in. She trained as a wireless radio operator, which to her was just another language played on its own instrument. With her French citizenship, she had no trouble getting assigned to go back undercover into German occupied France. She kept it all secret from her family. They were important to her, but this was her decision, and they had no need to know. They would only have tried to interfere.

Nadia went back into France to fight the evil Nazi barbarians. She met evil on its own turf and on its own terms. There was no way to pass through it unscathed. Evil was simply the triumph of human fear and greed. The only way to pass through it unchanged was to not judge it to be evil.

But the Nazis weren't barbarians at all on the surface. They were perfect gentlemen when putting on a show for the occupied people as long as their skin wasn't too dark and as long as they weren't Jewish. Nazis were just men in uniforms like any other men. At least they were capable of being like any other men, but they weren't. They were occupying most of Europe, enforcing fascism and anti-Semitism, and worshipping their false god, Hitler. They were imprisoning, torturing, and killing good, innocent people. They were monsters who looked and acted like ordinary gentlemen. They had torn Nadia's world apart, because the leader they idolized lacked tolerance, patience, compassion, and an understanding of common human ground.

How do otherwise civilized men look up to someone like that? she wondered to herself every time she encountered any of them. It ceaselessly amazed her how blind human beings could choose to be, and at the same time she worried, wondering what her own blind spots might be.

Nadia was back on home ground, courtesy of the English, but France was completely changed by the occupation. She quickly found her own people to work with as well. Reporting to the English was one thing, but the whole point of being there was to assist and prepare the French Resistance for an Allied invasion, so she connected with Claire Devereaux, a friend from her childhood, who was working with the resistance. Claire had relocated from Paris to Normandy. Claire was tall and slender with curly blonde hair, but a somewhat asymmetrical face that kept her from being described as pretty. Nadia traveled back and forth between Normandy and Paris coordinating with the resistance and maintaining her job reporting to the British by wireless. When necessary, they assisted downed Allied pilots in escaping Nazi occupied France back to England.

*

June 1943

The Narim family back in London had no idea what Nadia was up to or where she really was. She had told them she was being stationed in North

Africa. She had told them she would be safer there than in London, considering the bombing raids. They had no reason to disbelieve her.

Shortly after Nadia had left for Africa, Abdel began having disturbing dreams. He dreamed he was a woman trapped in an eight foot by ten foot cell. His hands were chained in front of him, and he had been raped. The walls of his cell seemed to be closing in on him. He sensed the worst was yet to come. He wanted to escape, but only did when he finally woke up.

Another night, Abdel dreamed there was some sort of catastrophic natural disaster that caused the ocean to rush inland and flood everything. There were people everywhere trying to run, trying to survive, and he was one of them. He grabbed onto something and used it for flotation. Salim appeared and joined him. They were being carried by the current. At some point, they were swept into a big, beautiful house that had been a mansion on top of a mountain with a beautiful view. Abdel saw a burning airplane fall from the sky and crash into the ocean; and then he realized that he and Salim were being swept into a room where they'd be trapped if they didn't find a way out.

Then Abdel dreamed he was a passenger in a motor car that went over a cliff and into a bay. He couldn't get the door of the car open to get out, and the driver, who he couldn't clearly see or identify, was yelling at him to get them out of the car. The door window was most of the way down, so Abdel went out that way, but when he reached the surface gasping for air, he realized the driver had not made it.

Upon waking each time he had one of these dreams, he carried with him into his day an ominous sense of foreboding. London was being bombed. All of Europe was at war, but still he knew something very bad was going to happen. He just didn't know what that something was.

*

Nadia knew that when she perceived difficulties resulting from the choice she would naturally prefer or whatever she thought was the right thing to do, she could deceive herself into choosing what she had decided would be the easier path. The evaluations she had received back in England before returning to France had alerted her to her own weaknesses. People tended to only allow themselves the options they perceived in the slanted light of the reflection in which they saw them. Nadia understood full well that through the unconscious, the inner self tried to guide us and point out which path to take, but she would have to recognize the guidance for what it was before she could make use of it. She tried to pay attention to her dreams and intuition, but she was under constant stress. Sometimes she just didn't have the luxury of a full night's sleep. Understanding was the first step, but the best choice was not always easy to make.

Chapter 7

Personal Victory
(The Chariot)

Truth always wins
It just simply is
To deny or accept
And thus determined

The truth simply is
That life moves on
The river keeps flowing
And dark turns to dawn

*

Brenda:

The Chariot card can lead us to personal victory based on the choices we make. Nadia had chosen to make her own decisions rather than wait for the men of her family to tell her what to do. She had chosen her work and her life. She had chosen to be in France.

The choice is the path of the journey. The Chariot is the destination or fruit of the journey.

*

Deception Past

October 1943
France

Nadia looked out across the French countryside as an internal wave of relief swelled up her spine. She was bicycling to Normandy, where she was supposed to lay low for a while. On the way to the coast, she recalled the previous time she'd been headed to a different coast to the south, running from the initial invasion with her family amid desperate throngs of refugees. The world had seemed to change overnight, and constant change had become the new normalcy.

The rhythmic motion of her legs pedaling while staring at the passing scenery gradually lulled Nadia into a state of daydreams. She recalled her vivid dream of the night before. She had dreamed she was with Claire Devereaux. Claire had taken Nadia to a chemist. Nadia waited at the counter until a stooped, elderly gentleman with rimless spectacles appeared from behind a curtain. He handed her two pills and a glass of water. She swallowed them both, inhaled and exhaled deeply, and then looked around for Claire, but Claire had vanished. Soon the pills took hold, and Nadia couldn't keep her eyes open any longer. The elderly gentleman showed her to the door. She cautiously looked around, a habit now to make sure she wasn't being followed, as she wondered what the dream meant.

When she arrived at the little farmhouse, Claire Devereaux was there to meet her. After they hugged, kissed each other on both cheeks, and exchanged greetings, Nadia assured Claire that she was fine.

"We're still waiting for the signal," Claire told her as they went inside. "It should be any night now. The men are ready to get the American pilot to the boat."

After being a refugee and an outsider in England, and then always having to look over her shoulder in Paris, it felt good to Nadia to be accepted and welcomed. Nadia's time in France was supposed to be a temporary assignment. She knew in her heart she didn't want to leave again, but after just a few months, her situation had become desperate. Most of the British agents she worked with had already been arrested. That had started as soon as she had arrived in Paris. She now relied solely on her French Resistance colleagues. This was her country, and she belonged here. All she wanted was to live among friends where she felt at home, but she wanted to live, and she wanted her country to be free. She knew she was in mortal danger. She had used the British to return to France, and they had certainly used her without even following their own procedures for protecting their own agents. She knew she would have to leave soon and return to her family if she was to survive. Her friends in the resistance were very concerned for her well-being. They warned her repeatedly the Germans were closing in on her. The Nazis intended to silence all communication with London.

Claire and Nadia, both dressed in black for concealment, waited in the dark moonless night on the shore listening to the sea. Nadia shivered in the night sea breeze. The oars dipping in and out of the water were counterpoint to the surf. Eventually, the rubber boat appeared out of the darkness, and the men climbed out and pulled it onto the beach. The men silently unloaded the boxes and carried them inland to the cottage while the women stashed the boat, camouflaging it with brush and branches. Inside the cottage, they opened the crates to find an assortment of electrical parts and radio tubes. Nadia picked out what she needed and set those aside. She and Claire sewed them into the stuffing of toy animals. There was a dog, an elephant, and a bear. Nadia would carry them back with her to Paris.

That night in the farmhouse, Nadia dreamed she was back in London living on the third floor of a four floor walk-up. She had become friends with most of the building's residents. She lived alone with her kitty cat, Clover, in a one-bedroom flat. Even though it was just a small apartment, she had accumulated enough stuff to fill all of the possible storage places—closets, shelves, cabinets, under the bed, etc.

One of her neighbors came across the information that their landlord, the building's owner, was planning to have the building torched to collect the insurance, even though the building was completely occupied. The word spread like wildfire throughout the building. Neighbors met with neighbors and discussed what could be done. It was generally agreed upon that everyone should be prepared at any time to flee the building. Throughout the four floors, residents were taking a good look at their possessions and deciding what was most important to them. Most were evaluating their own priorities and choosing what they should have ready and easily accessible to grab and take with them should they suddenly have to evacuate their homes. Nadia was not an exception.

While one of the apartments vacated because of the perceived threat, one of her downstairs neighbors decided to store some of his more precious possessions outside on the street. To this end, he bought a large cart which he parked outside the building and invited others to store some of their more personally valued things there also. The problem was that nothing on the street was very safe either. Mainly for that reason, Nadia didn't take advantage of his offer.

Meanwhile, she found herself pulling all of her clothes and things out of drawers and shelves, out from under the bed, and out of the closets, and laying everything out in plain view. She put all her photographs in a shoebox and set them, her notebooks filled with her writing, and her vina—the beautiful Indian instrument whose music was so precious to her—by the door. To those items she added Clover's carrier. Then she began sorting through the clothes. She laid out on the bed only the clothes she was truly fond of and packed the rest up into bags and boxes to give to charity.

After she'd given away the excess clothes and shoes, enough clutter was cleared out to leave living space again. She decided everything else was expendable. Like many of the other residents, she took to sleeping fully dressed.

One night, in the middle of the night, while she was sleeping, an air raid siren went off. She picked up Clover, once she caught her, and stuffed her into her carrier. She grabbed the shoebox of pictures, her vina, and her notebooks and headed off, considerably loaded down, out the door and down the flights of stairs. By the time she had joined the others already gathered outside in the street, she learned that there was no air raid, but the building was on fire. She realized that not only were her arms entirely too full, she was very lucky to have made it safely out of the building considering how long it had taken her to get there. The other residents had managed to evacuate much more expediently.

That was when one of the neighbors, a middle-aged gentleman from the second floor, stepped forward and announced, "The alarm was NOT triggered in response to an air raid or a fire. I hope you'll all forgive me for the disturbance, but I decided we'd be better prepared if we had an unexpected and seemingly realistic fire drill before any real disaster occurred. I took it on myself to set off the siren without telling anyone. This was just a drill."

Nadia was grateful as well as relieved. Since she was very tired, rather than have to carry everything back up the four flights of stairs, she decided belatedly to make use of her other neighbor's generous offer to use his cart. While she loaded her belongings into his cart with the other boxes and suitcases already there, the residents talked among themselves for some time and eventually decided that several of them would take turns at night watching the cart and the building from a doorway across the street. After agreeing to take the first watch the next night, Nadia climbed back up the stairs with Clover. Once back inside their little home, Nadia had a prolonged cuddle with Clover, and then set the kitty free and went back to bed.

A couple of nights later, after she'd returned to sleeping in her nightgown, a fire alarm rang out again in the middle of the night. This time when she woke up she smelled smoke. She immediately grabbed her coat and called out to Clover as she put the coat on, scooped the cat up as she trotted up to Nadia, and stuffed Clover inside her coat as she ran out the door and down the stairs into the street. She didn't care if the cart was still there or not. She realized that faced with the end of life, the only thing that mattered was the life itself. She woke up feeling chilled to the bone, but she had no time to consider the meaning of the dream.

Nadia made the return trip to Paris safely with her small, lifeless companions. Whenever thoughts of her latest dream surfaced, she had to push them aside. She absolutely had to stay alert. No one suspected; the soldiers even smiled at her. She slept poorly that night. She assumed it was just the job and the danger taking its toll on her.

The next day when she went out on foot, she noticed she was being followed. She diverted from her course many times until she was sure she no longer had her unwanted shadow. She knew she should seek refuge somewhere else, but she was tired and just wanted to go back to her own apartment, so she did.

He was waiting for her, dressed in a brown fedora, tan trench coat, and plain brown trousers and shoes. He confronted her in her own apartment. He was just as afraid and determined as she was. When she realized what was happening—when he told her he was turning her in to the Germans and that she was being arrested—she tried to run, but he had a gun and she didn't.

She was betrayed and arrested by a Frenchman. In times like those, who could ever be sure about anyone? She had been sold out by someone she thought was a friend. She never learned who it had been, but she surely had been stabbed in the back by someone. The problem with being betrayed was that she felt like it was all about her, when in reality, it was only about her betrayer.

Maurice, the Frenchman who arrested her, worked for the Germans. He had needs, and he had wants. Fear blurred the line between needs and wants—so does greed. Fear perceived need but didn't think. Greed only thought about wants but didn't feel. Evil was the triumph of fear and greed.

Rations, by definition, were limited in war time. Safety didn't exist. After she was locked up at Gestapo headquarters, she had time to wonder what caused someone to betray her. Was that person afraid for himself or for someone else? Had her betrayer already been caught himself and was just trying to stay alive? She understood, at the hands of her captors, how easily one could be coerced by cruelty or fear of cruelty.

Maurice and whoever betrayed her were just human. No human was made up exclusively of fear and greed, not even Adolph Hitler. All things good and evil are woven together by self-deception. Maybe someone were afraid of Nadia. They certainly had good reason to be. She was challenging Goliath without slingshot or stones. She was defying the Nazi monster in its occupied territory with, at best, a faulty escape plan and no one left in Paris who could or would dare back her up. She was doomed by simply being there. She had understood the risk when she returned to France, but deceived herself by believing she could beat the odds. She had to believe that maybe her betrayer was protecting someone else.

Whatever Maurice's reasons for working for the Germans, he had taken her totally by surprise. She shouldn't have been. She had known she had been followed, and knew in hindsight she should never have returned to her flat. Her own unconscious had tried to warn her. She should have stayed with Claire in Normandy, but there was no going back and redoing it. She sat in her cell and wondered if someone had deceived her by pretending to be her friend. Or had she deceived herself by believing she had friends she could trust in such a place and time? Nadia, her betrayer, and Maurice could well have been soul mates—three tiny fish trying to survive in a poisoned pond. All ended up as bait.

Nadia had time to realize she had sold herself out with her promise to return to occupied France. And she realized she was sold out by the British promise of a mission that could be accomplished. She deceived herself into believing it was her duty to be the mouse for the big cat to torment to death. There was never hope of evasion of capture, much less hope of rescue. Nadia came to understand that she sold herself out for blind faith in a system that valued only victory, not individuals. Her only comfort was that she had provided London with some information and had helped some pilots escape. She had traded her life for theirs. That was enough. She had done what she could. She had done nothing wrong.

Everyone was just trying to survive. Everyone in a war zone was shell-shocked. The trauma victim reverted to whatever comfort zone he or she could find. The captive either came to believe and trust the captors or else gave up realistic hope altogether. Nadia was an idealist. Realism wasn't her strongest asset. She held onto her ideals.

*

Deception Past

November 1943
Normandy

Claire Devereaux received word of Nadia Narim's arrest about three weeks later. Nadia wasn't Claire's first friend to be arrested by the Nazis, and she wasn't the only one of their friends to be betrayed or arrested by Maurice. Claire never knew who the informant was, but she knew their little cell of resistance against the invaders had been defeated. She knew that no one she knew who had been arrested since the Germans invaded had ever returned or been heard from again.

Now all that was left to do was to lay low and try to survive. Or not. One dark, rainy night after drinking too much wine, because she still had wine but no food left, Claire decided that if she couldn't continue to fight her enemies, she wasn't going to wait around to be captured by them. It seemed inevitable to her. It seemed black and white, and she only saw two options to choose from.

She staggered, barefoot and drunk in the rain, down to the beach, dropping her almost empty bottle along the way. She bent down and picked it up. That's when she saw the driftwood log. She dropped down on her knees into the sand and grabbed the bottle by its neck with both hands. As she raised the bottle over her head and back as far as her arms would go, the remainder of the wine poured down onto her head and ran down through her rain-soaked hair. Then, as she felt her heart shattering, her arms, along with the wine bottle, came crashing down onto the driftwood. With all her might she tried to thrust the broken bottle up into her abdomen. Her hands let go, and she crawled through the broken glass and sand toward the water. Shards and splinters of glass, wood, and broken shells, stung in her knees and the palms of her hands in harmony with her bruised belly. She looked up toward the ocean, and the rain stung her face with cold. The seawater was even colder as it embraced her body with numbing sleep.

*

After a brief stay in a cell at Gestapo headquarters in Paris, Nadia was sent to a prison in southern Germany. She was kept in chains in solitary confinement and kept busy knitting. She was grateful for the knitting. At least it was something to do while she wasted away alone and out of touch with everyone and everything she cared about. All she wanted was to live among friends where she felt she belonged. There was plenty of time to think and remember and wonder what was happening to those she had known and wonder what was happening elsewhere.

Nadia found her comfort zone in a Nazi prison cell of solitude and the constant, repetitious work knitting for soldiers fighting in bitter cold. By that time, it didn't matter what uniforms they wore, what language they spoke, or what atrocities they may have committed or prevented. All that mattered was that they were cold and needed comfort. She could help. She understood how it felt to be cold and alone with no source of warmth or comfort available. They were just trying to survive, and Nadia no longer had others around her pronouncing them to be evil. Nadia wasn't judging.

Maybe the most important thing she learned was that she could only accomplish anything one stitch at a time, and that it was more important to focus on making those stitches than what anyone else was doing or not doing. Accomplishment could only from the smallest details. Each stitch was more important than the finished product. The journey was more important than the destination.

Knitting was exactly what Nadia needed—calm, quiet, repetition with a clear sense of accomplishment. It calmed her nerves. It gave her mind freedom to wander. Each stitch was like the silent repetition of a mantra slowly weaving a soft, comforting fabric. She was contributing to the consolation of another suffering human being somewhere. It didn't matter that the suffering soul was wearing the uniform of the enemy she had tried to fight. It didn't matter that it was slave labor on behalf of the enemy that had taken her freedom and her future. She had, in a strange way, chosen to be there, and now she chose to willingly work each stitch into a pattern to warm some soldier in an enemy's uniform fighting to end her life.

Nadia reflected on the choices she had made that led to her being there. She missed her mother and brothers, but knew they would never understand her choice that ended up with her in prison. They would not understand her newly found freedom from material possessions and social status. Now she had nothing but time and solitude in which to realize the essence of her inner nature, and she found a quiet peace hiding deep within her being. She came to understand that when we made a choice in accordance with the direction we received from our inner self, the results led us to a sense of victory and accomplishment. Imprisonment was far from how she wanted to live her life, but sometimes victory was found in how we accepted the circumstances imposed on us. Harmony between our inner selves and our conscious choices was how we achieved the otherwise elusive state of happiness.

Nadia was allowed a brief walk outside in the courtyard of her prison every day. Between the chains and meager rations, those walks became gradually more laborious, but she loved the fresh air. It was the only way she had of sensing the seasons and passage of time.

*

September 1944
Germany

One day after what Nadia figured to be nearly a year, she was taken in chains by her captors to a train station where she and three other English women prisoners boarded a train full of German soldiers. The women were allowed to talk to each other. They spoke in English. It was great to share their company. Even in chains, Nadia enjoyed the sense of freedom allowed by having no idea where they were going, why, or how long it would take to get there. Facing the unknown was the greatest freedom there is. It was her final taste of life.

When they arrived at the work camp at Dachau, the women's clothes were taken, numbers were tattooed on their forearms, and they were separated. They never saw each other again.

Nadia was beaten and raped for what seemed like hours. One of her left fingers was broken. The pain and degradation were overwhelming. She had no sense of time and no idea how long the senseless ordeal continued. She knew they were going to kill her. She wished they'd just get it over with. Finally, she was dragged toward the crematorium. When the soldiers dropped her next to the brick wall just outside, as she fell into a kneeling position, her head dropped down onto the ground, and she instinctively and defensively tucked it under her body for protection. Then, without warning, she was shot in her upper back. She was helpless and in pain as they picked her up and carried her inside toward the heat and stench of one of the ovens to their left. She saw the glowing embers and bones and realized as they put her into the oven that they were going to burn her alive. The pain from the rape and beating and the physical shock from the gunshot wound were minor compared to the horror of seeing the remains already there. The heat and stench made her gasp for air at the same time her body tried to vomit. But at the last moment, she chose to take responsibility for her thoughts. She chose to choose her perception in her last moments in the physical world. She chose the personal victory of truth over her murderers and her environment. She chose her last thought. Her last thought as the oven wall burned the tattooed number off her right forearm was *liberté*. Freedom.

Chapter 8

Balance
(Justice)

Balance is not stasis
It is a practice of process
Troublesome but relentless

It's who we are
It's what we do
It's nothing new

*

August 1945

Salim had always been the more ambitious brother in the Narim family. He saw himself as the man of the family whose responsibility it was to provide for, direct, and take care of the rest of his household, even if they no longer lived under his roof. His very looks commanded respect. He was highly competitive and very sensitive whenever his older sister excelled over him in music or studies. Salim was the only one of his siblings with a competitive nature. He was also the only one of the three who was gregarious and outgoing.

Nadia and Abdel were more introspective and cooperative. Abdel was calm and quiet when the Narim family in London received word of Nadia's death, but Salim was histrionic as usual. Nadia had joined the British armed forces before telling the family, much less asking their permission. Now the war in Europe was over and they had finally received news that she had been taken prisoner by the Nazis in Paris, transferred to a concentration camp in Germany, shot execution style, and burned in the ovens. Abdel understood that Nadia had made her own choices in life, and now it was over; there was nothing to be done. It was over. She wasn't coming back, and her remains had already been disposed of. It was over.

Salim found it hard to let go. He was more like his mother who, after decades and a war, was still grieving for her lost husband. With only his reclusive mother and silent brother at home, Salim went to his friend in the apartment next door to vent his emotions.

Young Doctor Ibrahim Akbey was kind, refined, comforting, and philosophical. "No good is ever lost in the world," he counseled his friend. "Physical law tells us that nothing is ever lost; it merely changes form. Spiritual law also has its counterpart. Your sister's good will never be lost."

Doctor Akbey had earned his medical credentials in London during the bombings. His parents had come to England from Turkey. He walked with a limp and a cane, but he had learned to walk, which was more than his parents had expected considering the birth defect of a moderately deformed left foot. His was a placid personality that accepted people as they were and events as they happened. He pushed himself through it all, accomplishing what he could. He married Maria, his brunette English bride, one night in a bomb shelter during the Blitzkrieg.

Maria had lost her mother years before to illness. Her father had been killed in one of the earliest of the London bombings, and her brother died on the continent in battle. Ibrahim and Maria had met in the hospital where they both worked.

He poured Salim a glass of wine and tired to reassure him. "Nadia was shot and killed quickly," he told Salim. "Even the sadistic and fanatical Germans would not have put her into the ovens until after she was dead. It is natural for you to feel abandoned by your sister. It is normal you feel angry that she did not consult you before committing herself to fighting in the war."

Salim nodded. He seethed inwardly knowing she had fought while he himself had not participated. He was head of the family by right of birth and gender, and Nadia should have been his to direct.

"Actually," the doctor continued, "you should be proud of her. What she did took great courage."

Ibrahim Akbey understood that the order of their world had been upset and that the times were moving them forward toward different ways. Ibrahim had befriended both Salim and Abdel, though in fact, he identified more with Abdel, whose subdued nature was more akin to his own. But he actually spent more time with Salim who often sought out the doctor's companionship. Abdel Narim was younger and welcomed the changing times for the opportunities they presented.

Over the days and weeks that followed, Doctor Akbey tried to gently coax Salim into understanding this, but Salim was not one to let go easily, especially when his life's expectations and the privileges he viewed as his birthright depended on not letting go of the old ways and values. Salim was a stubborn man.

*

Brenda:

Justice, or balance, is only attainable by letting go of what we want to happen and accepting what is. It's an invisible force that we simply cannot control. Some try to create it through laws and rules, and no doubt society needs them. But the opposites that attract must also be balanced. It's hard for us to do that with forces we can't see. Something somewhere has to mitigate our choices.

True justice is never revenge or deliberate punishment. The law of karma balances all in its own time. What is done always returns to the doer.

*

1946

The Narim family, especially Salim, only perceived a lack of justice for Nadia. He felt betrayed that she had never shared with him the reasons for her choices, but he tried to understand. When she was awarded posthumous medals, he began to use her status as a hero to further the family reputation. In this way, he came to forgive her. What was left of the Narim family moved back to Paris, where Salim did his best to demand a return to their former lifestyle.

The Akbeys, of course, remained in London. When Maria became pregnant with the Akbeys' first child, she and Ibrahim moved to the United States, land of opportunity. They both applied for citizenship. Having not been ravaged by German bombs, life was easier there.

Abdel followed the Akbeys to the United States and left Salim to rebuild his childhood dreams in Paris. Abdel lived for some years in New York City before making his home upstate in the country. Both brothers eventually married and had families of their own.

Doctor and Maria Akbey settled in Warrington, Florida, on the northern shore of the Gulf of Mexico, where their first daughter was born. They named her Sophia. Maria was a housewife and a stay-at-home mother while Ibrahim worked as a civilian doctor at the Pensacola Naval Air Station. By the time their second daughter, Sonia, was born, they were all US citizens, and Dr. Akbey had set up his own private practice in Warrington as a family physician. Their third daughter, Isabel, was born mid afternoon of the last Sunday of January, 1952, in her parents' upstairs bedroom on Second Street. Dr. Akbey had bought the family a yellow brick, two story, four bedroom home on Second Street just south of Dexter in Warrington. The property was on the east side of Second Street on the bayou. Ibrahim built a pier and, several years later, a boathouse to protect his cabin cruiser. They had large front and back yards filled with tall pine trees and fire ant hills.

The girls all inherited their father's olive complexion, brown hair, and brown eyes, but Sonia was the only beauty. Sophia, instead, had inherited her father's brains. From a young age she had to wear thick glasses. Isabel would never be considered attractive because her face was skewed and asymmetrical.

While Isabel was growing up, whenever weather and time permitted, the family would take the boat out to Santa Rosa Island or Perdido Key for a picnic on the beach. Many picnics were filled with stories of London, the war, the bomb shelters, and Ibrahim's friends, Salim and Abdel Narim. Salim had become wealthy following in his father's footsteps, while Abdel had made his own name turning his land in upstate New York into a communal farm where young Sufi idealists came and lived, doing all the work in exchange for his wisdom, guidance, and personal favors. Ibrahim told his daughters the story of Nadia's courage, how she had died for the cause of freedom, and become a war hero.

Sometimes the Akbey family would take nets and go crabbing. Sonia loved to catch the crabs, and Sophia loved to eat their mother's crab gumbo, but Isabel was afraid of the pinchers. Then after seeing the helpless things boiled alive and hearing their screams, which everyone told her was just air escaping, Isabel couldn't bear to catch or eat them. The rest of the family laughed at her sensitivity and truly believed she would outgrow it, but she never did.

Sophia was brilliant and made straight A's in school. She never questioned what she was told to do and was her mother's favorite. Her mother felt the need to protect her more than the others because of her naturally poor eyesight.

Sonia was the beauty. She was popular, competitive in anything nonacademic, and witty, but often that wit turned into a sharp, sarcastic tongue. Still, Sonia was her father's favorite. He admired her spirit and her healthy, energetic, physical perfection.

Isabel was quiet and sensitive. She tried to keep up with her studies, and she did well, but never as well as Sophia. She had no desire to keep up with Sonia, but she would have appreciated more notice from their father. She resented her mother sending her to Sophia for help with school work, and she simply didn't get along with Sonia, who could be verbally cruel. She knew she was neither parent's favorite and isolated within her own family. From early on, Isabel championed the underdog, no matter the cause.

*

1965

One summer when Isabel was thirteen and Sophia had learned to drive the family car, the three sisters went to Pensacola Beach for the day. On the beach that day, Isabel met Patty Compton, who was the same age as Isabel and on vacation with her parents and older brother, George. Patty was fair skinned with straight brown hair that grew all the way to her waist. It was her most feminine feature. Isabel and Patty quickly became best friends.

When the Compton family went home to Huntsville, Alabama, after their vacation, Isabel and Patty exchanged many letters. Patty returned the following year and spent the whole summer with Isabel as a guest of the Akbey family. Patty and Isabel taught themselves to play guitar and sing folk songs, and soon they were writing and singing their own songs.

Ibrahim and Maria both found the songs and the singing annoying and sometimes even grating and disturbing. While Isabel and Patty became inseparable, Patty was getting on the older Akbeys' nerves. They found her outspoken, somewhat crude, and her voice was often too loud for their quiet tastes. Neither Patty nor Isabel had any sense of style when it came to their manner of dress, nor were they interested in being fashionable.

When Mr. and Mrs. Compton, at Patty's urging, invited Isabel to come live with them in north Alabama and go to school with Patty, Ibrahim and Maria were at first taken by surprise. Maria was against it.

"Patty will only further contaminate Isabel," Maria told Ibrahim. "She's already a bad influence. Isabel is gullible enough as it is."

"I want to know how Isabel feels about it," he responded.

"You're too easy going," Maria argued. "You need to stop this nonsense."

"I'm still the head of the family?" he chided her.

She nodded and left the room.

Ibrahim called his youngest daughter to him. "I'd like to know your thoughts on going to live with the Comptons. You know your mother and I don't want you to leave us."

"I know, but the last thing I want is to be in the same high school with popular and beautiful Sonia," Isabel explained. "I don't have friends at school. Patty's my only friend."

Dr. Akbey understood. He wanted his daughter to be happy, so at dinner that evening, he announced to the family, "I've made my decision. Isabel will go to Huntsville, Alabama, with Patty and live with the Compton family. They have generously offered to allow her to share Patty's bedroom."

Chapter 9

Flickering Streetlamp
(The Hermit)

When surrounded by darkness
Find the light within
Follow the wisdom of the heart
When you stumble, begin again

You can't escape who you've become
So simply take a stand
Defend yourself for all you're worth
And bloom where you've been planted

*

Brenda:

The 1960s and 1970s in North Alabama were a meeting of the past and the future in the present. There was a lot of turbulence and the times converged like the high and low atmospheric pressure systems that so often came together there to create storms and spawn tornadoes. It was a violent time in a place with a long history of violence—at least as long as the European/Christian presence had been there to keep a written record of it. The southern good ol' boys and the Ku Klux Klan, which had originated just a few miles north of the state line in Pulaski, Tennessee, came up against the liberal futurist idealists and the Civil Rights Movement.

101

Drug dealing and prostitution prospered, and scientists under pressure committed suicide. But strangely enough, the US manned space program only produced white male astronauts until the 1980s. General Robert E. Lee's birthday was still celebrated as a holiday, and liquor stores tended to close in honor of the occasion.

The United States had not quite learned from the mistakes it had made back during Prohibition in the first part of the twentieth century. Prohibition had outlawed alcoholic beverages and only created the gangs, black market, and violence required to provide the supply necessary to meet the public's demand. Even during Prohibition, marijuana and cocaine had been legal. Now the hourglass had been turned upside down again. Alcohol was legal, but the other drugs were not. Once again gangs, black market, and violence arose to provide the supply necessary to meet the public's demand. Once again law enforcement was overwhelmed and under resourced to deal with the problems created by outlawing mood-altering substances. Once again legislators had ignored the illness to treat the symptoms as crimes, and no one was looking for the reasons people chose to self-medicate or how to treat the underlying causes. Once again no one seemed to understand that they couldn't cure the disease by inflicting more pain on the patients.

The Hermit of the Tarot withdraws from the outer world to seek his true path by way of his own inner light. Once he finds it, he strives to light the way for others. The Reverend Dr. Martin Luther King Jr. was an example of one who followed the path of The Hermit card. He was no hermit, but he found his light within and followed that path in peaceful marches where he lit the way for others.

*

1968

When Sand was a teenager, her Aunt Virginia, her mother's sister with the red hair, brought Sand's grandmother to visit for a weekend. Aunt Virginia went into Sand's bedroom, where Sand was sitting on her bed working on homework.

"There's something you should know," Virginia told her. Sand put her book down and paid attention. "When Clarabelle was fourteen years old, she was raped by our father's brother, your great-uncle. You'll never know him or his name. Our Daddy, your late grandfather, severed all connections with his family as soon as he found out. Now, this is not something you should ever talk about.

"Your mother, Louise, never let herself believe it really happened. I think she just couldn't deal with it. Louise criticized Clarabelle for everything that happened, as if Clarabelle could have stopped it. She was very cruel. She still denies it ever happened. She's afraid that if people knew, it could ruin all of our reputations, and that's true. This must be kept secret at all costs for the sake of the family's position in society."

"I understand," Sand acknowledged. "What a terrible thing."

"Exactly," Virginia said. "I'm glad you understand." Then she left the room.

What Sand understood was that the Nelson family had no position in society, and that Aunt

Clarabelle had been forced to suffer in secret all
these years. If Louise just couldn't deal with it, how
did Clarabelle manage? She wondered how her
parents could blame Clarabelle for having been
raped.

Sand thought about how Louise could keep
the secret of Clarabelle's rape from her own self.
She not only didn't admit it to herself, she never
told Sand's father about the rape. Sand also
wondered how any of the Nelsons could have
deluded themselves into thinking they had a
position in society.

So, Sand realized Clarabelle's substance
abuse was self-medicating her secret pain. Her need
to be in control was considered inappropriate
behavior for a woman in those times, even though
her body had been violated against her will. *Of
course she wants to be in control,* Sand thought to
herself. *Of course she's afraid of ever being
overpowered and violated again.* In those days,
blame for the trauma of rape fell squarely on the
shoulders of the victim. Society's judgments often
forced victims of trauma to seek shelter
underground.

Not long after Aunt Virginia and
Grandmother's visit, Sand's mother took Sand aside
and told her, "Men are animals when it comes to
sex. Once a man gets turned on sexually with a
woman, he can't stop, so don't let any boys get
started with you by touching you where they
shouldn't. Once they start kissing and feeling
around, they'll go all the way no matter what. It's
the woman's responsibility to stop the man. It's all
up to you, and that's all there is to it."

Sand pondered the contradictory information
she'd just received from her mother as soon as her

mother left the room. She concluded that her mother must have truly believed she would have succeeded in fighting off Sand's great-uncle if he had forced himself on Louise instead of Clarabelle. Louise's defense against all that frightened her was denial.

Sand reasoned that denial was a way of ignoring what people didn't know how to deal with, and ignoring was ignorance. She wrote in one of her notebooks, "Denial walks down the aisle and betroths delusion, whose alias is fantasy. Many brides and grooms believe their spouse will protect and comfort them for better or for worse, whether or not they know how or are able."

Sand taught herself to knit that fall when she developed insomnia. All the yelling at home, all the conflict everywhere, and all of life's contradictions had finally caught up with her, and knitting was a quiet way of being creative. But mostly all the dream-memories, hormones, and flow of the unconscious were too overwhelming to deal with, so she stopped sleeping for a few days at a time for a couple of months.

Sometimes she would slip out of the house and walk down to the field at the dead end of Delaney Road and watch the moon set and the sun rise. Nature was surreal like dreams, or maybe it was the other way around. All the most important symbols in dreams seemed to Sand to come from Nature, so it made sense that watching it and being in it could act as substitutes to help the conscious and unconscious sort things out. That's how Sand figured out the knitting—her unconscious used it as a symbol to sort things out. Symbols in dreams were like yarn that the unconscious used to stitch together patterns, themes, and substance.

Sand liked the way the blanket she chose for her first project seemed to materialize out of nowhere, and she liked knowing she was making it happen. For the first time in her life, she had a tangible sense of accomplishment that wasn't open to anyone else's judgment. She chose a variegated pattern of orange and browns and made six strips, each a foot wide and six feet long, which she later sewed together with the same pattern yarn and a darning needle. It was all a straight knit stitch, as she hadn't figured out the purl stitch yet. While she was avoiding the intensity of the unconscious, like taking a break from the dream world, she decided the purl stitch was more moonlike. Sand came to associate the knit stitch with consciousness and the warm orange of the sun.

In the daytime that summer, she mowed other peoples' lawns to make some money, which she saved in a miniature combination safe Jody had given her for her last birthday. That also gave her a sense of accomplishment while getting her out of the house. And she could think things over while she mowed. She wondered if her mother's art of denial was really any comfort to Louise. She began to wonder if Louise had denied Sand's past life memories because, by that time in her life, denial was the only way she coped with anything new or unusual.

*

Deception Past

October, 1968

    A month after school started, Sand's biology teacher announced to the class he had been drafted. It was then that Sand realized no young men were safe, and the war, which had been going on far longer than the Korean conflict, World War I or II, or the Civil War, could go on forever. That's how it seemed. No one could ever explain to her satisfaction exactly how a civil war in such a small, agrarian, faraway land could threaten the safety of the United States of America. Nothing was ever gained by it, but lots of lives were lost, and lots of families were torn apart on both sides of the Pacific Ocean. Sand was grateful she was female and not faced with being conscripted into a life of violence and killing she neither wanted nor understood.

    It was early in her first year of high school that Sand started having dreams about betrayal. These dreams were nothing like the vivid, repetitive nightmares of her early childhood, but they were disturbing all the same—very vague, dark dreams in which she was always someone's prisoner and being interrogated. She had this overpowering sense of desperation and longing to be accepted, appreciated, and approved of by her interrogators. Every dream was different, but in every dream Sand always told the men holding her captive whatever they wanted to know. When she woke up, she could never remember what it was they wanted to know. Then in another dream, she clearly saw Patty Compton, a girl at school, accusing her of having betrayed their friends. She didn't understand what it all meant.

*

Mitch, Candace, and Sylvia Masterson went to the
same public schools as the other kids Sand knew,
but they lived in the trailer park on Madison Pike.
The trailer park was almost directly across the street
from the original entrance to Sherwood Park, but it
wasn't considered part of the same neighborhood.

Sherwood Park was constructed of
permanent housing. Families that lived in the trailer
park couldn't afford to own their own house with a
foundation. An apartment complex had also been
built on the same side of Madison Pike as Sherwood
Park, just down the road to the east of the trailer
park, but the apartments weren't considered part of
the neighborhood either. Still, people who rented
apartments were considered a cut above the people
who lived in trailers. The traditional notions of
some people being better than others just because of
where they lived or how much money they had
made no sense to Sand; however the Masterson kids
were very aware of it.

Mitch and Sylvia were blonde and nice
looking, but Candace, who was between them in
age, was dark haired and downright gorgeous.
Sylvia was Sand's age, and they were in the same
English class together that first year when Sand got
to high school. Sylvia had four younger sisters, but
Sand never got to know any of them. Sand thought
trailers were cool, if not a bit crowded for such a
large family, but the elder Strasbergs said that
people who lived in trailer parks were trash. Sand
knew that wasn't right. Her parents said lots of
things she knew weren't true. Sand and her parents
didn't have a very trusting relationship from the
start, and that relationship became even more
strained during Sand's teenage years. Sand never
understood thinking of people, or animals, or plants,

or any living creatures for that matter, as trash. Well, maybe spiders and cockroaches. It just seemed so Nazi-like. The only drawback Sand could find to living in a trailer, besides the lesser space, was that they were so easily destroyed by tornadoes, and there were many tornadoes in North Alabama.

Sylvia's dark-haired older sister, Candace, who could have been a beauty queen if the family had enough money for entry fees, was outgoing and a lot of fun. Sand liked her, and Sylvia alternated between adoring Candace and being jealous of her. Candace was a light-hearted, free-spirited teenager whose happiness beamed through her entire body right down to her fingertips. Being popular was important, especially to teenage girls from a poor family. Their escape from poverty traditionally hinged on marrying up, which meant finding a husband who would be a good provider, rather than seeking achievement of their own. Even in those days, women who sought achievement of their own were looked down on by society. Candace and Sylvia were raised to seek popularity and good husbands.

Their older brother, Mitchell, by contrast, was always reading strange books and talking about symbolism, duality, and the underlying meanings of dreams and events. Mitch would say, "When you get caught up in worldly events, it's like riding on the rim of a wheel. One minute you're on top, but the next you're being dragged through the mud. But if you find your center inside yourself, you're at the hub of the wheel. You see all that's going on around you, but you're still safe in the center of the storm."

Nobody paid much attention. Mitch was the eldest, but he'd never even been out on a date. He preferred going to the library over going to dances. His sisters thought he was just compensating for his lack of social life and social standing with a lot of mystical nonsense. Candace dated every boy she met, while Mitch read books by Carl Jung, practiced yoga that he taught himself from books, and read Tarot cards. Sylvia joked that Mitch was searching for the meaning of why he'd been burdened with six sisters and no brothers.

As soon as Mitch finished high school, he grew his blond hair long and a beard and mustache as well. Their fair-haired dad, Mr. Masterson, was a landscaper and worked at a nursery. He worked hard and never complained. Mitch, like his father, was destined for a blue collar life.

Their mom was dark haired, overweight, a chain smoker, and a chronic complainer. It didn't matter who you were or how old you were, she'd fill your face full of smoke and your ears full of woes that just never seemed to be anything important to anyone but her. What was important to her was that it was all about her. Her husband's job was to provide for their family, and hers was to deal with all the kids' problems. She just wanted somebody to listen to her problems, but her husband was too tired when he got home in the evenings to be bothered, and on weekends he was always busy fixing something. Besides, anybody that made the mistake of listening to her go on and on nonstop once wasn't likely to do it again.

The Masterson family went to the same Catholic church as Louise Strasberg's family, but Sand's parents didn't socialize with Mr. and Mrs. Masterson, because they lived in the trailer park. Louise considered that socially beneath her.

Rick McDevitt and Sylvia Masterson had been in the same class in public elementary school and in the same homeroom in middle school, but then Sylvia failed the seventh grade. Rick had passed. Rick was also fair haired and would have been considered handsome except for the pock marks left on his face by a bad case of childhood chicken pox.

Sand learned from Rick that Mrs. Masterson's younger sister, Kate, had once been a nun and taught at the Catholic elementary school, but had left the convent to get married around the end of Sand's fifth-grade year. Sand didn't tell either Rick or Sylvia what she had seen during her fifth-grade year in the same Catholic school, but she wondered how much the Masterson family knew. She wondered what Kate had been up to in the years since, and if she had molested any more young boys.

*

Brenda:

Sand was growing up during the steady and lengthy escalation of a war that technically was never declared in a place that had not been important enough to learn about in public schools. Americans were told that Viet Nam was crucial to defending democracy and protecting the United States. No doubt on some level to someone it was. When the war was finally lost, democracy was fine and the United States was no less secure.

Meanwhile, as the undeclared war was being fought, few Americans could credibly defend it as necessary for the safety of the United States. It was an extension of the Cold War paranoia that held the nation in the grip of fear that somehow communism could overthrow their government from afar. Like self-destructive, frightened people, sometimes an entire society could create the very situation it claimed to fear just by blindly reacting to that fear. It was the bully syndrome. A bully would strive to create fear so that the fearful would do the bidding of the bully.

Those years were a time of social unrest and increased criminal activity on the part of the American government in the name of protecting national security. When the government didn't follow its own laws, the rest of the country felt less inspired to be law-abiding. Trust between the government and its people had been broken.

Many understood their society had gotten off track somewhere and wanted to find a way back to their true path. Many were searching for the path back to peace. They were searching for The Hermit to shine his light, but most failed to realize it was inside themselves the whole time.

*

1969

Michael Latimer was in the same class as Sand when she went to public high school in tenth grade. He was the only white kid Sand knew who wore his curly dark brown hair in the style of an afro. He was proud of his hairstyle, as it allowed him to grow it longer than the other white boys in school and still not break the dress code, which required a male student's hair to not cover his ears or collar. He lived on the next street over, a block east of the Strasbergs. Michael was the first person Sand shared any of her poetry with. It started with a valentine she made for him one Valentine's Day. It wasn't about love or even about Valentine's Day. She just wanted to make him an original card. It made him smile. "This is great!" was his exact response. Encouraged, she began the practice of giving poems to her friends for birthdays and special occasions.

Michael declared the creation of his own country in his bedroom and seceded from the United States. His secession was not to preserve slavery or discrimination, but to end it, at least in his little kingdom. In Michael's room, the concepts upon which the United States was founded and that students were taught in school were always open for debate and free discussion. There was no racial or gender discrimination in Michael's country and no military draft. Teenagers, who outside Michael Land could be drafted but not vote, could vote but not be drafted in his country. Michael was an idealist.

And it wasn't just hype. Michael's parents were probably the only nonracists in the neighborhood, at least in practice, and kids of Asian and African descent were just as welcome and likely to show up. When Sand met the Latimer family, she felt that somehow their inner selves shone through to the physical world so brightly they could reveal that light to others to help them find their own way down their own paths. In many ways, the Latimers were like The Hermit lighting the way for others by finding their own light within themselves. Idealism was contagious, and Sand liked it better than religion.

Sand's good looking, muscular, childhood friend, Jonathan Moreau, was a year ahead of Sand and Michael at the same high school. Jonathan was on the school football team and very popular. The girl he started dating was mocked by the cheerleaders as a plain Jane. He had met her in one of his classes—Patty Compton, whose best friend, Isabel Akbey, had come up from Warrington, Florida, right next to Pensacola, to live with Patty and her family. Jonathan and Patty seemed an odd match, but both were creative, played guitar, and liked to write songs.

Sand started dating Rick McDevitt, who was also a year ahead of her in school and also a friend of Patty Compton. Rick and Patty had known each other for years. Sand and Rick would often go out on double dates with Jonathan and Patty to a movie, dance, or party. Sand's parents didn't want her to date yet unless it was a double date. Her mother felt she would be safer that way. Sand knew her mother was trying to protect her from what she wouldn't admit had happened to Aunt Clarabelle. Sand also knew she had nothing to fear from Rick McDevitt.

Rick's best friend was Matthew Barnes, who was also a friend of Patty Compton. Matty was one of the tallest kids in school but played no sports. He was blond with what could be described as an Irish mug for a face. He was also very introverted and didn't smile much.

It was customary to start school assemblies in the gymnasium with the high school band playing the US national anthem. It was expected that everyone would stand as a show of respect when the Star Spangled Banner was played. But at a school assembly, Matthew Barnes remained seated in silent protest when the national anthem was played. After the assembly, some of the other kids expressed admiration for Matty—that he was cool or brave for not standing. Rick McDevitt and Michael Latimer were among them.

At first Sand thought it didn't really matter whether Matthew Barnes stood or sat during the playing of the national anthem, as it didn't change the country or the war one little bit. She also thought it was fine with her if he chose to sit it out as a matter of free speech. She figured he had his reasons and they were his business.

Matty Barnes was the same age as Rick McDevitt, Jonathan Moreau, Patty Compton, and Isabel Akbey. His father was a senior noncommissioned officer in the army and stationed at Redstone Arsenal. Matthew was opposed to the US participation in the Viet Nam war and was very vocal about it.

Later that day at lunch time, Jonathan patiently explained to Sand, "Matty's opposition to the war is really his resentment of his father, Sergeant Major Barnes. Matty's dad treats him like a buck private in boot camp."

"I disagree," Patty contradicted.

"Me too," Rick jumped in. "Matty is simply expressing a legitimate political belief. I agree Matty's father is obnoxious at home, using his military demeanor in place of parenting. Anybody that's ever been to their home can see that."

"I agree," Patty added. "Even Matty's mother knows Matty's father is a serious problem. Of course, his father doesn't see it that way. But Matty has a right to his political beliefs."

"All I'm saying," Jonathan continued, "is that for Matty, the United States Army and the Viet Nam war are all representative of his father."

"It's kind of hard to separate your life from your beliefs," Sand commented.

Meanwhile, other kids at school were all discussing the pros and cons of fighting in Viet Nam and whether Matty actually had the right to sit through the national anthem. None of the teachers or school administrators mentioned it, but it was in conversations wherever there were students.

That afternoon on the school bus, Jonathan warned Sand, "The football coach was very upset about what Matty did today. The coach took it as a personal assault on the country and got the team all fired up about it."

"An assault on the country? With what … his ass? So why didn't you just explain his relationship with SGM Barnes to the coach?" she asked him.

"How would that matter? SGM Barnes represents the country. He wears the uniform. It would only have made things worse. Things are bad enough as it is."

Sand didn't understand Jonathan's warning.

Matty didn't show up at school the next day. Rick told Sand and their friends before school, "Matty was beaten up after school yesterday by some of the football players, who wanted to teach him a lesson for being un-American."

"What?" Sand reacted. "Has the Bill of Rights become un-American as well?"

"This is the South," Jonathan countered.

She turned her anger toward him. "The South is dead. It's NOT rising again. It lost already. You knew and you didn't bother to warn Matty. You took part in the violence by proxy." She knew Jonathan hadn't been there, because he had ridden the bus home with her.

Jonathan was just as outraged at her accusation. "I tried to warn Matty by telling you." Then he walked away.

"What?" she shouted after him. Then she turned back to her friends. "He only told me the coach had the team all fired up about defending the country. What does defending the country have to do with beating up Matty?" It had never occurred to her that her own fellow students would beat up one of her friends for sitting down when they were standing. And a coach had instigated it. It was all so very wrong.

Sand couldn't understand how Jonathan could continue to be part of the football team after that. What difference did it matter that Matty didn't stand up? It didn't change the country or society or the grand scheme of things. Sand felt it was stupid and petty to become violent over something that didn't even affect anything. Matty could have had a sore foot, even though he didn't. Sand saw the coach and football players as having committed the crime of assault because of what they believed was in the victim's thoughts without due process. That seemed pretty un-American but, as Jonathan had pointed out, they were. They still believed in the Confederate States of Stupidity. *And how dare Jonathan blame her for his not warning Matty.* She didn't understand how conflicted he felt about Matty's small protest after his own brother had died in service of their country.

Matty was back at school the following day, but the bruises didn't show. The jocks had been careful to avoid hitting his face. Matty was no less vocal about his opposition to the war and the military after that. If anything, he seemed encouraged and ready to fight passively for his beliefs, but he didn't bother to go to the police or press charges against his assailants. He knew overall public opinion would be against him just like it was against the Civil Rights freedom marchers and still was against the antiwar demonstrators elsewhere in the country. In North Alabama, Matty didn't even have a movement, much less his own parents, behind him. He was a loner and he was pretty much alone but, then again, he and Rick were still best friends and often quoted the recently assassinated Dr. Martin Luther King Jr.

*

Sand became friends with Isabel Akbey in gym class that spring. Neither was athletic, neither was noticed by the more popular students, and neither had a lot of close friends. Sand already knew Isabel's roommate, Patty Compton, who was dating Jonathan Moreau. In their small circle of friends, composed mostly of the more artistically inclined at the high school, Patty was popular. She played guitar, sang, painted, and took drama class. Patty, Jonathan, and Isabel were a year ahead of Sand in school, but that didn't matter to them. Patty and Isabel talked about each other all the time whenever they were apart.

Isabel's family was in Florida, but she had come up to go to school for the year and stay with Patty's family. They never said why and Sand never asked. Sand thought it was cool that Isabel's parents and Patty's parents would allow her to do that. Sand hung out with Isabel and Patty a lot the next two years. Isabel and Patty were very close, and Isabel and Sand became close friends.

Patty never treated Sand like an equal; she was very patronizing. Sand always thought it was because she was younger than Patty, or maybe because Sand was an old friend of Jonathan's and Patty resented the time Jonathan spent talking to Sand.

Sand had saved her money from mowing other peoples' lawns the summer before and used it to buy a guitar. Isabel taught her what she knew, and Jody showed her how to read music. Soon Sand was teaching herself classical as well as popular music. Jody and Jonathan were extremely complimentary of her playing, and that gave her more confidence in herself. Jonathan even told Patty and Isabel that Sand could play better than any of them, himself included.

Sand liked boys and hadn't learned anything yet about jealousy, possessive relationships, or sexual relationships between members of the same gender. She knew that Isabel and Patty slept in the same bed, but she hadn't yet realized they were the first lesbian couple she knew who lived together. She had read about lesbians in Greek history, but never thought about the possibility in the present. In those days, coming out about being homosexual just wasn't common due to fear of prejudice and retaliation, and most heterosexuals never mentioned such things. Hatred of homosexuals could be even more violent than racial hatred. Sand had no clue that Patty resented the time Sand spent with Isabel.

Sand had gym class with Isabel that semester. Isabel had a birthmark just above her navel. Sand noticed it in the locker room when they were undressing. The mark was bright pink and looked to Sand like a comet streaking across Isabel's abdomen toward her left. It was quite prominent against her olive skin and very noticeable. The first time Sand saw it, she asked Isabel what it was. Isabel told her it was her birthmark. Sand wondered what sort of death would cause such a mark, but kept that thought to herself.

Patty was definitely the dominant, assertive one of the pair. Sand hung out with Isabel a lot more. Isabel was less opinionated, more accepting, and more open minded. Sand hadn't yet realized that it was because Isabel was hiding behind other people's identities. Isabel was there for the first semester that year, and then she went back to live with her own parents in Florida.

Right before Isabel left Huntsville to go home, she confided in Sand, "Florida isn't the paradise one might imagine. You know, I first attempted suicide when I was eleven."

"No way!" Sand exclaimed. "Why?"

"My parents always preferred the company of my two older sisters. One's my father's favorite, and one's my mother's favorite. I'm the extra nobody needed. Nothing I could ever do would ever be good enough for them, except for leaving. I just wanted to please them by disappearing from their lives forever. The problem was I didn't know how to tie a proper noose. I'd never sailed or been in Girl Scouts and earned a knot tying badge, so when I tried to hang myself with a scarf, the knot came undone. Nobody noticed. I felt like a complete failure. No one ever commented or asked about the big bruise it left on my neck."

Being a disappearing child herself, it didn't seem the least unusual to Sand that no one would have noticed. Maybe that's why Isabel wanted to be someone else and belong to another family. "So then why are you going back to them?"

"Can't stay here," was the answer.

Sand was already sad at losing her friend. Now she was depressed because of what Isabel had told her. Life was cold and cruel it seemed. She thought about the way her own family treated Aunt Clarabelle. She thought about how Matty's family treated him, and how the school seemed to think violence was patriotic. Where did it all end?

That night Sand tried swallowing a bottle of muscle relaxing pills from her parents' medicine cabinet, and then she told them what she'd done, because she knew they'd never notice otherwise. They got mad, yelled a lot, and ordered Sand to go outside and wait in the car for her father to drive her to the hospital. She did as she was told. She waited. When it seemed a long time had passed and she was becoming drowsy, she meekly went back inside. Both her parents were sitting at the kitchen table. She asked them when her father was going to take her to the hospital, but her mother said he'd refused. Her father was silent. She went to her bedroom and fell asleep as soon as she lay down on her bed.

She dreamed that night she was walking through the woods wearing a necklace of sleigh bells and being followed by a pet dog. They weren't going anywhere in particular, and Sand found it very pleasant in the company of the dog, who accepted her unconditionally as she was. The sleigh bells jingling with every step was a happy sound. The next morning she got up early and found some sleigh bells in the hall closet with the Christmas decorations. She strung them on a string, and wore them around her neck to school even though it was after Christmas, and all the decorations had recently been put away. When she got to school, she ran into Rick McDevitt in the hallway, but he didn't seem to notice anything had happened, so she decided everything was perfectly normal. And it was.

That afternoon she learned her mother had put some leftover penicillin capsules into the bottle with the one muscle relaxer that was left. At least Sand had a good night's sleep. Her father told her to never do anything like that again and to never tell anyone as it would ruin the family's reputation.

Sand told Isabel what had happened, and Isabel offered to take her back to Florida with her to live with her family. They had a good laugh. It was like two invisible children from two dysfunctional families could somehow cancel out the disappearing effect. Or maybe, while they were together, they actually cancelled each other out and were invisible to the rest of the world.

After Isabel went back to Florida, Sand had only an occasional nightmare. The most vivid, frightening dream that stayed with her a long time was one where she was at school and everyone was in the hallway because it was in between classes. Patty was pointing at Sand and loudly denouncing her as a traitor. Patty said Sand had *given them up,* and in the dream, Sand was very upset, because she didn't want it to be true. It was really a most unpleasant feeling to wake up with. She tried not to think about it because it was so troubling, but the more she tried not to think about it, the stronger the recollection of it became. She wished Isabel was there so she could talk to her about it, but decided it was best not to mention it in a letter.

Patty Compton was far less tolerant of Sand after Isabel went back home to Florida. Sand didn't have much in common with Patty except that they were both close friends of Isabel Akbey and Jonathan Moreau. Patty never initiated a conversation with Sand, so just to break the ice, Sand would ask Patty, "Have you heard from Isabel lately?"

Patty always responded loudly with great annoyance and a dramatic shake of her head with its extremely long, straight hair, "No, I have not heard from Isabel. All everybody wants to know is if I've heard from Isabel."

Even though Sand never actually sought her out, she couldn't avoid Patty altogether because they knew the same people. Sand endured her encounters with Patty by being inwardly amused at how Patty would actually tilt her head back before speaking to her, literally looking down her nose at Sand. Sand and Isabel never considered themselves popular, but it made Sand smile to know that everyone was asking about Isabel instead of Patty. She wrote a letter to Isabel to let her know.

Throughout that year, Patty's boyfriend was still Sand's friend Jonathan, who was still a high school football player. Sometimes Sand and Rick McDevitt still double dated with Patty and Jonathan. Patty and Jonathan's relationship was all for appearances as near as Sand could tell. Jonathan never seemed to notice Patty's friendship with Isabel. He was busy hanging out with the guys. Patty didn't seem to miss him when he wasn't around, but everyone in school understood that Jonathan and Patty were a couple. Maybe that's why no one seemed to notice Patty and Isabel's relationship.

Patty broke up with Jonathan that spring and went to live with Isabel Akbey's family in Florida for the summer. Jonathan didn't seem too broken up about it. He saw Sand in the neighborhood that summer and told her, "I got a letter from Patty."

Sand was excited at the news. "What did she say? How's Isabel?"

"She says they cut their long hair short."

"Why?" Sand asked innocently.

"Butch and the Sundance Kid," was his answer. "You wouldn't do that, would you?"

"No, of course not," Sand reassured him. She liked her long hair. Once again, she failed to grasp what Jonathan was actually telling her.

Chapter 10

Going in Circles
(The Wheel of Fortune)

The world is whole just as it is
And it is ever changing
We ride along for good or bad
The wheel is always turning

The choice of how we ride is ours
The centered keep their balance
And all the Universe will share
With beauty, love, and kindness

*

June 1969
Warrington, Florida

Back in the Florida panhandle at her parents' house, Isabel dreamed she was walking the streets holding her cat in her arms. She ran into Patty Compton and Sand Strasberg, only in the dream, Patty's name was Claire, and she had curly, shoulder-length blonde hair instead of straight, medium brown hair. Claire said she knew a place where they could all get free beds for the night, but it was first come, first served, so they needed to get there soon so they could find beds. The three of them went into the building and up to the desk, where Isabel signed in first. She was still holding her beloved cat. They found empty chairs in the waiting room, where they sat down.

Isabel had drifted off to sleep when motion around her woke her up. Her cat had gotten loose from her arms and was on the floor heading for the door. Isabel jumped up and ran to catch it just as everyone around her was moving toward the back of the room, down a hallway, and into a large dormitory where beds were being assigned. Isabel caught the cat just as she realized Sand and Patty were no longer in sight. She asked the lady at the desk where she should go since she was the first name on the list, and the woman behind the desk directed her to follow the crowd.

When Isabel found Claire at her newly assigned bed, Sand was nowhere in sight, and Claire was with someone else. That was when Isabel suddenly realized the cat she was holding wasn't hers. She let the cat go, and as it scampered off, she cried out for someone to help her find her precious cat, but no one responded. Claire told Isabel she needed to find a bed, but by then all the beds were already taken.

*

Brenda:

Nature teaches us by example that the natural, and therefore most harmonious, state of physical matter is change. It's often uncomfortable, but apparently necessary from a larger perspective. We live in a world made of physical matter and in bodies made of physical matter, or at least that's how we see it. Anyway, like it or not, our bodies and our world are always changing. Children are naturally more in tune with this reality because their bodies are growing, developing, and continually changing. By the time children become adults though, they've been taught to "settle down," to seek "stability" and routine. It's frequently the beginning of unhappiness and the loss of awareness of communication with that free inner spirit. That's often how dreams become dormant and unfulfilled.

But the wheel of life, called The Wheel of Fortune in the Tarot, is constantly turning. By the time an adult has passed the zenith of physical prime, a natural awareness of that unconscious inner being begins to reawaken. One realizes there is more to life than material creature comforts and the external physical environment. Adolescence, however, is on the opposite side of that curve.

*

July 1969
Huntsville, Alabama

Sand often daydreamed she was walking down the path through the woods where the neighborhood kids had built a tree house in an old pine tree. In her daydreams, she just kept going with no destination in mind, no obligations, no one with unrealistic expectations of her to please, and nothing to prove to anyone. Sometimes at night, the daydream took over her sleeping dreams.

One night she dreamed she was trying to get away from Isabel, her good friend. In the dream, Isabel was trying to make Sand wear someone else's clothes so Isabel could wear Sand's. Sand wanted to wear her own clothes. Isabel and her best friend Patty were drama students; they enjoyed costumes and getting into character and being someone else other than themselves.

127

Sand never took drama class, and she'd never been in a play. She was having enough trouble just being herself without adults criticizing the life out of her. The last thing she needed or wanted was to have to be someone else or wear someone else's clothes. It didn't occur to her to question why Isabel, or anyone for that matter, would want to wear Sand's clothes or walk in her shoes.

Sand ran down the footpath looking over her shoulder every few steps to see if she was being followed. Once she was satisfied there was no one following in her footsteps, she slowed down to a more leisurely pace. She was enjoying her clean escape and her total lack of destination, but mostly she was actually enjoying wearing her own clothes. She was enjoying being herself because she was by herself without the threat of consequences caused by other people's interference.

When Sand woke up, she saw the day in a new light even though it was still dark. While the rest of the house slept, Sand walked down to the field where the street she lived on dead-ended as a street but continued on as a foot path. She watched the full moon set, and then she turned around to the east and watched the sun rise before going home to get some breakfast.

At long last, the American astronauts beat the Soviet cosmonauts to the moon. For the first time in her short life, Sand felt the world was united. She also felt it would have been more sporting of the Americans if they had planted a Soviet flag next to the US flag at Tranquility Base in honor of all the astronauts and cosmonauts who had died in the process of realizing that dream, but then it always seemed to be more important to men to be first in something. She figured if women had been in charge, things might have been different. She wished Gus Grissom had lived to see the big event.

*

August 1969

Isabel and Patty were back living with the Compton family by the end of the hot, humid summer so that Isabel could stay through their senior year of high school. Sand finally began to realize the actual nature of Isabel and Patty's relationship. After that, Patty's attitude toward her began to make more sense, but it was cool with her now that she understood what was going on.

It was during that summer that Sand dreamed she didn't feel well. She went into a drugstore. The pharmacist gave her some pills, which she took, and they instantly made her sleepy. Since it was early evening, the pharmacist warned her that she'd better not drive. He told her there was a place to stay just a block down the street from his store.

Sand found the motel, signed in at the desk, and was waiting in the lobby to be shown to her room when she found herself surrounded by a family with a young girl. The little girl came and sat next to Sand. She took Sand's hand in hers. The family then rose to their feet with Sand in the midst, and Sand was also forced to rise, even though she was quite tired. Together they all began walking slowly toward the motel's front door, all the while crowding closer and closer together. The older woman whispered in Sand's ear, "We're mourning her death," and nodded toward the little girl who was still holding Sand's hand.

*

Once back at school, all of Sand's friends were talking about the Woodstock Festival that had taken place in upstate New York the month before. Matty Barnes and Rick McDevitt claimed to know a girl from a rival school who had attended. They repeated her stories of how cool it had all been being with so many people of their generation all bathing together in a stream and, of course, the music. All the top musicians of the day were there, including Sand's favorites, Jimi Hendrix, Cat Stevens, and Jefferson Airplane. Matty and Rick actually sounded jealous to Sand of this girl they knew. Sand didn't understand what was supposed to be cool about so many people crowded together in the rain and mud, or why bathing together outside was supposed to be cool. Sand was interested in the music but couldn't imagine anyone wanting to have been there.

Sometime between Thanksgiving and Christmas, Jonathan and Jill Moreau's father suffered a fatal stroke. Having lost both his brother, Nathan, and his father, Jonathan told Sand, "I've become aware of a need for something meaningful in my life. My religion is everything to me now." Sand listened patiently as he continued, "I've always gone to church and been a devout believer. I've decided to make a greater spiritual commitment. I'm now 'born again.' This is the biggest thing that's ever happened to me. I know who I am now. No matter what happens, I can handle anything now."

Jonathan and Sand saw each other more frequently once he was no longer seeing Patty Compton. They talked about many things during their frequent walks through the neighborhood. He often told Sand that he had come to realize his father and brother were in a better place. Sand understood it was necessary for Jonathan to believe this just to get through each day, as well as to help his mother and kid sister, Jill, cope with their losses.

Jonathan asked Sand one afternoon, "Do you believe in an afterlife?"

Sand thought carefully before she responded, "What I tell you is not about proving or disproving anything. It's not about anybody's beliefs. It's just about me. That's all I know. I only know what I remember. I hold on to my memories because there have to be others who, like me, forgot to forget, and because so many who did forget are looking in all the wrong places for their lost memories. I'm just affirming the simple truth that I'm not alone in remembering. So with me, and others who remember, it has nothing to do with belief or faith."

What she said made absolutely no sense to him, so he never brought up the subject with her again. But Sand understood his silence as an answer that he, like just about everyone else in her life, didn't remember anything from before he was born. She wasn't going to spell it out for him so he could argue with her about it. She knew he was trying to find a way to get her to go to his church, but she wasn't interested. What she really wanted to tell him was, "It's not a matter of belief. I REMEMBER living BEFORE this life," but she knew he wouldn't understand.

She understood that for Jonathan, church
was like family—unconditional love. Jonathan's
was a kind and loving family, but for Sand, church
was like family—constant rejection and
denunciation. To Sand a kind, loving family was
one that didn't yell all the time, ignore you
whenever you asked a question, hit you with a fist,
or throw heavy, solid objects at you that made dents
in the wall behind you when you ducked. Still, she
didn't trust churches that didn't know about people
being reborn into new bodies after the old ones
died.

*

Sand dreamed one night that she was in her
mother's church. She could smell burning candle
wax. The candles everywhere were still burning
while rivers of melted wax spread outward in all
directions. Sand's mother was always soft spoken
and well behaved at church and at Sand's school.
She had the clergy and teachers convinced that she
was such a sweet, mild-mannered lady and
wonderful parent. They never saw the crazy, out of
control woman Sand lived with at home.

The priest came out onto the altar, only he
wasn't a priest with a Roman collar. He was a
protestant minister in a suit and tie. Only it wasn't a
minister, it was Jonathan. Jonathan commanded the
congregation to sing, and they sang. He ordered the
believers to pray, and they prayed. He directed the
faithful to stand and raise their arms upward to
heaven, and they stood and reached for the sky.
Sand realized Jonathan had total control over his
audience. That was what religion was about—total

control. The congregation raised their hands while their pockets were emptied.

Families were also about love or control, only Sand's had neither. Sand never told Jonathan about her dream. He would have taken it as a sign from God. She took it as a warning not to get robbed.

She understood that for Jonathan nothing that happened in the present ever mattered. It was all about the heaven he would be in when he left this world. Jonathan was in love with his perception and experience of God. And he sang so beautifully, Sand wanted to believe every word, at least until the performance was over. But Sand had to deal with the imperfect world she lived in. She had to stay aware of the present to survive it, because you never knew where you might end up next time around. Things could always get worse, and after her recent childhood experiences, she was in no hurry to have to go through childhood again any time soon.

*

After thinking over Jonathan's question and his silence in response to her answer, a few weeks later Sand asked Isabel straight out, "Do you remember living a different life before you were born into this one?"

Isabel answered, "I read a book about an American woman under hypnosis recalling a past life in Ireland, even though the woman had never been to Ireland in this life. It was a true story. Further investigation revealed that the woman she claimed to have been had actually lived a life much like the one described under hypnosis. They had similar interests and personalities, and close comparison of the faces showed similarities in the bone structure.

"There was also an American psychic named Edgar Cayce who told many people about their past lives. They might be different genders or races from life to life. Most of the world's people accept the premise of reincarnation as fact as opposed to the relatively smaller number of Christianity's population, but even some Christians, Jews, and Moslems also believe in reincarnation. In the Christian New Testament there's a verse, 'Who sinned, this man or his parents that he should be born blind?' He'd have to have lived before to have sinned to cause himself to be born blind."

Isabel never actually answered Sand's question, but she gave her a lot to think about, which Sand followed up on by checking many books out of the public library. For Sand it was like doors and windows being flung wide open all at once to let the daylight shine in on her little world for the very first time. At least now she felt she had been proven right after so many years.

Eventually they talked again about reincarnation. Sand told Isabel about her dreams and memories as a young child and about how her recounting of them was so poorly received by her mother and her mother's church. Isabel said as a matter of fact, "Then you're just remembering what you lived."

Before talking to Isabel, Sand had no idea anyone else ever talked about such things, but Isabel pointed out again how so many people in Asia not only accepted reincarnation, but took it for granted. It was part of their way of thinking and their way of life. Isabel was the first person to ever accept Sand's memories as fact. Sand felt reassured that she wasn't alone after all. So she decided to go a step further and tell Isabel about her recurring dreams of Patty accusing her of somehow betraying the rest of them.

Isabel laughed. "Patty's always been jealous of you," she revealed. "Haven't you noticed that? Your subconscious is probably just warning you not to trust her."

"I wonder if she was in my past life," Sand thought out loud.

"Maybe she betrayed you?" Isabel suggested. "Who knows what different roles we play in our different lives?"

Then Sand understood that Isabel saw reincarnation as an actor going from role to role rather than a more specific set of memories. But she also took Isabel's warning seriously that she should be careful around Patty. If anybody understood Patty, it was Isabel.

That spring Sand learned from Rick McDevitt that he also believed in reincarnation. Sand couldn't believe she had been afraid to mention it for fear he wouldn't go out with her anymore, but they had never discussed it before. When she asked him if he personally remembered living before, he didn't laugh at her or mock her. He answered, "No, but only the present matters. Living in the past is a distraction, and dwelling on the future is delusion."

That school year was Isabel and Patty's senior year. They took drama class together. Isabel admitted to Sand that she enjoyed taking on alternative personas and escaping into someone else's identity, while Patty craved an audience and applause. By this time neither Isabel nor Patty bothered with any pretense of interest in males.

Sand didn't sign up for drama class even though Isabel kept urging her to. Sand felt like she had enough drama to deal with every day without concerning herself with entertaining other people or trying to pretend she was someone else. Still she wondered if there wasn't some sort of fun she was missing out on. Why else would the drama students put themselves through what she perceived as so much stress? But Isabel and Patty never seemed to be enjoying themselves when they were memorizing or rehearsing their lines. Instead Sand tried to get onto the school newspaper staff, but she didn't make it. Her grades were just too average, and she didn't have any friends already there to help her. The only friend Sand had at the school that wasn't looked down on by the kids on the newspaper staff was Jonathan Moreau, and that was because he had been on the football team.

Jonathan had already quit the team by the end of January when he found out his mother was dying of cancer. It had started in her stomach and spread to her liver. By the time she became ill and the cancer was diagnosed, it had already metastasized. In those days, a cancer diagnosis was terminal at any stage. There was nothing the doctors could do for her but try to make her comfortable and minimize the pain with medication. Jonathan and Jill had already lost their father and Nathan, so that pretty much left Jonathan to take care of Jill. His mother died of cancer at the end of March.

Sand was keenly aware of Jonathan's loss, but she didn't know what to say to him other than that she was sorry and understood he was grieving. She tried to be there for him just to listen, but any attempt she made at conversation was met with his declarations of faith and invitations to pray with him or come to his church. His religious obsession made Sand and most of the friends they had in common, uncomfortable. They began to avoid him, and Sand saw very little of Jonathan after that.

*

May 4, 1970

It was spring and already hot outside. Just after the fifth-period starting bell had rung, a girl in Sand's American history class, who often talked about smoking pot, came running into class all upset about something.

"You won't believe what's just happened," she announced to the class. "There was an antiwar demonstration at Kent State in Ohio. The National Guard was called in to keep the peace, but the demonstrating students started throwing rocks at the National Guardsmen, and then the National Guard opened fire and shot and killed four students."

"What were they thinking?" Sand exclaimed.

"They're soldiers. They're trained to kill, and they killed four Americans," was the answer.

"No, I mean the students," Sand explained. "What were they thinking, throwing rocks at people with guns?"

The girl looked at Sand totally confused. "They were demonstrating against the war. The National Guard was the enemy."

"Why were they throwing rocks at people with guns? How stupid is that? And why were they throwing rocks if they were demonstrating against violence? And when did the National Guard become the enemy?" Sand asked.

The teacher called the class to order. Sand thought about what she might do if she had a gun and someone threw rocks at her. Well, that was a no-brainer. She'd run away. But the National Guardsmen were trained men, and men were more likely to shoot. As the teacher was speaking, Sand wondered why it was some people always had to have an enemy to hate.

The Kent State shootings were all over the news that night. It was just last summer the whole world seemed united over the moon landing. It was just last month that Apollo XIII was in the thoughts and prayers of people all over the planet. Now the country was divided yet again. Sand was becoming aware of just how quickly peoples' emotions could flip.

*

Before Isabel, Patty, Jonathan, Rick, and Matty graduated, Isabel and Patty seemed to no longer enjoy their togetherness as much as they had before. When the school year was over, Isabel went back to Warrington to live with her parents. Patty enrolled in classes at the University of Alabama in Huntsville, or UAH, that summer. She moved into the spare bedroom in her brother George's apartment. George Compton was also enrolled at UAH.

Chapter 11

Grasping at Space
(Strength)

Courage for the challenge
Is not found in anger
But in gentleness

*

Brenda:

Strength is often found in gentleness and imparted by kindness. The picture often used to represent it in the Tarot is a woman gently closing the jaws of a lion rather than provoking it with confrontation.

*

1970

Sergeant Major Barnes tried to force his son, Matthew, to learn to drive during his senior year, but Matty refused because cars polluted the environment. Since Huntsville, Alabama, had no form of mass transportation at that time, Matty was forced to walk any place he wanted to go. Matty's father threw him out of the house after graduation, so Matty got a job washing dishes at a restaurant.

He lived with Rick McDevitt's family until he had enough money saved up to pay the deposit on a cheap, efficiency apartment about a mile from the restaurant where he worked. He put a mattress on the floor for a bed and bought some pots and pans and dishes. Matty didn't require much in the way of material possessions. He never got a phone, so gradually he lost touch with most of his high school friends.

Sand never understood Matty's father. It seemed to her the man didn't understand that not everything could be conquered by force. He didn't even understand that the might of the United States armed forces couldn't even conquer tiny North Viet Nam. How could force work as a parenting strategy? Neither Matty nor his father was gifted with gentle persuasion.

Sand and Rick never officially broke up their relationship. They just saw each other less and less. Rick hadn't asked Sand to the senior prom because the event just wasn't meaningful to him. Sand understood that as a signal their dating was over, even though it didn't have much meaning for her either. They still saw each other that summer whenever their friends got together as a group.

Sand's mother, Louise, was angry about it. Going to the senior prom was an all important event to Louise and her imaginary position in society. She took it as a dreadful social insult.

Rick had a fortunate birthday in the draft lottery. He didn't think his conscientious objector status would have done him much good, so the lottery worked out well for him. A lot of southerners were against lotteries for fundraising causes because they called it gambling and said it was sinful, but they didn't raise any objections to the draft lottery, which was gambling with life instead of money. Still, it was better than only the economically less fortunate having to suffer the losses it entailed but, in Sand's opinion, it was still gambling with human life. Those with lucky birthdays, like Rick, were allowed to keep their lives. Many viewed the draft as service to their country, but many others saw no benefit to their country from blind service for a lost cause in another country that was no threat to the United States. Many loyal Americans saw it as another country's civil war that the US was interfering in big time and didn't understand why. The answers they received didn't justify the murderous meddling. Sometimes acting on the perceived need to prove one's strength to others only served to prove the fallacy of the delusion to oneself.

Denial of the constant change of reality is a problem for most people, Sand discovered. It wasn't limited to her mother or her family. One day she wrote in one of her notebooks, "Striving for a defined goal of a static condition will always result in disappointment and disillusionment until one realizes the innate transitory nature of that condition."

Sand came to view the Cold War as trying to reach such a static condition defined as victory over communism. She wrote, "The government and the military tend to define their goals by static conditions that, by nature, cannot persist. It is inevitable that if idyllic conditions are achieved in the physical world, they will not last. Communist revolutions of the twentieth century succeeded, but they can't stay that way forever. The Allies in World War II achieved victory over the Axis countries. Then everything changed. The United States seems to always be toppling other regimes it once supported. There is no permanence in politics, but still governments continue to tear families apart for temporary solutions to temporary, often invented, problems usually rooted in monetary schemes. The governments are temporary and made up of ordinary people. The politicians are temporary and just ordinary people. Our very lives are temporary. Even our appearance, age, and health are temporary. Since the common denominator of all the world's great religions, which are made up of ordinary people, is the teaching of love and compassion, it makes sense that the mantra, 'Make love, not war,' resonates around the world. Many practice the first half of that mantra, but most forget to practice the second half."

That fall, after Jonathan Moreau, Patty Compton, and their class graduated from high school and Sand was starting her senior year, Patty was living in her brother George's apartment. Patty and George were both enrolled in the university, but UAH had no dormitories at that time. George was majoring in political science, while Patty studied art. Both were vocal against the war in Viet Nam that had never been officially declared but had gone on for years, and for lifetimes for the families whose sons never came home or came home as damaged goods—maimed and broken. Not that Huntsville ever made the national news for antiwar protests. Sand, on the other hand, preferred to keep uneducated opinions to herself.

*

Brenda:

Many families in the United States were tired of allowing their government to throw away

142

their sons' lives in the civil war of an obscure country on the other side of the Pacific Rim that posed absolutely no threat to the United States. Most of the World War II generation, now the parents, had never even heard of Viet Nam when they had been in school, but it had invaded their living rooms via the evening news every night for more than a decade. The choice to fight or not to fight wasn't about patriotism or loyalty. It was about the credibility of the elected politicians who were supposed to represent their constituents instead of forcing unwanted military action on them. Nobody in the news media ever talked about whose investments were involved or how it all got started. By the early 1970s, the rest of the country had its share of antiwar protests and demonstrations, but in Huntsville, not so much.

Strength is force. Light is a force that can only be blocked by physical density, but like any true force of Nature, it cannot be stopped. Everyone knows that to get what one wants, one has to make it happen. The force of choice is the most pervasive and gentle force in the universe. It works through individuals only, and no matter the options perceived, there is always another possibility.

Choices are limited only by perception. The United States perceived only the choice of fighting until military victory was achieved. By 1970, young American men of draft age had recognized that being drafted was not their only option. Those that realized they had a choice were not viewing global events in the same light as their government. Gurus and teachers from India, China, Japan, and Korea had been coming to the United States and Europe for decades teaching yoga, meditation, martial arts, and Buddhism. The years of Americans dying in

Southeast Asia had only served to shine more light on Asian cultures and alternative philosophies. The odd effect of starting a war with another country is that the country that starts it becomes inundated with the culture it attacks. Adolescence craves new information and experiences. There was a new emphasis among American youth on harmony and the inner self. Any individual choice must be arrived at individually to achieve the desired effect of inner harmony with one's natural self. The right choice can't be rushed or influenced by others. The most successful decisions are arrived at gently and peacefully in the quiet space of one's inner being.

*

Matthew Barnes never bothered to register for selective service. He would have opted for prison time rather than serving in the military if it had ever come down to that. Since Matty had refused to even learn the convenience of driving a car on the moral objection that automobiles with combustion engines were polluting the planet's atmosphere, he certainly would never have picked up a gun, even just to shoot at a paper target. That was before the days of recycled paper.

Sand was never close to Matty. She just knew him from school and because he was Rick's best friend, but after that summer she simply lost touch with him.

*

One night after watching George Compton clean his growing gun collection of varying firepower and listening to him talk about resisting the draft in a less than nonviolent way, Patty had a very vivid dream. She dreamed she met the actor Peter Fonda on campus. He was playing Frisbee with some other students, and Patty joined them. Somehow they all ended up at Peter's apartment. It turned out they were a revolutionary cell preparing for an inevitable showdown with the Federal Government by stockpiling weapons and explosives. Peter taught Patty how to load and shoot a rifle.

There was a knock on the door. It was a neighbor warning them that the Feds had finally found them, were gathering outside, and beginning to surround the building. One of the guys volunteered to set the explosives in the back entryway. He was volunteering to stay and die to ensure the explosives went off just at the moment the Feds rushed in. Patty said adamantly that she was staying with him to cover the front door. Peter and the others disappeared down into the basement hoping their secret exit would get them out to freedom.

The front door burst open and Patty opened fire. She was sure the two of them were about to meet a glorious end in a firefight or explosion. She was going to keep shooting until her friend behind her set off the explosion, and then it would all be over.

Her automatic rifle jammed. She desperately crawled to the back hallway as fast as she could. After her friend fixed her weapon, Patty crawled back to her corner where she could see the open front door. To her horror, she saw there were bodies piled on the floor just inside the door, and she could see some outside in the hallway as well. They were all in a varied assortment of civilian clothes. There were no badges. Even worse, none were armed. The only weapon in sight was Patty's, but it was too late to undo what she had done.

Not knowing what to make of things, Patty kept her rifle pointed at the front door. Then a middle-aged black man appeared on the threshold. He was dressed in army battle fatigues with the name "Star" on his chest above his right pocket, and his arms were raised in the air. There was no firearm in either hand or visible on his person. He said nothing. Patty hesitated as he slowly approached, and then she fired. The moment before he fell, blood appeared on his chest where his name had been. His eyes, still open and looking directly at her, glassed over. He dropped to the floor dead.

Just then, Peter Fonda and the others reappeared through the secret exit. Peter asked Patty, "What have you done?"

"I thought I was supposed to," she responded quietly, almost in a whisper. "How was I supposed to know they were innocent people?" The tears began to flow down her face. "What do we do now?"

"Well, we can't get away. We're surrounded, and there are just too many innocent bystanders in the building now to set off the explosives."

Patty put the weapon down on the floor. "I'll tell them I did it all," she said.

"Yes, you did," Peter acknowledged.

Patty turned herself in to the waiting law enforcement officers. Her hands were chained behind her back, and her feet were shackled as well. She was led away and put into the back of a police van. At the jail, she was booked and put into a cell much smaller than she had imagined with three other women. There were two sets of bunk beds with a toilet in between the beds. The cell was the same length as the bunks, and the only unoccupied floor space was between the bunks—the width of the stainless steel toilet plus a couple of inches on either side. The other three women were of African American descent. They didn't wait to start making rude comments about her being a lily white southern belle, a plantation mistress, and a slave owner. The walls began to close in on Patty. There was no escape. She was going to be there for the rest of her natural life.

When Patty awoke, she lay still trying to figure out the dream. She'd never pictured herself in jail before. She had never thought about what it would really be like to be imprisoned. She had been taking her freedom for granted. But then she realized that she wasn't free in the dream before her arrest, because she was robotically doing whatever she thought others expected. Was she really like that? She had always pictured herself as a free spirit, a rebel against conformity.

And why Peter Fonda???

???

Peter Fonda???

Peter Fonda. An actor???

What did he represent in the dream? What did she know about him? Well, he was an actor. Patty imagined herself as an actor as well as an artist, but what did the dream really mean? Was she following him because he was popular or famous?

Peter Fonda???

???

Well, he was also male. Maybe she should avoid men altogether? No, that just wasn't possible or practical.

???

Maybe she should try to avoid doing what men seemed to expect of her.

But Peter Fonda???

What else did she know about him? Well, let's see. Peter Fonda was Jane Fonda's brother. Jane Fonda was against the Viet Nam war.

???

Peter Fonda was Jane Fonda's BROTHER.

Later that morning, Patty called Julie, a petite, pretty girl with short, mousy brown hair who was in Patty's English literature class. After a lot of small talk, Patty asked Julie to meet her at a coffee shop downtown that was a popular hangout for the college kids. They met, and a relationship was born. About six weeks later, they rented an apartment together, and Patty moved out of George's place and away from all his guns.

When George got his draft notice, he fled to Quebec, Canada, leaving his weapons behind in his vacated apartment.

Chapter 12

Snared
(Hanged Man)

Changing times bring changing ways
And some catch on too late
Opposites compete for space
But only forgiveness can overcome hate

*

Brenda:

Not all problems could be solved whenever anyone wanted. Our perceived problems were probably just part of some universal balancing act. Solutions didn't always seem to present themselves. Sometimes we found ourselves in situations where we'd made choices that led us so far away from our natural course that it was best in the long run to stop trying to correct things and allow things to balance themselves of their own accord.

Sometimes all a person could do was let go and surrender to the circumstances at hand. Sometimes that was the only way to find one's way back to the path one was meant to be on. That's the message of The Hanged Man, who hangs upside down by one foot. Awkward situations could be opportunities to see things from a different perspective.

*

Franki deMerle

September 1970

Sand's senior year of high school turned violent. The high school football team called themselves the Rebels, and there was a giant Confederate flag painted across the back wall of the school gymnasium. It was six years after the Civil Rights Bill had been signed into law, but people only change when they're ready. Legislating people's beliefs is contrary to human nature, but sometimes it's best to try while keeping in mind that people may still choose hate if that's their habit. Tolerance and patience must be learned, and it's a long process. Extreme tolerance and patience are often required of mere humans on the receiving end of hate. People have different breaking points.

If the law had been enforced, Reverend Martin Luther King and his supporters wouldn't have had to march, and they wouldn't have been beaten and jailed by the officers and deputies sworn to enforce the law. White history buffs were too busy claiming that the Confederate flag was part of their history and heritage to care how it made the descendants of slaves feel having it waved in their faces every day. Of course, those same white people were still claiming the Civil War had been fought over states' rights rather than slavery. They almost made the bloodshed sound romantic, but it was just semantics since the states' rights they were fighting over were the states' "rights" to allow slavery to exist. The Confederacy was nothing more than a class system financed by the social elite minority. No one was entitled to "rights" who wasn't of their social standing. The vast majority of those who had fought and died for it really died to end any hope of regaining "rights" they'd lost by leaving the Union.

They were really dying because they had so little to
live for. Elitism makes life miserable for everyone
not part of the elite.

In support of the high school football team,
the school band always played the song *Dixie*, the
infamous old Confederate anthem with its
degrading insinuations for those with darker skin, at
the pep rallies and football games. A lot of students
were tired of all that reveling in a very ugly, bloody,
and bitter past. Not all of them were descendants of
slaves, but most were. They were ready to move on
into a promised free society where they could have
the same opportunities as everybody else sharing
the great American dream.

A group of students met with school
officials and got the officials to agree that the band
would stop playing *Dixie*. Sand wasn't at the
meeting, but it was publicized on TV and in the
newspaper, and Sand was happy with the decision.
She and her friends, both black and white, felt
relieved that the issue had been resolved.

Pep rallies were gatherings of students to
show support for ball teams. The students, faculty,
and school administrators would get together and
shout a lot and try to will the team to win. Sand
figured that it made the participants feel like they
were more than spectators at a spectator sport. That
encouraged them to actually come to the games. It
also gave them something to shout about. Shouting
was easier than actually participating in the sport,
and not everybody could anyway. It was a social
thing, kind of like going to church. People came
together to share something they believed in, only
the churches were still segregated while the school
was not. Everybody that participated in a pep rally
brought with it their own symbolism and what the

school, the people, the team, and life in general meant to them. The kids in school at that time had grown up with strong feelings, both pro and con, about the Civil War and the Civil Rights Movement.

At the first football pep rally that school year, the band played *Dixie*. Sand was standing at the top of the stairs near the school offices and heard the music blaring up from downstairs. Sand didn't like to go to pep rallies because they were noisy and pretty much all alike. She'd been to them before. That was enough for her. She still felt stung by the way the football coach had directed some of his team to beat up Matty Barnes her first year there.

As Sand stood there and watched, a group of black students came up the stairs and were met by the principal, who had just come out of his office. The students respectfully asked, "May we speak to you, sir?"

He told them brusquely, "Y'all get on down to the pep rally where y'all belong," as he walked past them and down the stairs to the pep rally.

At first the students just stood there stunned, looking at each other. One of the girls shrugged and started down the stairs. The others followed after her. By the time they reached the foot of the stairs, the principal was on the stage addressing the students saying, "Let's show 'em who's boss."

That's when Sand saw the white guys at the foot of the stairs attack the two girls leading the black kids who'd just come down the stairs. It started with grabbing, and quickly escalated to fists. Knives came out, students were stabbed, and it quickly became a riot.

Sand didn't go down the stairs. She froze. Other students already downstairs were brave enough to try to pull kids out of the fight. One of them was Michael Latimer, idealist and one-time founder of Michael Land. Sand watched from the top of the stairs. Once the knives came out, went into other kids, and there was blood, she'd seen enough. Fear overcame her and she ran. She hid in a corner by the pay phones until a girl she knew came by. They decided to use one of the phones to call the local newspaper to alert the paper to what has happening. Her friend did the talking and was perfectly clear that the white guys had attacked the black kids at the instigation of the principal.

When the ambulances and police arrived, only injured white students were allowed in the ambulances. Michael and some of his friends realized what was happening. There were more white students than black, but there were more injured black students than white. The real teamwork came when Michael and his friends managed to sneak the more seriously injured black kids past the police, through the parking lot, and to a car parked in the neighborhood behind the school, because the student who parked it there hadn't bothered to get a parking permit for the school parking lot, which was now barricaded by the police.

Sand followed her friend who had made the phone call and helped from inside the school, passing the injured off to another friend waiting at one of the back doors. It was like an assembly line or an underground railroad. The first carload of injured kids was taken to the Latimer home, where Michael's mother took charge and arranged for other cars driven by adults to assist. Eventually the injured got the medical care they needed, and there were no fatalities.

After the news got out that there was fighting in the school, parents started showing up at school to take their kids home. Sand's mother came to the school, but Sand refused to leave. The riot was over. The local news media, in spite of the earlier phone call made by Sand's friend, blamed the black kids. That was expected but wrong.

*

It was ugly that school year. Police turned police dogs loose on kids in the parking lot who were just trying to leave a basketball game where fighting had started. The police did more to inflame tension and tempers than the principal.

Somebody threw black paint on the Confederate flag on the back of the gym wall. Sand was ecstatic when she saw it. She had always hated that flag. A federal judge down in New Orleans, Louisiana, ordered it to be painted out anyway. Sand was glad when it was gone. She also hated the song *Dixie*. She didn't like school very much either, and she was definitely not a football fan.

After the first big riot, smaller ones followed. There was no predictable pattern to the occurrence as far as Sand could distinguish—except for the presence of groups of both races. Sand learned early on that whenever the police were around there would be trouble, but fortunately there weren't enough police on the force to be a constant presence. Their uniformed presence was meant to keep order, but of course, it consisted solely of white males who had been raised during segregation.

Deception Past

One day during lunch time when Sand was avoiding being in the commons area, which served multiple functions such as pep rallies in the morning and cafeteria at lunch, she walked the upstairs hallways for lack of anything better to do. The building was built of three triangular sections, a center, and an administrative area. The library was above the commons area in the center. The way the building was laid out, it was easy to walk around in triangles in lieu of circles indefinitely. No one's mind could possibly be on studying, or at least Sand's wasn't. Usually there were only a lot of people in the halls when classes were changing, so she felt safe. At this time, students who didn't have lunch had class, and students who had lunch tended to be downstairs in the commons area. The halls at this time of the day were usually pretty much deserted, so Sand walked the halls like a zombie in shock. After all that had happened, she was emotionally numb.

Then Sand turned a corner only to find two mobs of students, one black and one white, facing off against each other. The tension was palpable. Sand had white skin and black friends. Most of the white students there referred to Sand as a "nigger lover," but most of the black kids in the other mob didn't know her. She had been walking almost hypnotically for so long that she just kept her pace, said, "Excuse me," and walked straight through the narrow space dividing the two groups. Once she'd turned the next corner, she looked back over her shoulder and saw both mobs had dispersed. The next day she went back to spending her lunch time in the commons area with some of her friends.

*

Sand had begun that school year taking physics for her science class, but the male teacher had encouraged the few girls brave enough to elect his class to drop it by only explaining concepts in sports metaphors. He refused to acknowledge any female student who had a question, and treated the girls like they weren't there. They got the message. Sand was one of the first to go. She didn't like being where she wasn't wanted. She was devastated, as she was truly interested in learning physics, but didn't see that she had any other option. She knew better than to try to protest to the school administration.

Her parents tried to console her by telling her that physics class just wasn't appropriate for ladies. Sand resented that but kept it to herself. She switched to earth science. The assistant principal who changed her schedule assured her that she had made a wise choice as the earth science teacher was female. Somehow that made the subject more appropriate for her.

On one of the quieter school days that year, the pride of the school administration in their modern space-age, windowless building was deflated a bit by the lowly custodial staff. It was hot and humid outside, but at least there was shade and an occasional breeze to be found. It was hot inside, and the air was stifling and still. The custodial staff had gone on strike that morning and had turned off the air conditioning system before they left. Everyone was peeling off whatever clothing they could get away with and fanning themselves with papers and notebooks.

While Sand was sitting in her third period earth science class that morning, an announcement came over the school's intercom, "The air conditioning has been turned off, but it will be turned back on as soon as we locate the switch. All emergency exit doors are to remain securely closed and locked. No doors will be opened, and no one is allowed to leave the building."

Sand's earth science teacher was Canadian. She had moved to Huntsville, Alabama, because her husband, a US citizen, had landed one of the much sought after jobs at Redstone Arsenal. Sand's teacher stared at the loudspeaker in total disbelief for a few moments before walking over to the classroom's emergency door and propping it open. This was in the days before surveillance cameras in schools.

"I will not allow my students to be roasted in an oven," she declared. "If you need to leave, do so quietly, and don't get caught."

Sand gathered that Canadians didn't much care for excessive heat or nonsense that flew in the face of common sense. She loved Canadians from that moment on and for the rest of her life.

*

Sand saw pretty Sylvia Masterson in the hallway between classes from time to time that year. Sylvia and her sisters were more interested in moving up in society than challenging it. Their only hope for a decent future was to marry a good provider. Sylvia's older sister, Candace, had managed to snag a husband that was not only a good provider, but handsome and popular. He was a rock and roll guitarist. The Masterson sisters wanted to survive, so they didn't involve themselves in politics. They knew they wouldn't be going to college, so finding a husband in high school was their sole mission. As a senior without a steady boyfriend, Sylvia was running out of time.

One day Sylvia asked Sand, "Why were you hippies demonstrating at lunch yesterday?"

"What?" was all Sand could think to say. She never thought of herself or her friends as hippies. Yes, they were out of step with the racism of the past and present, and yes, they were opposed to unnecessary war. Well, if that made Sand a hippie, then so be it. She'd been labeled, but demonstrating?

"Everybody's talking about the sit-in at lunch yesterday," Sylvia bubbled. Sylvia loved gossip. Maybe it filled a primeval need for storytelling that was void in the lives of those who didn't read books.

Whatever, Sand thought. Sylvia clearly wanted to get the scoop on the big event so she could give her friends the inside story. Sand thought back to lunchtime the day before. Then she remembered. "The table and chairs where we usually sit were missing, and the commons area was crowded, so we sat on the floor," she explained to Sylvia. It had seemed a practical enough solution at the time.

"But what were you protesting?" Sylvia persisted, only listening for a more sensational answer.

"There weren't enough chairs, so we sat on the floor," Sand tried again.

"OK. Have to go." Sylvia ran off smiling as if she'd heard what she wanted to hear. Sand shook her head as she watched Sylvia disappear into the crowd down the hall. She wondered what the next misconception had just become.

*

Sand took to skipping school two and three days a week. Her homeroom teacher never marked her or anyone else absent anymore unless a student advised her in advance they wouldn't be there. Some of the teachers were sympathetic to the stress the students were experiencing and the fear they had of being there. The fair-skinned police patrolling the halls occasionally only seemed to antagonize the underlying tension. White kids sensed the police were there as their personal protection and that the black students would be the scapegoats for any trouble. It's the way it had always been in the Deep South, and that was certainly the way it appeared to be playing out to students of both races and to the public at large who relied on the reports of the local news media. White kids were taken away in ambulances while black kids were taken away in police vans. One result of all of this chaos was that illegal substances began to be exchanged and used freely by the white kids in the school lavatories and parking lot. Sand learned that marijuana smelled like the girls' restroom and the southwest side of the parking lot. She wondered where it all came from, but not enough to ask. Except for those she considered friends, she wasn't inclined to talk to anyone.

*

Franki deMerle

1971

On a warm day in February while Sand wasn't in school, she walked through the field at the end of Delaney, the street she lived on, to the woods and the tree house. There was a familiar sweet but heavy smoke in the air surrounding the old pine tree.

"Hey!" she called up, not wanting to climb up without knowing who was there.

Michael Latimer stuck his bushy head out, smiled, and yelled, "Hey!" back down to her.

She climbed up. He showed her how to smoke marijuana, and they took turns taking tokes off the joint. The smoke clouded Sand's brain and senses, and she drifted into a giggling stupor. Michael turned the joint around, put the lit end into his mouth and brought the other end to hers, and blew. He almost blew her over the side of the tree house. She loved it. "It's called a shotgun," he instructed her.

"Let me try," she giggled.

"Be careful not to burn your mouth," he cautioned.

She took what was left of the joint and returned the shotgun. After that, whenever Sand was with people who were smoking pot and she didn't want to, she would take the joint that was passed to her and do shotguns to everyone else, trying only to inhale the secondary smoke.

When the joint was finished, the two of them cuddled together. Hands wandered. Sand was in too much of a relaxed stupor to flinch at Michael's touch. She felt safe. It helped that all was quiet. They were safe and alone high up in a tree in

160

the deserted woods. She loved the feel of his soft, dark curls.

He kissed her and she kissed back. Tongues intertwined, warm, gentle, moist, and sensitive. They unbuttoned each other's shirts together and unzipped each other's jeans. Sand enjoyed stroking his erection and exploring his genitals with her hand. When Michael explored her own, she melted. All inhibitions had been cancelled by her body, and he climbed on top of her and gently slid inside her. All it took was a couple of thrusts and her body turned into an explosion of blazing heat and pleasure that seemed to continue forever until he was finished. Afterward they fell asleep in each other's arms. It was the first time she had felt totally relaxed in a very long time. It was the first time in her life she had experienced any degree of physical affection and intimacy. It was a new experience for her and she completely surrendered herself to it. She fell in love with Michael in a special way that would always last but never have any strings attached.

*

By March, Sand had become good friends with Chrissie Jackson, a sophomore. They bonded over their love of poetry. Chrissie was an avid fan of Emily Dickinson. She had read everything she could find in the library that mentioned the famous poet's name. Sand had only read the Dickinson, Frost, e.e. cummings, and others required for English class, but had continued amassing her own original collection. Chrissie was over-the-top, exuberant, dramatic, and an incredible optimist and romantic. Chrissie was petite, dark, and of African

American descent. Sand and Chrissie agreed that the whole concept of race was paper thin and totally subjective. Whenever they were asked the race question on a form, Chrissie and Sand learned to just write Human.

The Civil Rights Act of 1964 had abolished segregated drinking fountains and segregated public toilets. Huntsville didn't have any city buses other than school buses, but even though the black kids were no longer required to sit in the back of the bus, it was still too dangerous for Chrissie and Sand to sit next to each other. Boys got beat up for doing that, and girls got raped for it. There would have been separate, segregated buses if the town had enough to go around. "Separate but equal" was a favorite slogan of Southern white politicians, but it really meant that the impoverished blacks got whatever they could afford while the whites kept them on the bottom rung of the economic ladder. At least in Huntsville, Sand and Chrissie were allowed to ride the same school buses as long as they didn't sit together. Sand wasn't supposed to bring Chrissie home with her either. Mostly they would talk at school or meet in a secluded spot at a park on weekends.

Chrissie fell in love that year with a guy in Sand's English class, but he turned out to be homosexual. Still, he went out with Chrissie to keep up appearances. At least he took her to the prom. On weekends in the park, the two of them liked to act out scenes from Shakespeare. Sand was usually the audience.

Chrissie started bringing poems to school that, at first, she said she'd found in her notebooks or on scraps of paper at home, but later admitted she'd discovered that she had written them in her sleep. They were written backwards, right to left in mirror writing, and they were fun to decipher. Chrissie could read them just as if they'd been written normally.

Sand thought Chrissie's poetry was pretty good. Neither Sand nor Chrissie used much punctuation, but they both had rhythm and rhyme (neither rigid) and some interesting thoughts. While Sand studied German, Chrissie was in French class. One day during lunchtime, Chrissie was even more excited than usual. Sand didn't even have a chance to ask why before Chrissie sat down across from her at the lunch table, pulled a piece of paper out of a notebook, and showed it to her.

"I wrote one frontwards," Chrissie said proudly, and then she proceeded to read it out loud to Sand.

> "Pourquoi dois-je faire des vers?
> Qu'est-ce que je devrais être?
> Laquelle est plus importante—
> Etre une poète ou être une amie?
> Ce sont l'une et l'autre partie de ma vie
> Si j'étais une poète
> Je serais toujours seule
> Je ne peux que faire des vers
> Quand je suis seule
> Les autres hommes revivraient ma vie
> Mais je l'écrirais seulement—mais si
> Je cherche à être une bonne amie
> Je ne serai jamais seule
> Je suis une poète mais
> Je ne voudrais pas être seule
> Ainsi fais-je des vers pour mes amis"

"That's beautiful," Sand commented even though she hadn't understood a word of it. "You're bilingual as well as bidirectional. Truly multidimensional."

Chrissie didn't have any brothers or sisters, and her only friends were her pseudo-boyfriend and Sand. Sand was angry that she couldn't invite Chrissie over to her house occasionally. Sand had broached the subject once with her mother, who was horrified at the notion. Sand didn't want to bring Chrissie home only to have her mother create a scene and make Chrissie feel unwelcome.

Sand was very interested in the dreams Chrissie was having when she wrote poetry and encouraged her to pay attention when she first woke up every morning to try to remember what she had been dreaming, and then to write down whatever it was.

"It's easier once you teach yourself to lie still when you first wake up," Sand explained. "Once you move, it's harder to remember."

Chrissie Jackson was a quick study. At first what she remembered were stanzas of poems. Then she started telling Sand about how she was dressed while she was writing, wearing an ankle-length dress. Eventually, bit by bit, after piecing together many different dreams, she was able to tell a more complete story and describe the whole house where she would write in her dreams. It was a large, two-story red brick house on a hill surrounded by wooded land. The house faced south. There was a flower and herb garden in the back of it on the east side. Her bedroom was upstairs. She lived with her family. They were all white.

Someone she cared about a great deal, maybe more family, lived in a smaller home down a path through the woods to the west. To enter Chrissie's house, one went up several porch steps. The room where Chrissie dreamed she was writing was to the right of the foyer. She would sit at a small desk and write at night. Chrissie guessed by the furnishings, the lack of electricity, and by the style of her dress that she was dreaming she was in the nineteenth century. Her dress was usually brown or some neutral or earthy color. She insisted it was New England. Sand asked her how she knew, but Chrissie said she just knew.

She also said she knew that she was single, and that there was a single bed in her bedroom upstairs. As she continued to explore her recurring scenario, she became aware that a war was being fought to free the slaves, that she was in favor of abolishing slavery, and that she was a free white woman—at least as far as women were free in those days. Chrissie preferred the night to the day because it was quiet and peaceful. It was a good time to be with her thoughts and write them down.

Chrissie remembered living with her family, and they had a good life. She played piano, tended her garden, cooked, and wrote poetry. She wasn't active in any organized religion and didn't attend church. Even in this life, Chrissie wasn't one to take church too seriously.

Chrissie preferred daisies over roses. She wrote poetry about trees, flowers, birds, animals, rocks of different colors, snow, and the play of sunlight and moonlight. She always dreamed of the family having their own piano and her sister had a sleigh bed. She loved the colors and the sounds and the seasons. Chrissie was somewhat nearsighted, and her glasses were always dirty and smudged. Sand always wondered if Chrissie was more nearsighted with or without them, so from time to time Sand would clean them for her.

As Sand approached her graduation date, she wondered what different directions she and Chrissie would go in and if they would continue to see each other or gradually lose touch as seemed to happen to so many good school friends.

*

Sand, Chrissie, Michael Latimer, and the rest of the student body learned shortly before graduation that after the original agreement not to play *Dixie*, there had been an unpublicized meeting in which somebody decided it was alright for the band to play *Dixie* if they also played a Negro spiritual. The people involved in the conspiracy of the private meeting just didn't bother to tell the people affected by their decision. They couldn't have been concerned about how others would feel about it since they were self-elected representatives, and that's probably why they didn't want anybody to know. That sort of lack of communication caused one hell of a misunderstanding. Maybe everybody at the meeting thought everybody else would tell the students. The principal didn't bother to tell anyone who asked to speak with him that morning before the riot. He didn't believe he needed to explain anything to any colored kids. Maybe he didn't feel he was required to explain anything to any kids. By his standards, the "coloreds" were lucky just to be attending his school at all. No one seemed to know if he was aware of the private meeting or if he even cared. He didn't bother to listen to what the students wanted to say to him for that matter. Maybe he was just in a hurry to get to the pep rally that had started without him.

A lot of kids, including Sand Strasberg, Chrissie Jackson, and Michael Latimer, thought the principal was making a white supremacist comment about who was boss when he got downstairs and took the microphone on stage, and that his comment was intended to lead the majority of students to subdue the school's minority population, but unfortunately that was also a misunderstanding. The principal was just trying to run a pep rally and support the football team. He wanted his school's team to show the other school's team "who was boss." After all, ball teams were a source of income for schools.

The police didn't understand the changes in society any better than the high school students or the school principal. Everyone was afraid, and adrenaline flowed freely and ruled the day. It was hard to reason with one's own biology when one was busy being manipulated by it.

Sand didn't bother to attend her own graduation even though it was supposed to be mandatory. She was afraid it would end up being another race riot. She would always be afraid of large groups of people after what she'd seen. She was happy just to have survived in spite of having white skin and black friends. Everyone else in her class was presented a high school diploma at the graduation ceremony. Sand didn't really care about the piece of paper, because the school records showed that she'd completed high school, but her mother wanted the diploma. Sand knew the school had to have made one up for her and reasoned it would be kept in the administration office.

School was over for graduating class once the graduation ceremony had taken place, but there was one more day left in the school year for the underclass students to receive their final report cards. Sand went to the office that morning and asked the secretary if she could pick up her diploma. The secretary walked over to an almost empty bookshelf on the far side of the office and picked up Sand's diploma. She carried it back across the room and laid it on the counter across from where Sand was standing.

"Why weren't you at the graduation ceremony?" the secretary asked.

"There was a death in my family," Sand lied.

"I'm so sorry. Please give my condolences to your family, and please wait while I clear this with the assistant principal," the secretary said.

"Sure," Sand agreed smiling back at her. Just as the secretary walked into an adjoining office, the front double doors behind Sand opened, and a mob of teachers poured into the office. They seemed angry.

The teachers, some of whom Sand knew, were all talking at once demanding their missing paychecks. No one was even looking at Sand. She decided not to wait around to find out what was going on. She didn't care to get caught near any more riots of any kind, so she reached across the counter, grabbed her diploma, and ran out a side door as fast as she could.

Louise Strasberg was very pleased to receive Sand's high school diploma. The newspaper reported that summer that the high school principal had mistakenly deposited a large amount of the school's money into his own personal bank account.

It was also announced that the principal had decided to retire. There was no prosecution. It was, after all, just a mistake.

Chapter 13

Transitions
(Death)

Find your passion and pursue it
Live your feelings and transmute them
Pain feels like a death
A cicada climbs out of its skin

*

June 1971

Sand moved through the woods and
undergrowth that bordered the highway being
careful to remain out of sight. She was grateful for
the moonlight through the clearing of the road that
gave her just enough light to maneuver through the
chaotic growth. Occasionally she would stumble
into a spider web, but the adrenaline rush from each
such encounter only pushed her forward. She was
counting on Nature to quickly recoup and
extinguish the traces she left behind. But once the
moon set, she had only the options of moving
blindly with the risk of falling and injuring herself
or stopping to rest.

She hoisted herself up onto a tree branch and
then another and, closing her eyes, settled her back
against the trunk. When she awoke, it was daylight
and traffic along the highway was constant. She was
exhausted, but the grumbling in her empty stomach
wouldn't stop long enough to let her doze off again.
She ate a couple of crackers and swallowed two big

mouthfuls from her water bottle. That bought her enough quiet to let her sleep until late in the day. There was still too much traffic on the highway to risk being seen, but her back, neck, and legs were stiff, so she climbed down off her perch and stretched on the far side of the tree, away from the road. She had no idea where she was, how far she had come, or how long she'd been doing this. She moved further into the woods until the sounds of the highway were barely discernible over the din of birds above and crickets and cicadas all around.

It was dusk when Sand came upon a stately old oak still wearing the remnants of a tree house high in its branches. There were just enough oddly shaped pieces of wood still attached to the far side of its trunk—moss covered and almost invisible, but there nonetheless—for her to make it up to the lowest branch, and after that, alternating attached wood and branches as footholds, she climbed into the remains of the roofless structure. She spent the night there, and in the morning began the work of finding a nearby stream for water and various edibles in the area. She found dandelions, mullein, and Queen Anne's Lace in a clearing just downstream. "When you're tired and hungry enough, odd tastes can be acquired," she mused to herself.

She wasn't successful in her attempts to carry fallen branches up to her new nest to make a roof, so she decided the living branches of the oak would have to suffice. After numerous days (she lost track of how many, probably because she wasn't counting), the cracker supply that had once filled her backpack was gone. She sampled various evergreen barks and even considered the protein of bugs, but decided not to go there. Her clothes were getting loose. The days were getting shorter, and the nights were definitely becoming downright cold. Realizing the red canopy of leaves she was now living under wouldn't last much longer, she decided to take her empty backpack and freshly filled water bottle and move on.

Sand followed the stream at her own now much less energetic pace, as it widened into a small river. Occasionally she'd spot a house, cabin, or tended field through the trees, and a few footpaths coming down to the river, some on the opposite bank and some on her side, but she never ran into anyone else. There was a deer at one point and at another a cat. She heard barking one night but never saw the dog. The river widened and the trees thinned.

Sand was tired. There were blisters on two of her toes. Her feet hurt and her head was swimming. She took off her shoes and put them in her backpack. There was no particular reason, but she'd walked so far—not in any measurable units because she had no idea how far—in those shoes they now seemed a part of her. She put her arms through the straps of her backpack one last time and waded out into the river.

The water was cold. She was chilled to the bone, as they say, but it felt good to no longer have to walk. It felt good to no longer have to unscrew the lid of the water bottle just to swallow a sip. She thought about getting out of the water to take off her clothes, now even looser and very heavy, and to empty the water bottle, but the undercurrent was too strong and she had too little strength left. She was still conscious as the river swept her into a much larger river where she was barely able to see the shore in the distance. She watched a bridge pass way above her between the water and the endless sky.

Sand was amazed, though not quite certain of what she was seeing, as she passed the side of a metal giant. She thought maybe she was an ant on a tree trunk. Then, as close as it had been, the monstrous ship shrank into the distance. There were no more horizons. The light faded from Sand's eyes as the darkness closed in all around her and swallowed her like a fog swallows all sense of direction. The alarm clock brought her out of it.

*

July 1971

Chrissie Jackson was physically as well as emotionally exuberant. She always greeted Sand with a hug. By this time in her life, Sand had learned to control her urge to cringe and back away when touched by a friend, but she had to work hard to learn how to actually return the hug she was given. Her sexual encounter with Michael Latimer had been a big help. Chrissie offered Sand lots of opportunities to practice this new skill.

Michael and Sand never actually dated. Making love in the tree house was just a onetime, spontaneous event. Sand didn't tell anyone else about it. She preferred to keep the cherished memory to herself.

After Sand finished high school and started classes that summer at UAH, the local university, she and Chrissie continued to spend time together outside of class. Chrissie introduced Sand to a non-profit, alcohol-free club where teenagers could hang out. It was supervised by young adults and as such was interracial. It was called The Gathering Place. Chrissie would go there on Friday and Saturday evenings unless she was home reading or writing. The Gathering Place was cheaply furnished with a small stage and an old upright piano. Soft drinks and snacks were sold. Sometimes Chrissie would play piano. Sometimes someone would bring their guitar and sing for entertainment.

Sand was surprised to learn that one of the occasional performers was Patty Compton. When Patty was there she was always accompanied by her girlfriend Julie. They were inseparable. Sand didn't know Julie, but she remembered how inseparable Patty and Isabel Akbey had been and wondered what had gone wrong. She never forgot Isabel's warning that she should be careful around Patty.

Then one Friday night at The Gathering Place, Chrissie introduced Sand to Steve Fernandez. He was only an inch taller than Sand, had brown eyes, black hair, a neatly trimmed beard, and wore a denim cap his mother had made for him out of worn out blue jeans. Dressed just like Sand that night, he was wearing a T-shirt and black jeans. It was love at first sight for both Sand and Steve. Sand spent the rest of the evening talking and listening to Steve. They agreed they must have known each other in a past life. He did most of the talking. Steve saw a beautiful woman, and Sand had found someone she felt comfortable and safe with. She didn't even notice when Chrissie left.

Even by the 1970s, there was virtually no noticeable Latino presence in Huntsville. Steve was born in Texas on a fortunate day that would be drawn as number 362 in his year for the draft lottery. His mother was unwed and pregnant when she came across the border into the United States from Mexico. They had settled in Birmingham when he was a little boy. She worked as a motel maid. Steve moved to Huntsville on his own when he finished high school. His mother was still living and working in Birmingham.

Steve worked as a custodian at Huntsville High School across town, but his true calling was his art. His preferred medium was anything three-dimensional. He worked as a custodian to support his sculpture habit. After their initial encounter, Steve and Sand met every Friday and Saturday evening at The Gathering Place and stayed until closing.

Sand's parents were not pleased. They didn't like Steve Fernandez. Not only was he merely a custodian, but his mother had come from Mexico. She and Steve spoke Spanish. Her parents complained to Sand that he was of the wrong ethnicity. The Strasbergs' prejudice against Steve angered Sand even more than her parents were angry with prejudice. Sand's grandmother came from Germany and spoke German. As far as Sand was concerned, twentieth century German history was nothing to be proud of. Besides, more people in the world spoke Spanish than German. For that matter, more people in the western hemisphere spoke Spanish than English. If anything, the Strasbergs were the outsiders. At least Steve's parents were born on the same continent, and he came from a Roman Catholic background. That should have at least made Louise happy.

Sand wondered what the point was of her parents spending so much money to send her to a Catholic elementary school with integrated textbooks if no one was going to learn anything from it. Custodial work was honest, and Steve was also a very creative artist. He had talent and was willing to work. The Strasbergs' hypocrisy made Sand all the more determined to marry him. Sand saw him for his values and charm. She had read a projection in the newspaper that by the end of the millennium white males would no longer hold a solid majority in the United States work force or US politics. She looked forward to that day.

*

August 1971

Jody, like most of the young men he knew, had no desire to go to Southeast Asia and fight in the jungle in a civil war that caused no threat to his country or way of life, but he wanted the veterans' benefits to pay for more schooling. So he enlisted in the army hoping that speaking fluent German would help him be sent to Europe and a Germany that was divided between the West and the communist Soviet Union instead of Viet Nam. It worked. First the army sent him to its language school at the Presidio of Monterey in California and taught him to speak Russian, and then he was stationed in Berlin, the divided city in the middle of East Germany, the German Democratic Republic. He stayed there for the rest of his four-year hitch with the army. Even though he never saw action, he came home emotionally damaged. He was probably emotionally damaged before he ever enlisted, but being thrown into a world he didn't understand, didn't like, and wasn't prepared for didn't help. Life had a way of being like that for many who grew up defensive and afraid and without adequate self-esteem or confidence. Fear could cripple. For some, the fight or flight reflex was damaged early on and only responded as freeze.

*

October 1971

Jill Moreau, Jonathan's sister, over whom he had inherited guardianship, was just a year younger than Sand. After Sand started college that summer, Jill had eloped with a man named Clifford, who had been a friend of Jody's and Nathan, Jill, and Jonathan's late older brother. Clifford had a birth defect, a deformed left foot, which had rendered him unacceptable for military service.

Jill and Clifford got married across the state line in Ardmore, Tennessee. At first Jonathan was devastated. He felt that he had somehow failed not only Jill but the entire Moreau family in heaven as well. He turned to his Christian faith for solace and began writing songs of faith.

Once Jonathan was free of guardianship over Jill, he deeded the Moreau home in Sherwood Park over to Jill and Clifford. Jonathan relocated to Nashville, Tennessee, to take advantage of the music industry opportunities there. Jonathan had inherited what savings and life insurance his parents had stashed away, which was enough for him to buy enough equipment to set up his own recording studio in his new home in Nashville. He enlisted in the Tennessee National Guard and became a chaplain's assistant. He also performed and recorded his songs, and went on to become a pioneer in the American Christian pop music industry. Jonathan made his living, such as it was, traveling from church to church performing his original, heartfelt songs. He was very persuasive.

He wrote, performed, recorded, and lived for his personal ministry. By the time the Christian popular music industry hit the big time in the 1980s, Jonathan was right in the middle of it. Through it all, he sang out his heart and soul with a golden voice to anyone who would listen. That was his chosen profession—to share his talent for the Lord.

Jill was eight months pregnant when she and Clifford were in a fatal car crash that left no survivors.

*

Brenda:

Death is like exfoliation. The natural state of existence in all worlds is change. Physical death is the ultimate, though inevitable, transition. Identities are temporary. Individual lives are just short stories comprising larger volumes that cannot be read on our microscopic scale. Old cells die. Our appearance is continually changing, and yet we learn by recognizing and remembering patterns. Life is temporary, and death is no different than a snake or June bug shedding its skin.

*

January 1972

During her second term in college at UAH, Sand went to work part-time for her Aunt Clarabelle. Clarabelle now ran an accounting business out of her home in southeast Huntsville. She hired Sand as her secretary and gradually began to teach the business to her. Most of her business

was doing federal and state income taxes for clients.
Sand worked four hours a day, three days a week
for Clarabelle while taking a full load of classes.
She still lived with her parents and used their
second used car to travel back and forth.

Chapter 14

Alchemy Through Moderation
(Temperance)

Mind and body
Death and life
Duality inherent
In dual sight

Even the boundaries
Sands and tides
Are blurred together
And lost in time

*

Brenda:

My Temperance card is depicted by an angel
balancing two goblets of water. It symbolizes the
eternal balance between elements, water and fire,
water and air, or body and spirit. Asian wisdom
would show it as the balance of yin and yang.
Conflict arises because this world is in a constant
state of change, while we are left constantly seeking
balance that cannot be maintained.

*

Deception Past

March 1972
Warrington, Florida

At their two-story, yellow brick home on Second Street, Isabel Akbey's father, Ibrahim, talked his daughter into applying for a position at the hospital as a ward clerk. First she had to complete a training course, but it was no problem. Isabel was top of her class. Having made the top score, she was given first choice of assignment both for ward and shift. She chose the evening shift, partly because it put her on a different schedule than her parents and partly because everyone else in her class had spouses or children and hoped to get hired on for the day shift. She chose the cancer ward, which was also commonly referred to as the terminal ward, because she knew no one else in her class wanted to work there. Competition was greatest among the trainees for the opposite end of the spectrum. Most of the newly trained ward clerks wanted the obstetric ward with the nursery. Birth was more popular than death, but Isabel felt strongly more empathetic toward death. She was very popular with the ward clerk staff. She was also the only ward clerk from her class that didn't have a husband, children, or grandchildren at home. She tried to make friends, but between the differences in family situations and religions, she just didn't have anything in common with the others.

Sometimes Isabel had to work weekends, but she didn't mind. She really had nothing better to do and no personal aspirations. She liked her job, and she was paid an extra shift differential for working the evening shift, which was 3:00 pm to 11:00 pm. Her duties included answering the phone at the nurse's station, answering the patient intercom, directing visitors and flower deliveries, transcribing doctors' orders, scheduling x-rays and laboratory tests, ordering patient prescriptions from the pharmacy, and paging doctors and emergency medical teams.

Because of her work schedule, Isabel had lots of solitary personal time. She tried frequenting bars, but she couldn't seem to connect with anyone she liked. Instead she was just pestered by men who didn't interest her. She saw herself as a misfit and became a loner. She would take long walks or drives at night. Sometimes she would take a rowboat out into the bayou. Sometimes she would go to the beach and just sit and listen to the sound of the surf and watch the tide. She kept to herself. She bought a used car so she wouldn't continue to be dependent on her parents' cars and so Maria could have more freedom as well.

When Isabel finally had enough vacation days saved up to take a week off from work, she drove back to Huntsville, Alabama. She didn't call or write anyone in Huntsville to let them know she was coming. She told her parents she was going to visit her friends, and they assumed she had made the appropriate arrangements. But instead, she just went, and when she got there, she wondered why. She felt like her life had gotten off to a false start somehow, that somehow she had gotten off the track and couldn't find her way back.

Mrs. Compton was understandably surprised to see Isabel, but she invited her in for tea and a snack. They talked about old times, and Mrs. Compton filled Isabel in on George leaving for Canada. Mrs. Compton gave Isabel Patty's college class schedule, apartment address with directions, and phone number, but when she mentioned Patty's roommate Julie, Isabel knew not to call or visit.

Isabel stopped by the restaurant where Matthew Barnes had been working as a busboy and washing dishes. Matty still worked there, but he wasn't allowed to stop and talk as he'd already had his break. Isabel didn't want to get him into trouble, so she left with the feeling that she'd gotten him into trouble anyway. She went to a different restaurant. After she was seated at a table, a friendly black waitress with a name tag that said "Chrissie" appeared and asked to take her order. The conversation began with a discussion of what was good on the menu and digressed to places and faces Isabel remembered. By the time she'd placed her order, Isabel had discovered that she and her waitress, Chrissie, had gone to the same high school, and both knew Sand Strasberg. The food was fine, and Isabel was grateful to Chrissie for the company, but by the time she left the restaurant, she felt lonelier than ever.

Chrissie called Sand on the phone that evening and told her about Isabel's visit and their conversation. Sand regretted not having seen Isabel and was deeply hurt that Isabel had apparently made no attempt to contact her while she was in town. They had long since stopped writing, and Sand couldn't remember why.

Steve Fernandez comforted Sand by telling her, "These things happen all the time. People get busy and just move on with their lives. After all, you've moved on with yours. Isabel probably has a whole new circle of friends and just didn't have time."

The drive back to Warrington seemed twice as long to Isabel as the drive to Huntsville. On the drive north Isabel had been vaguely optimistic and had been looking forward to visiting with her other family and seeing her long-lost soul mate, Patty. On the drive south she had absolutely nothing to look forward to, and any unexpressed or unconscious dreams she may have harbored were shattered forever.

Once she was back home, she put on her smile and pretended to family and coworkers that she had a wonderful vacation visiting with old friends and reminiscing about their school days. But deep down she knew all she had was a flight of fancy and a conversation with a stranger who happened to have had a once-mutual friend.

*

Isabel never returned to Huntsville, Alabama. She continued to work at the hospital. She never requested a change of shift or change of ward. She watched patients check into her ward, and occasionally she watched them leave the ward still breathing, although she knew they would either return or pass away at home. At night she continued to watch the sky and listen to the water. She never paid any attention to the news or kept up with television or entertainment.

She began to read the books in her parents' library and developed an interest in the more liberal, mystical aspects of her ancestral religion, Islam. She especially liked the Sufi writings and the work of the Lebanese poet Khalil Gibran. Gradually she came to feel that she was filling up the empty spaces in her soul.

Isabel felt she was balancing her life by pursuing her spiritual reading and meditations while working at the hospital where the physically ill were treated. She believed that by becoming more spiritual, she would somehow become better at her job, and that she would somehow better help the terminally ill patients that came through her ward to make an easier transition from the material world into the after life. Maybe she did. Comforting others comforted her as well.

Temperance was a balancing force. Water tempered fire. Air tempered earth. Moderation was a path of balancing. Isabel was trying to find her path.

*

May 15, 1972
Huntsville, Alabama

Sand was in Morton Hall at UAH when she heard that Governor George Wallace had been shot. She actually cheered, but then she was immediately ashamed of her own reaction. Maybe the bully finally got what he deserved, but truthfully, no one deserved to be shot. He was human and had a family. Still, at least it might shut him up for a while, especially since he was running for President of the United States. He didn't have much of a chance of winning, but if he did, Sand knew it would be a disaster. She had to admit that not liking him was no reason to wish him harm.

*

November 1972

Sand was eligible to vote in her first presidential election. She understood the importance of the responsibility. She also wasn't going to let anyone, including Steve, influence her vote, even though he was concerned if they didn't vote the same way, they would cancel out each other's vote. She couldn't vote for Richard Nixon because she didn't trust him. He wouldn't let women visitors to his White House wear trousers. Even Sand's high school had lifted that dress restriction her senior year. She couldn't vote for George McGovern because she didn't know anything about him except that he was from South Dakota. She'd never been to South Dakota, but from what she'd read, there was just as much prejudice there against Native Americans as there was in Alabama against black people. She knew she didn't understand the Viet Nam War and wanted it to end because she didn't like friends coming home in caskets. She also didn't understand the Cold War and wanted it to end. She knew the United States was the only country that had ever used atomic bombs on another country, so it made sense to her that the communist countries were afraid of the United States. She wondered what the point was of spending all that money on weapons instead of helping people. Sand had been taught in Catholic school that communists were evil because they wanted to destroy religion. She knew nothing about economics or how communist governments ruled, so since she didn't care much for religion, she had no reason to hate or fear communists. Sand chose not to vote.

*

1974

Sand continued to go to classes at UAH, work part-time for her Aunt Clarabelle, and knit blankets whenever she was watching television, listening to music, or talking on the phone. And she continued to see Steve Fernandez.

Usually when she was working at Clarabelle's house, she was really studying, doing homework, or writing papers for class, because there was actually very little to do at Clarabelle's. When she was there, Clarabelle usually went out to run errands, telling Sand how nice it was to have someone to answer the phone for her while she was out. Sand was instructed to raid Clarabelle's refrigerator whenever she felt like it.

The only time there seemed to be any actual work was during tax season, January to April every year. Sand couldn't imagine how Clarabelle was managing financially, but she was grateful for the paycheck and the time to study without interruption while getting paid. Clarabelle was not judgmental about Sand seeing a young man who worked as a custodian, and that was a refreshing change from her parents.

On the evening of April 1, Sand's father took her to a concert at Huntsville High School. Her mother opted to stay home. Louise was working on a dress and wanted a quiet night of sewing. It had been warm and windy that day, and the weather forecast predicted a drop in temperature, so Sand took a jacket with her even though it was already April.

The performance was by a visiting flute and piano duet. Both William and Sand were enjoying it very much when the concert was interrupted by an announcement that a tornado had just touched down in Sherwood Park. Without saying a word, William stood and headed for the exit. Sand followed.

The drive home was eerie. The street lights were out, it was still raining, and there was no moon or starlight from the cloud-filled sky. Not only was the power out on the west side of town, but as they approached Sherwood Park, they began seeing through the car's headlights that there were power lines down on the ground.

William cautioned Sand, "If for any reason we have to get out of the car, be very careful. Everything is wet, and we have to assume the downed power lines are live. There's a very real danger of electrocution."

Sand understood, but fortunately they were able to get through in the car. Trees were down in yards, and there were occasionally large branches in the street they had to drive around in the dark, but they made it home safely.

Louise was fine and still trying to sew by candle light. "I was sewing," she explained, "and then I heard what sounded like a freight train pass over the house right as the lights went out."

Two days later, Sand noticed the trees were blowing in circular patterns just like they had been during the day two days earlier. She called her father at work and told him, "There's going to be another tornado."

"You're overreacting," he patronized her. "Everything's fine. It's understandable you're still upset from the other night."

That evening, the family was watching TV when the broadcast was interrupted by a weather alert warning that there was a tornado on the ground just west of Sherwood Park. Then the station went off the air. Sand opened the sliding glass door onto the patio on the west side of the house and heard the roar. The three of them headed into the hallway as the doorbell rang. One of their neighbors with two little children said her husband was out of town on business and they were all frightened. Sand grabbed the mattress off her bed and put it in the bathtub for the kids. The adults huddled in the hallway. Sand quietly worried about Steve Fernandez.

After the roar passed over and the power went out, the battery powered radio warned that another tornado was heading north up Memorial Parkway from the Tennessee River. The radio station went off the air, and then they heard the roar coming from the south. They passed the evening that way in the dark, listening to distant but approaching roars, until one by one, they nodded off to sleep.

The next day the Strasbergs learned from the radio that at least six tornadoes had come through the area the night before. The Parkway City Mall on South Memorial Parkway was gone. The tornadoes had come up from Mississippi and wreaked havoc in Huntsville and on Redstone Arsenal before heading north to do more damage in Kentucky and Ohio. It was days before the power was restored, but everyone managed without it.

Chapter 15

The Shadow
(Devil)

Shadows only fall
When light encounters obstacles
Time gives a security
That something new will follow

Habit turns obsession
Trying to control
A feeling, a sensation
A need for something more

Free will blindly follows
Giving up control
To madness and delusion
Lost in shadows' hold

*

Brenda:

      Some of the trailers in the trailer park on Madison Pike had been blown away, but Sand learned later that the Masterson family had survived with no injuries. Otherwise, I might not be here to tell you her story. As it turned out, Sand didn't know anyone personally who had been hurt by the tornadoes.

      Services were restored, debris was cleaned up, and life went on. Isabel Akbey heard about the devastation from the national news in the newspaper. She took it as a sign that her past had been blown away.

The Devil is the card of temptation. It is our shadow, our dark side. It represents recognition of the crazy things people do to fulfill their desires. For Isabel, the past was a temptation. The winds that blew it away from her grasp helped her let go.

*

During high school, Chrissie Jackson waited tables at a restaurant on weekends, Mondays, and Wednesdays for a couple of hours right after school to save money to help with her intended college education. But when Chrissie graduated from high school and started college, she was disappointed with what she found there—all the politics, the religion, and a desperate lack of romance. Every time Chrissie thought she'd found true romance, the man turned out to be seeing someone else. She quickly became disillusioned.

College didn't live up to her expectations, so she dropped out after her first year and found three part-time jobs waitressing. Tips were good. Sand stopped by one of Chrissie's restaurants one day for lunch only to learn that Chrissie had quit a couple of weeks before. After some investigating, Sand found Chrissie serving at her one remaining work site. Chrissie's father had died of a heart attack and left a decent inheritance for both Chrissie and her mother. Chrissie had taken her part of her father's financial legacy and bought a small house on a secluded, wooded lot up on the mountain.

The foothills of the Appalachians included a lot of small mountains that met the Tennessee River Valley at Huntsville, Alabama. Lots of little mountains (relative to the rest of the Appalachians) were to the north and east of Huntsville, but only one in particular was referred to as the mountain. In Huntsville, the mountain meant Monte Sano Mountain. Monte Sano was the natural eastern boundary of Huntsville, while the Tennessee River was the natural southern boundary. There was also Drake Mountain to the north and Green Mountain to the southeast, but Monte Sano was the mountain.

Chrissie Jackson bought her home up on the mountain so she could write. The only income she needed was for food, clothes, taxes, utilities, occasional transportation, and medical insurance. In other words, she still needed income. What she didn't need was a social life, so she left that behind. Eventually she landed a receptionist position for a local TV station that was conveniently located on the mountain. After that, her trips into town became fewer and farther between.

Sand had always imagined Chrissie Jackson being the one person she knew in high school who would stay in school forever until she had earned her doctorate. She had always pictured Chrissie as a high school professor, keeping her students' avid attention with her sheer enthusiasm for whatever piece of literature they were studying. But that wasn't to be. Sand couldn't foresee which way Chrissie's path would take her, and Chrissie wasn't at all concerned with looking ahead. At least part of Chrissie's fountain of energy, if not all, had its source in her innate manner of living in the moment. For Chrissie there were no regrets about the past and no worries about the future. For Chrissie there was the joy or sorrow of the moment. For Chrissie life wasn't about the destination but the journey. It was that chronic attunement to the present moment that kept Chrissie true to herself and on her own path while others around her were digressing and wandering. She lived her solitary life, but she also stopped sharing her poems with anyone. She wrote but never published. She totally withdrew from the world of people. Nature was her only friend.

*

Sand continued to see Steve Fernandez regularly. Her parents continued to resist accepting the relationship. They began restricting Sand's use of their car to only the days she worked for Clarabelle, but that only resulted in the two sweethearts keeping the Strasberg telephone busy for hours at a time every evening and on weekends.

Then Steve managed to get hired as part of the custodial staff at the university. Sherwood Park was separated from UAH only by what used to have been the cotton fields and what had become Research Park. So Sand walked to school by cutting across the fields to rendezvous with Steve in the Humanities building where he worked. The chairman of the art department allowed Steve free use of the space and equipment in the sculpture studio, and the chief custodian allowed him to spend any free time on the job there. Everyone in the building always knew where to find Steve. Sometimes he would walk Sand home from school after he finished work, but he never went past the woods that bordered the field at the end of Sand's street to avoid any possible confrontation with Sand's parents.

Sand earned her bachelor's degree from UAH in English at the end of 1974. By the following February she landed an entry-level job at the *Huntsville Times*, the larger of the two local newspapers. It didn't hurt that Michael Latimer's maternal uncle, Thomas James, was an assistant editor, and that Sand had used Michael as a reference. She had to leave Clarabelle without a secretary, but by this time it was obvious to Sand that Clarabelle only had a handful of clients. With what she had learned from her aunt's instruction in bookkeeping and taxes, Sand couldn't figure out how Clarabelle was paying the bills, but they were getting paid. Clarabelle would always buy more of everything than she needed, and she was a heavy drinker. Clarabelle had offered to take Sand out to the nightclubs with her on weekends, but Sand preferred talking to Steve.

*

1975

     Sand's new boss at the *Times* was what William Strasberg referred to as an odd duck. He was a nice looking man, tall and slim with short dark hair, but he had the palest skin Sand had ever seen. He was always nicely dressed in a suit with a stylish tie, but his mannerisms were distinctly different. He had a way of swaying and tilting his head while looking you right in the eye that made a lot of people uncomfortable, but he seemed nice and polite enough. Since he had no children of his own even though he'd been married for at least a couple of decades, Mr. James's primary status in his family was that of an uncle, and he was adamant about the mandatory use of his complete given name. He would never ever respond to any shortened version of it. He was quiet for the most part, but had a reputation for becoming overly familiar with his female employees. Sand knew that Thomas James was aware Sand was a close friend of his nephew Michael, so she wasn't worried. Michael had told her if his uncle ever got out of line with her to just let him know.

Meanwhile, Michael Latimer had ended up enlisting in the Alabama National Guard in Birmingham so he could continue his studies at the University of Alabama in Birmingham (UAB). After she started working at the *Huntsville Times*, Sand only saw Michael a couple of times when he was home visiting his parents and dropped in at the paper to see his Uncle Thomas. Sand still enjoyed Michael's company. The lack of resemblance between the Latimer family and her new boss was striking. Thomas James was no idealist.

Sand was surprised to learn that the secretary, who preferred the title office manager, was Sylvia Masterson Clark Hatfield. Pretty Sylvia had managed to snag a husband by getting pregnant. She married Jimmy Clark straight out of high school, who then divorced her when she started seeing Wendell Hatfield. Jimmy had been a laborer for the Hatfield Construction Company, but Wendell was part owner in his family's business. Sylvia was still marrying up. Sylvia and Wendell, who hated it when she affectionately called him Wendy, had custody of Sylvia and Jimmy's son, Charlie, as well as their own daughter, Michelle.

For Sand, it was nice to find a familiar face at her new place of employment. She found it ironic that Sylvia, who always wanted to be the first to get the scoop on any gossip, had ended up working for a newspaper.

After Sand started working at the *Times*, she started having a recurring dream. She was in the woods when darkness suddenly fell. Then she heard a voice saying, "Run from the shadow." She woke up, realized it was just a dream, and then fell back asleep. She was in the park where she used to meet Chrissie. An ominous, dark cloud would appear and come toward her, and then a voice would say, "Run from the shadow." The dreams continued off and on for about ten days.

By March, Dennis Johnston had moved in with Clarabelle. Before moving in, Dennis had visited the office/home when he was running errands for Clarabelle, usually driving Clarabelle's Cadillac, so Sand knew him. On one occasion, he had offered to sell Sand some marijuana, but Sand declined. Sand couldn't imagine being so indiscreet as to risk her parents finding out she was buying an illegal drug in her aunt's house. Sand also couldn't figure out how Clarabelle's business was making enough money to support both her and Dennis. That's when Sand realized the real income that was supporting all the booze was illegal. Clarabelle told everyone Dennis was her new partner, and that he was a certified public accountant. He was just a few years older than Sand's brother, Jody. Dennis was from Arab (long "A", short "rab"), where his parents and sister lived. Dennis stood a couple of inches over six feet, though he preferred to sit or lie around. He had receding, thinning blond hair and a pronounced beer belly. Like Clarabelle, he liked his alcohol.

Sand knew from previous conversations with Clarabelle that Dennis was someone her aunt had been partying with for some time. Clarabelle also told her he was on parole after doing time in prison for possession of marijuana. Clarabelle confided in Sand things she didn't want shared with Sand's parents. Sand kept her secrets to avoid starting yet another fight in the Strasberg household.

Sand and Steve Fernandez planned their wedding for May. Rather than spend a lot of money unnecessarily, they were married in the field at the end of Delaney Road. Michael Latimer was best man. They were married by Steve's Unitarian-Universalist minister, and Sand wrote the ceremony. It lasted exactly one minute, but it was framed before and after with very special performances by her old friend Jonathan Moreau, who came down from Nashville just for the occasion.

Much to everyone's surprise, William and Louise Strasberg bought Sand and Steve a house as a wedding present. It was a two bedroom, white clapboard house next to the corner of North Rose Drive and 9th Avenue, just a couple of blocks from the middle school where Sand had attended ninth grade. There was a gas furnace for heat in the very center of the house and big concrete front and back porches. In the back yard was a two-story garage that Steve converted into his very own sculpture studio. North and South Rose Drives ran parallel to each other with a park-like area dividing them. Down the center of it ran a small creek with stately old oak and sweet gum trees scattered on both sides of it. Sand loved the view from the front porch of her new home. Steve and Sand pooled their money and bought a used, green and white 1962 Volkswagen bus.

Mr. and Mrs. Strasberg also bought another home for themselves and sold their house on Delaney Road in Sherwood Park. Their new home was down the street from Clarabelle on the southeast side of town. Sand had a bad feeling about the new house, and she expressed that to Steve.

His response was, "What's wrong with it? It's much bigger than the one they had and in a nice neighborhood. Your mother will be close to her sister."

"My mother doesn't get along with her sister," Sand commented.

"I know. I don't get that. They're family."

"What don't I like about the house?" Sand repeated the original question. "The bedroom windows are up high and they're wide but too short. Mom likes that for privacy, but all I can think is, what if there's a fire? They could be trapped back there."

"I didn't think of that," Steve said.

Clarabelle's and Louise's houses were mirror images of each other, and the only floor plan of that kind in the neighborhood. Each house had a circular driveway with both the kitchen and front doors opening onto the carport in front of the house. Sand's family had always referred to the kitchen door as the back door, but on these houses the back doors were on the front. There were also sliding glass doors on the back. The Fernandez house had a front door on the front of the house, and the kitchen door opened onto the back porch, so it really was a back door.

Even after the Strasbergs moved in down the street, Louise didn't see much of Clarabelle. Steve told Louise and William like he'd told Sand, "She's still family."

Louise said, "We don't approve of Dennis living in Clarabelle's house. It isn't proper. He's young enough to be Clarabelle's son, for heaven's sake."

But Sand knew Dennis Johnston and Clarabelle weren't lovers. They weren't sleeping together. Clarabelle had her bedroom and Dennis had his. Occasionally that summer, Dennis would bring a boyfriend home for the night.

Clarabelle confided to Sand when Sand came to visit one evening, "I'm thinking of putting a deadbolt on my bedroom door."

Sand had never heard of such a thing. "Why?" she asked as they sat in the office.

"For protection," Clarabelle answered. "I've also bought a pistol." She got up and went to the back of the house. When she came back, she was carrying a small box. She took the lid off and showed Sand the pistol. "I have to take care of myself as long as I'm playing ball in this town," Clarabelle explained.

Sand was shocked. She didn't know what to say, so she said nothing. Clarabelle was creeping her out. Guns creeped her out. "Well, time's getting away from me. I have to be going," Sand said, excusing herself.

"Come back anytime," Clarabelle invited.

After that, Sand avoided seeing Clarabelle. She wasn't comfortable around guns. She didn't like the sound of Clarabelle "playing ball in this town," whatever that meant. She talked it over with Steve, and he agreed that the people Clarabelle and Dennis associated with were not the kind of people they wanted to be around.

"Maybe your parents were right," he said.

"So why did they move almost across the street from her? I have a bad feeling about this." It didn't make sense to Sand that Clarabelle could consider getting a gun and putting a deadbolt on her bedroom door instead of changing whatever it was in her life that had led to such fear. She rationalized that maybe it was some sort of paranoia stemming from her childhood rape.

"You've been saying that a lot lately," Steve observed.

*

August 1975

Jody moved back in with his parents that summer after returning home from Germany and the army. He didn't know what he wanted to do with his life, so he went home. Jody didn't like or appreciate what he'd seen of the world through the army's eyes, and he was very bitter about his experience with the army.

When Sand tried to pin him down about it, he just ranted, "I don't want anyone ever again to have such control over me or my life and how I live it. I saw too many corrupt officers and too many hateful, angry noncommissioned officers. I don't want any part of that anymore."

Sand asked, "What do you mean by 'corrupt officers'?"

"Selfish, arrogant, idiotic bullies. Greedy, thieving officers who do whatever they please while controlling everybody under them."

Sand could see he was angry and out of control, so she dropped it. Then she realized, even though he didn't go to Viet Nam, Jody had sacrificed his freedom by serving in the very institution that was supposed to defend freedom. It seemed a contradiction to her. Once again Sand was greatly relieved that by being female she at least had a choice of what to do with her life. She hoped

Jody could overcome his bitterness and depression that resulted from his experiences, whatever they may have been.

*

September 8, 1975

It was the second Monday in September. Around three in the morning, Sand woke suddenly and woke Steve up with one sentence, "Someone's at the back door and he's trying to get in."

In an instant Steve was on his feet and running to the front door. After listening a moment and hearing nothing, he went back through the kitchen, picking up a butcher knife along the way, and out the back door. He circled the house a couple of times before coming back in and telling Sand there was no sign of an intruder or any disturbance. He realized she had been dreaming and asked her to tell him everything she could remember.

Sand sat on the bed shaking in terror for a few minutes. Then she said, "Someone had broken into the house through the back door, only it was on the front of the house. I was trapped. I was lying on the floor and there was a man leaning over me. He was wearing a hat, and I couldn't see his face, but I knew he was about to do something unspeakably horrible to me. He was smiling. I could see him smiling, but I couldn't make out what his face looked like. I was so terrified I couldn't move. I knew I needed to run away, but I was frozen with fear. I couldn't move a muscle. I was trapped anyway, because he was between me and the only way out. Then I heard it—an almost metallic sound, 'click, click, …… click.'"

That was all she could remember, but it was enough. She was shaking and scared to death. Steve held her and tried to calm her down. No matter how hard she tried, she couldn't go back to sleep. She was just too afraid. Even after Steve nodded off and started to snore, she just snuggled up close to him and waited through the early morning hours for the alarm clock to sound.

Chapter 16

Struck by Lightning
(The Lightning Struck Tower)

Devastation shudders
Walls have crumbled all around
After the dust settles
A ray of truth is found

Overwhelming darkness
Obliterates the stars
When questioning arises
Things are seen for what they are

*

Brenda:

The Lightning Struck Tower symbolizes an event that strikes unexpectedly like a bolt of lightning. It's only after the rubble is cleared away that we can see what we couldn't see before. It's only after the dust settles that we can truly appreciate the transitory nature of existence. That transitory nature is what we fear most, because most of the time we just can't see what's coming—at least not consciously.

Some people drink to silence their unconscious. Some people drink to drown their fear. Fear can be used to induce the weak willed to do terrible things they wouldn't even think of on their own. Dennis Johnston didn't think of much on his own with what was left of his brain. He'd been drinking while smoking marijuana and taking pills for years.

Fear constricts the focus and skews perception. The conscious remembers, has premonitions of fragments, and tries to cope with the present. The more afraid it is, the narrower its focus, the more acutely it focuses on fear.

Sand was afraid of fire.

*

After the alarm went off, Sand and Steve got out of bed, dressed, and had a hurried breakfast. Usually Sand drove Steve to work and dropped him off at the UAH Humanities building before reporting to work herself. This morning was different. She was still shaken from her nightmare and afraid to be alone, so Steve drove her to work and then took their VW bus to UAH. Sand was at her desk around 9:15 that morning when she got the call from Jody.

"There was a fire at Clarabelle's house," he told her. "She and Dennis are dead."

Sand was stunned. She thought of her nightmare. "What happened?" she asked quietly.

Jody continued, "Mom and Dad had already left for work. I heard sirens and noticed a fire truck go by, so I went out for a walk to see what was going on. I didn't even make it past our own driveway before I saw the fire truck, police cars, and ambulances all in front of Aunt Clarabelle's house. I started asking questions and was told that the neighbor across the street from Clarabelle's house had noticed around 7:30 that Clarabelle's kitchen door was partly open, and black smoke was coming out of it. She called the fire department.

Firemen went in looking for anyone who might be in the house as well as the source of the fire. They found both, but they won't say any more than that. It's roped off as a crime scene, and the police are investigating."

Sand shuddered. "Call Mom and Dad."

"Of course I will," he agreed. "I thought you might have heard something since you work at the paper."

"No, nothing. Thanks for telling me."

"Sand," Jody said before she could hang up. "You need to know this." He took a deep breath before continuing. "She was the source of the fire. Clarabelle was the source of the fire. They haven't even taken the remains to the morgue yet. They're both still in there. Dennis was identified by his driver's license picture; his face wasn't burned. He was slumped over the tub with his hand on the faucet. He never managed to turn it on."

When Jody paused, Sand said, "She was in the hall."

That took him by surprise. "I thought you said you hadn't heard?"

"No," she corrected, "it was a dream I had last night. Go on."

"The police asked where to get her dental records. I had to tell them she wore dentures; she didn't have any teeth. I gave them her doctor's name and contact information. Maybe he can help them identify what's left of her."

Sand remembered her dreams telling her, "Run from the shadow." She thought about the black smoke. She remembered her recurring nightmare from childhood where there was no fire but lots of black smoke and the feeling of imminent mortal danger. It seemed so long ago. She

205

remembered what woke her and Steve early that morning. She remembered the sinister face that she couldn't quite make out. She remembered looking up and knowing he was smiling. She remembered her frozen terror. She remembered, "click, click …… click."

When she hung up from talking to Jody, Sand called the UAH music department secretary. "It's a family emergency," she said. "Please, please, find Steve right away and have him call me." Her voice was shaking.

Sylvia Masterson overheard and came straight over to Sand's desk. "Whatever's wrong, Sand?"

"My aunt who lives down the street from my parents has been killed," she explained. She was starting to cry.

"That's terrible," Sylvia said loudly, attracting the attention of Mr. James as she put her arm around Sand's shoulders. "Tell me what happened," she continued, handing Sand a couple of tissues. Thomas James came closer, just close enough to listen in. "It's best to talk about these things," Sylvia continued. "Go ahead and just tell me all about it."

It wasn't long before Jody, out in the street in front of Clarabelle's house, was being harassed by a Huntsville Times reporter and photographer. Before that, he had thought things couldn't get any worse.

Meanwhile, Thomas James had stepped in and was asking questions—as a professional, not a friend. She couldn't believe how bloodthirsty her boss was acting. Hers was a stunned silence broken only by her desk phone ringing.

When she answered, all she said to Steve was, "Clarabelle's been murdered. Please come get me right now."

*

William and Louise Strasberg came home early from work after being called by Jody— William from the Arsenal and Louise from the bank downtown where she worked as a secretary. They learned from the police that any funeral arrangements would have to wait until the investigators released Clarabelle's body. No one could say when that might be. They were still trying to make a positive identification, and there was nothing further the family could do to help with that. The wristwatch and ring Clarabelle always wore were not on her wrist and finger. The Strasbergs wondered if it had been a robbery.

That evening, the story was the headline on the front page of the *Huntsville Times*. "Double Suicide," it read.

That evening Sand and Steve joined Jody, William, and Louise at the Strasberg home down the street from the crime scene. "How could you tell them this?" William accused Sand, throwing the paper down in front of her.

She picked up the paper and saw the headline. "NO!" she protested. "I NEVER said anything like this. This is unimaginable."

"Well, that's right," William said in a much calmer tone. He sat down on the sofa. "This whole nightmare is unimaginable."

None of them could comprehend how anyone could possibly believe Clarabelle and Dennis had set themselves on fire deliberately.

What a horrible way to die. Sane people just wouldn't do that. Clarabelle and Dennis had their problems and spent a lot of their time inebriated, but they weren't insane.

Sand quickly learned that family members didn't sleep well right after one of them has been murdered. It was like the victim's blood poured into the family well of unconsciousness, and no member could take a drink from that well without the vivid, bitter, rancid taste reenacting the whole scene. It occupied waking thoughts and conversation to the point of obsession, until eventually the living world trickled back in like the sun burning away a thick, putrid fog. In the days and weeks to come, Jody, Steve, and Sand would find themselves pulling the pieces apart and trying to put them back together again in different ways, trying to make them fit so they could understand what had actually happened.

*

September 9, 1975

When Sand got to work, she immediately confronted Thomas James. "Are you out of your mind? How could the *Times* print such a thing?" She demanded an explanation.

"Buddhist monks in Viet Nam practice self-immolation on a daily basis," he responded coolly.

"You have got to be kidding! This isn't Viet Nam and my aunt and Dennis weren't protesting the war."

Sylvia came up to Sand to try to calm her down. Sand pushed her away. "Get away from me."

"You're just upset because your aunt has died," Thomas offered.

"Ya think?" Sand shot back.

"Look," Thomas continued, "nothing in the house was burned but the bodies. No one else was there. Take some time off."

"Then why was the kitchen door open?" Sand asked as she turned and walked out.

That evening the *Times* headline read, "Murder-Suicide in Southeast Huntsville." The Strasberg family still couldn't believe it. The *Times* article suggested Dennis had murdered Clarabelle and then killed himself by setting his own back on fire.

Once the investigation finally concluded, the police's murder/accident version was far more credible, but still there were still unanswered questions. Clarabelle's remains had been found in the hallway just outside her bedroom door with her head pointing toward the den that she used as her office, which had the window that looked out into the carport. The kitchen was just beyond that, and the door had been left open. The police surmised that it had either been left open accidentally, or it had been left open deliberately to create a draft in hopes that the house would burn and destroy any evidence.

The office phone on Clarabelle's desk was off the hook. Dennis's fingerprints were on it. Dennis lived and worked in the house. The police didn't say what other prints were on the receiver. Clarabelle's had to have been, but they never mentioned that.

In the central bathroom where Dennis's body had been found, there was a book of unburned matches on the floor. Dennis was only burned on his back. Except for the bodies, the only part of the house that had burned was the floor underneath

Clarabelle's body. Clarabelle's body had been doused with Varsol, a solvent used in copy machines. Clarabelle's office copier and supplies were kept in the room meant to be the small third bedroom directly across the hall from the central bathroom. The police found a partial container of Varsol in Clarabelle's bedroom, and some of the liquid was on her bed sheets. They said it was clear that she had been in bed when she was doused with the Varsol. The Varsol-free area of the sheets formed an outline of her body. When Sand learned this, she thought of the deadbolt Clarabelle had never gotten around to putting on her bedroom door.

The police had also found Clarabelle's ring and watch in the crawl space under the house. The floor had burned through just under her left hand and they had fallen through. The watch had stopped at five minutes to seven that morning, apparently from the fire. The police determined that Dennis had deliberately set Clarabelle on fire, and then had accidentally caught fire himself. The official police ruling was Clarabelle was murdered by Dennis, and he died accidentally.

*

When the Johnstons, Dennis's family in Arab, learned what had happened, they couldn't believe it either. It was bad enough for such a gruesome thing to happen, and it was bad enough they'd lost Dennis, but they were publicly stigmatized by the guilt of his alleged crimes.

After the police finally released the crime scene over a week after the murder, the Strasberg family went into the house. Sand didn't want to, but the family had to deal with it, and it was easier on everyone to deal with it together. Everything in the house was covered with black, oily soot. Sand would never forget that smell as long as she lived. The worst part was that the shape of Clarabelle's body was burned into the floor in the hallway.

The hall and central bathroom had taken on sinister connotations for both Sand and Jody. In their parents' house, the mirror image of Clarabelle's, the whole back part of the house— hallway, central bath, and all three bedrooms—were now dark, eerie, and foreboding places. William and Louise's bedroom corresponded to Clarabelle's. Jody's counterpart was Dennis's room. Both houses were now darkened by a shadow.

The autopsy report showed Dennis's blood alcohol level was more than three times the legal limit. There were over a dozen bottles of Valium in Clarabelle's medicine cabinet. The police left the pills for the family to flush down the toilet. There was no way the sober Strasberg family could have predicted what would happen when reason was sacrificed to chemically induced reaction. Sand wondered how people under chronic stress, like fire fighters and police, coped with the aftermath. She figured they were just as much victims, having to witness what had happened, breathe the soot in the air, and deal with the morbid details as well as the grieving families.

When the Johnston family arrived at Clarabelle's house, William blocked them from going in. "You're not welcome here," he told them.

Dennis's sister answered politely, "We'd just like to collect Dennis's things, if that's alright."

"It's not."

"We're his family," she said, starting to cry.

Sand, standing in the doorway behind her father, noticed the sister's strong resemblance to Dennis. She felt sorry for her and ashamed of how her father was treating the Johnstons, but she didn't interfere.

"We have a right to his things," the sister insisted.

"You have no rights here," William contradicted. "Those rights were forfeited when he murdered my sister-in-law who had allowed him to live here."

Sand had to speak up. "It wasn't their fault, Dad. They're grieving too."

The sister turned to Sand. "Can we at least have Dennis's gold cigarette lighter, please? It has sentimental meaning for us."

"I'll look for it," Sand assured her. "When we find it, I'll get it to you."

"Thank you so much." The Johnstons got back into their car and drove away.

The Strasbergs went back into the house. They searched, but no one could find a cigarette lighter of any kind.

Everything in Clarabelle's house was saturated with black, oily soot. Everything that came out of her house reeked of the same rancid smell. Louise took the curtains from Clarabelle's bedroom and had them cleaned. She simply wanted to give the expensive drapes to Sand, who didn't have any. They were thick, expensive, off-white draperies that shut out all light and sound from the outside world.

One day Sand came home and found that her mother had been to her and Steve's house and hung those curtains over their living room windows.

"I don't want them here," Sand told Steve.

212

Steve shook his head. "This is a gift, and we should accept graciously. Your mother has given us a gift. She could have kept them, or sold them, or given them to someone else. We must accept graciously."

Sand understood that her mother had just lost her sister, but to Sand they were thick, black, sooty walls of dark, shadowy clouds, blocking out light, life, and escape from pain and death. They were shrouds, but she didn't argue with him. It had been too much.

Sand and Steve went to bed at the usual time that night. At some point in the middle of the night, Sand woke up and took the curtains down. Steve came out onto the front porch where she was sitting with the offenders in a cardboard box. He said nothing and went back to bed.

When she gave the drapes back to her mother, Louise wailed angrily, "But I spent so much money having them cleaned, and they were expensive to start with. I thought you'd want something of hers."

Sand shrugged and told her, "I can't deal with seeing them. I appreciate the gift, Mom, but everyone grieves in their own way and time."

*

Sand refused to discuss any of what had happened with anyone at work. She couldn't trust them and blamed herself for not realizing it in time. It was a newspaper, after all. Murder was a headline story. They were just doing their jobs, and she still liked hers.

Steve, on the other hand, talked about all the details with his friends and coworkers of the

213

janitorial staff. One of the other men had a brother who sold solvents, office supplies, and cleaning supplies for a living. Steve was introduced to the salesman. He explained, "Varsol has a higher ignition temperature than comes from a match. I'll show you." He poured a small amount of the chemical into an empty ashtray. Then he took out a book of matches. One by one, he lit each match and dropped it into the Varsol. Nothing happened. When he ran out of matches, he emptied the ashtray and then poured some more Varsol into it. "Now watch," he told Steve. He pulled out a cigarette lighter, lit it, and touched the flame to the Varsol. The ashtray ignited.

No one had found Dennis's gold cigarette lighter.

Chapter 17

The Art of Time
(The Star)

The Dreamtime frees our hearts to soar
To fly among the stars
In waking when we've closed the door
Trust visits in the dark

Sometimes the world offers no way
We have to close our eyes
To follow the road of our dream
And trust in changing Time

*

    A week or so after the funeral, Sand got out
of bed before Steve one morning. It was still dark,
but she didn't turn on a light because she didn't
want to wake him. He still had about twenty
minutes to sleep before the alarm would go off. She
walked into the kitchen, intending to see what she
could cook for breakfast, but instead Sand saw
Clarabelle standing there in a cloud of black smoke
saying, "Look what they've done to me."
    Steve was awakened by Sand screaming.
About the time he managed to calm her down, the
alarm went off. They both managed to get to work
on time anyway, though with severely frayed
nerves. Neither had gotten a good night's sleep
since the murder.
    Sand eventually came to realize that "me"
and fear together are what create true hell. After

some months had passed, she was able to drift off to sleep without trying to force her mind not to think about Clarabelle's death out of the sheer terror of reliving it in another nightmare.

Sand continued to receive sympathy cards in the mail at home. One of them read,

> "For every day there is a season
> To every life there is an end
> For every crime there is a reason
> Though we may not comprehend

Love,
Chrissie Jackson"

*

While the Strasberg and Fernandez families sorted through and distributed the belongings in Clarabelle's house, Jody, being unemployed, took on the unpleasant task of cleaning the place and having the floor repaired so the house could be put up for sale. The whole family was anxious to be rid of it and to put the nasty occurrence behind them. Sand wondered how her parents could continue to live in their own mirror-image house, but they stayed. No one could sleep. No one could get the wretched smell out of their minds and nostrils.

Jody wore a bandana over his nose and mouth whenever he was inside the damaged house. Virtually every inch inside the house had to be scrubbed to get rid of the black, oily soot and its smell. So it was Jody who came upon the fat nine-by-twelve inch manila envelope backed up against the wall up on top of the high cabinets above the washing machine in the laundry room behind the kitchen. Stuffed inside the envelope were pages of accounting ledgers and photographs. Names on the ledgers and faces in the photographs included Huntsville and Arab city council members, a state senator, the Madison County sheriff, Dennis Johnston, and the man Clarabelle first worked for years ago when she moved from Memphis to Arab. The ledgers appeared to be records of payments made by this man to Dennis, various others, and the sheriff, as well as receipts from the senator, city council members, and numerous other people.

Jody gave the package to Sand, who showed it to Steve. "We should take this to the police," Steve stated.

But Sand disagreed. She pointed out, "There are notable people in this package, and they might not want anyone to know about it. This might be dangerous."

"I agree," Jody chimed in. "I don't want any part of it. No one should know it exists. We should just destroy it before it anybody else gets hurt," he said emphatically. "I just wanted you two to know there was more to the story than the police report and news versions."

"OK," Steve agreed. "Maybe it is dangerous. Let's not tell your parents anything about this. It would only upset them more, and nothing would be accomplished."

They all agreed. The final decision was to do nothing. The only living souls that knew it existed were Sand, Steve, and Jody. They promised each other never to mention the envelope's contents to anyone.

Without telling Steve or Jody, Sand took the package to work and locked it in her desk drawer. She just didn't want it in her home, and until she decided what to do with it, she felt better hiding it more or less in public. At least she finally understood how Clarabelle had been paying her bills and where Dennis had gotten the marijuana he was selling. It was a dark world they had lived in, and she had worked as Clarabelle's secretary in the middle of it without realizing it. She wanted to forget it had existed. She was grateful to have a job to escape into.

Steve poured himself into building abstract sculpture. He would enter competitions in Huntsville, nearby Scottsboro and Albertville, Birmingham, and Nashville. Occasionally he would win prize money, and he kept a collection of ribbons he'd earned.

Sand was proud of Steve's art. He was creative and talented. She found herself feeling comfortable again with her life and happy with Steve. Clarabelle's tragic death seemed to have brought her parents closer to her and her husband, but she still worried about Jody. He didn't have a job or a hobby.

Jody had started going back to church with his mother, who now belonged to a parish in southeast Huntsville. He became active in helping Catholic Charities and delivering Meals on Wheels. Once he found enough charities to hold his interest and occupy his time, he stopped going to church again.

Sand worried about Jody's lack of interest in employment, but was glad he was spending his time helping others instead of falling into the darker ways of drugs or alcohol.

She was also relieved he was living with their parents during the aftermath of the murders. She felt they were safer while he was there.

*

July 27, 1976

One night Sand and Steve decided to go camping south of Huntsville by Guntersville Lake. They wanted some fresh air without the usual daytime heat and humidity, and they also had decided it was time for Sand to face her fear of fire, which centered on Clarabelle's murder, her nightmares, and her memories of the past. They found a campsite, built a fire, and stayed up late that night just watching the fire and keeping it going. It was a clear night, and the stars were spectacular without the city street lights. Steve drifted off to sleep.

As the night grew long and the temperature dropped, Sand tried to stay focused on the positive aspects of fire: how fire had been necessary for human survival over the centuries, its comfort of light and warmth, and its utility in cooking food. Then she noticed the dancing shadows that the flickering fire was projecting onto the trees nearby. As she stared at the shadows, they weren't sinister or threatening. They seemed to paint patterns as she watched. After a while, a Chinese man emerged in shadow form against the trunk of a pine tree. To Sand he appeared reminiscent of the Buddha, and he appeared to be reading from a book as thousands of smaller figures paraded before him. It occurred to Sand that he was reading from the Book of the Dead, and what he was reading were the names of the smaller figures passing before him. Then she saw that the light, which was all one light, was reaching down into the smaller figures' physical bodies like thousands of fingers from the hand of God. It seemed to Sand that as the large shadowy man read each name, the finger of light withdrew from the body back into God's hand, and the body passed into the shadows to become one with the greater darkness.

Eventually Sand fell asleep, and when she woke up, Steve was already up and ready to head home. On the drive back to Huntsville, Sand tried to explain to Steve what she had experienced in watching the shadows before she fell asleep.

"You still have issues to resolve," Steve commented.

"I disagree."

Rather than argue about it, Steve switched on the car radio. The news broadcast was telling about a large earthquake that had struck China. Thousands were believed to have been killed.

"You know," Sand observed, "it makes sense that if the fingers are all connected to one hand, then damage to one finger could be sensed in some way by another."

*

August 1976

Sand amused herself at work by listening to the office gossip about her boss, Thomas, and Sylvia. Sand's coworkers referred to Thomas behind his back as "The Undertaker"—only in part because he kept the thermostat set so cold. He apparently had started his career writing obituaries.

Thomas James boasted, "You know, I'm related to the outlaws Frank and Jesse James."

Sylvia shot back with, "Well, my husband Wendell's paternal grandparents moved to Madison County, Alabama, from the mountains of western West Virginia. He's a Hatfield of the infamous Hatfield-McCoy feud."

Easygoing Wendell Hatfield, his laid-back brother Olsen, and their quiet, hardworking father, Robert, hardly seemed to Sand like the type to get into bloody battles over pettiness, but they were all true sons of the South, and the McCoy family fighting for the Union had been at least part of the problem back then. The Huntsville Hatfields were Confederate flag-waving good ol' boys. Sand liked Wendell and Sylvia, but she cringed every time one of them parked a truck or car in the *Times* parking lot with a Confederate flag on the bumper or back windshield.

As for Thomas's family history, Frank and Jesse James had also fought for the Confederacy, and Frank had spent time in the Madison County Jail down on the courthouse square in downtown Huntsville overlooking Big Spring Park. He had also escaped from that jail.

Sylvia Hatfield was rumored to be Thomas James's latest lover. Sand personally felt that newspaper staff should verify their facts before spreading rumors, but they were all just human. She also thought maybe it was Sylvia's karma for all the rumors she had started with her own gossip over the years. They were all just human, Sand rationalized. The rumors were the least of Sylvia's problems. Wendell quit his job to play golf for a living. As nice a guy as he was, he was no athlete. Sylvia and Wendell seemed to be living the American dream.

Sand visited their home occasionally and noticed they had expensive standards. Sand thought they must be living on credit because their income, at least what Sand knew about, wasn't enough to cover it.

Meanwhile Thomas's wife, Danielle James, a short, stout, dark haired registered nurse, bought her husband a brand new sports car, a bright red Mitsubishi Eclipse, for a birthday present, only she had it delivered to the *Huntsville Times* with a giant white bow on it. Sand wondered why she didn't just have it delivered to their home. Danielle was obviously trying to make a statement, and it was clear that statement was intended to be public and noticed by more than just Thomas.

Then one day Sylvia failed to show up for work. Thomas was in meetings all morning. It was Sand who took the call from Wendell. "Sylvia's been taken by ambulance to the Huntsville Hospital emergency room, and I'm out of town," he said. "The children were getting ready for school, and Sylvia went to take a shower. They heard her scream. Our oldest, Charlie, found Sylvia on the bathroom floor. Water was everywhere, and the water in the shower was still on. Everything was steamy, because the hot water was blasting out of the shower head at full force. Sylvia was unconscious. Fortunately Charlie knew to call 911 for help. He also turned off the water and covered Sylvia's nude body with towels."

"Where are you?" Sand asked.

"Fort Lauderdale, Florida." He was close to hysteria.

"OK, I'll check on her. Where are the kids?"

"With my parents. Sylvia was taken to the hospital by ambulance," he repeated.

"It's OK, Wendell," Sand tried to reassure him. "I'm sure she's in good hands. Just get back home."

"Right," he said and hung up.

Sand told the boss, and together they went to Huntsville Hospital. When Sylvia regained consciousness, she was in shock. Sand and Thomas were told she was burned over two-thirds of her body, and a large part of that was third degree. Her face was spared, but her neck, chest, and right arm weren't. When a police detective arrived at the emergency room, Thomas spoke to him. Then Thomas told Sand, "The burns were caused by the hot water from the shower."

Sand had never consciously realized before that a person could be burned by tap water. Steam, yes. Boiling water, obviously, but a shower? No. Sand soon learned that if the water was hot enough, it only took a fraction of a second to cause third degree burns. Regardless of the source, a burn was a burn. Sylvia almost died.

To prevent infection, Sylvia had to endure brutal scrubbings with what she described to Sand in her more lucid morphine moments as wire brushes. It sounded like some medieval form of torture. Sand asked Wendell and Thomas repeatedly why Sylvia wasn't transferred to a hospital with a burn center, like one in Birmingham for example, since there was no burn unit in Huntsville, but Sylvia was kept at Huntsville Hospital. Sand wasn't family and therefore had no influence over Sylvia's situation.

When it was all over and she had survived, Sylvia told Sand her health insurance wouldn't cover plastic surgery, even for burns. She was badly scarred for life, but she had survived, and eventually she returned to her job at the newspaper. In the meantime, rumors and allegations flew around the Times about Wendell resetting the temperature on the hot water heater to get rid of her, but Sand knew that was ridiculous. Wendell would never have risked hurting the children, and it could just have easily happened to any one of them. As if ugly rumors weren't bad enough, when Sylvia came back to work physically scarred, some of the newspaper staff actually suggested behind her back that she had done it to herself deliberately because, the warped story went, she and Thomas had a falling out and she was trying to make him feel sorry for her or possibly guilty. Then there were those who tied the rumors together and said Sylvia had done it to herself to frame Wendell so she would be free for Thomas, scars and all. None of it made any sense to Sand.

The actual police investigation eventually revealed that the hot water heater was faulty and had simply malfunctioned. It was a potentially fatal accident. Sylvia lived cheerfully with the scars because she knew those scars had spared one of the children a painful death. A child's odds of surviving Sylvia's experience would have been far lower.

*

October 1976

Mitchell Masterson, Sylvia's older brother, also worked as a custodian at UAH, though at Morton Hall instead of the Humanities building, and Steve and Mitch became friends. Morton Hall was the first building the University of Alabama built in

Huntsville. Sand didn't get to know Mitch until after she had started college at UAH.

Mitch Masterson had simply declared his homosexuality openly when he registered for the draft, and as a result, the military didn't want him. After Steve and Sand had gotten married and Sand was working for the Times, Mitch would come over to the Fernandez house from time to time. Sometimes he would join them for a movie, and sometimes he would pick Steve up in the morning, and Steve would ride to and from work with Mitch, leaving Sand to drive their VW bus.

Mitch loved to talk about the play of polar opposites, the yin and yang of Nature, and the anima and animus in everyone and everything. Steve loved to talk about positive and negative space and how important it was to view the negative space of sculpture, even though most people only saw the positive space or actual physical form. They would get into lengthy discussions of light and shadow and how important it was to look at what was not present in a situation in order to understand what was present.

Mitch met Gregory Phillips through his brother-in-law, Wendell. Greg Phillips had not been called for military service. Greg worked construction for the Hatfield family business and, though clean shaven, wore his straight brown hair in a long ponytail. Mitch and Greg moved in together. Their place wasn't much more than a four room shack on the eastern outskirts of town on the eastern side of Monte Sano Mountain, but they fixed it up and made it pretty cozy. They were in love and determined to be lifetime companions.

Greg Phillips wasn't the deep thinker Mitch Masterson was, and in contrast to Mitch, he was a

quiet man. Sand and Steve saw Greg as a gentle
soul. He was kind and generous, loved animals, and
had a green thumb with flower and vegetable
gardens. After a hard day's work, he and Mitch
liked their beer. They probably drank to excess, but
they were in the privacy of their own home and not
hurting anyone.

Sand learned that beautiful, outgoing
Candace Masterson, Mitch and Sylvia's sister, who
was in between them in age, had fallen in love
while still in high school with Stacy Campbell, the
local bad boy rock and roll lead guitarist. Stacy was
dark, handsome, and had lots of confidence.
Teenage girls adored him. He had dropped out of
high school early on to play with various rock bands
until he finally started one of his own, the Stingrays.
Everybody knew he was destined to be a rock star
idol. Candace believed it too. They had gotten
married downtown in Big Spring Park while Sylvia
and Sand were still in high school.

At first, the Campbells led a very bohemian
lifestyle, but after playing in clubs and for high
school dances all over North Alabama, the
Stingrays started going on tour. Stacy would be
gone for months at a time. Meanwhile, Candace,
who had given birth to a precious baby girl about
six months after they'd married, stayed home with
Brenda, their daughter. The Campbell family
eventually moved into the two bedroom blue house
next door to Sand and Steve Fernandez on North
Rose Drive as renters, but usually just Candace and
Brenda were there. Brenda was a carbon copy of her
beautiful mother. Stacy only showed up on rare
occasions, and when he did he usually hung out
more with Mitch, Greg, and Steve rather than
spending time with his wife and daughter. That was

how Sand came to be one of the first adults in Brenda's life outside her family.

*

Brenda:

The Star of my deck is the grace that flows to those who manage through all of life's tragedies to keep their hearts open to trust in the universe, or at least in their own inner natures. Candace heart' was still open in those days. My mother believed her husband was destined to be a star. If she could only have seen the truth, she would have run away from him.

*

April 1977

Sand ran into her former high school boyfriend, Rick McDevitt, in two of her and Steve's favorite shops. One was a bookstore and the other was an ice cream parlor. The two shops were on opposite sides of the town square. Rick worked in both places. Steve and Sand would wait for Rick to get off work, and then they would walk down to Big Spring Park where Rick taught them to sing Sufi songs and dance. Sand liked the words that evoked pleasant, uplifting thoughts, and it was fun. Sometimes Rick's girlfriend, Valerie, would join them. Sand liked her and thought she was perfect for Rick. Valerie was kind of plain looking with light brown hair, but she was a happy, level-headed person with a lot of common sense. They seemed like a good match.

Sand and Steve attended Rick and Valerie's wedding and reception. Then for their honeymoon, Rick drove his bride to an estate in upstate New York that was owned and operated by Abdel Narim. It was a commune. The residents gave up their personal possessions and worked at the discretion of Abdel Narim and the hierarchy he had established. That meant they were assigned their jobs and had to work all of their waking hours for Abdel's benefit.

Some of that old-time religion, no matter how deep and mystical, could be downright unfriendly to a woman's self-esteem. It certainly put a crimp in Valerie's expectation of a honeymoon. A lot of women would sacrifice their own soul to please their man. A lot of women throughout history had to just to survive. But Valerie lived in a time and place where she didn't have to, and she had the sense to know when to say, "Enough." Women had already come through the feminist bra burning. Sand was proud of Valerie when she returned to Huntsville alone, but sad for Rick at the same time. She understood Rick had heard the calling of a mystical religion out of the past, but he was a masculine sun who couldn't see how it all looked from the perspective of his moon bride. Valerie had the marriage annulled, and Sand never heard from Rick again.

*

September 1977

At work Sand was assigned to assist Jennifer Emerson, a no-nonsense, all business *Times* reporter, who was checking on the status of six unrelated missing and abused children. Sand stopped by the social workers' offices for updates and then went with Jennifer to each of the children's neighborhoods, where they interviewed family members and neighbors.

In the afternoon, they attended a press conference given by the relevant social workers and police. Two of the children had been found. One, a fourteen-year-old, was arrested for breaking and entering and burglary and was still in custody. The other, age eight, had voluntarily returned home. His name was Jamie. Jamie's father was accused by his neighbors of physically abusing the boy, although none of them admitted to having actually witnessed any abuse or having any evidence.

Sand went back to the neighborhood with Jennifer to talk to the family. They knocked on the door and the father opened it. He was bald on top and slightly overweight. They saw Jamie standing behind his father, and he looked fine. He bore a strong resemblance to his father with his hair in a crew cut.

Jennifer showed her press ID and started to introduce herself and Sand, but Jamie's father interrupted saying, "No press, please," and closed the door.

As the neighbors learned the boy had come home, a crowd gathered around his home and demanded that the father come out and face them. Sand and Jennifer stood in the street and watched it all unfold. Sand was uncomfortable in the presence of a crowd. She had a very bad feeling about the developing situation.

Finally, father and son appeared at the door of their home together. When the neighbors started shouting, the father came outside, obviously bewildered. Suddenly, above the roar of the crowd, there was a gunshot, and the father dropped to the ground. The crowd was silenced. Sand jumped at the sound and then saw the look of horror, sadness, and fear on little Jamie's flushed face. As most of the crowd quickly dispersed, several men wrestled the woman holding the gun to the ground.

By the time the police arrived, Jamie's father was dead. The woman responsible was Jamie's mother. Sand and Jennifer learned that the mother and the now deceased father had been divorced less than a year, and the father had been awarded sole custody due to the mother's mental instability. She was an elementary school teacher at a public school and was also a former Catholic nun. She was also Sylvia, Mitch, and Candace's maternal Aunt Kate. This was the same woman Sand had witnessed molesting a boy about Jamie's age now all those years ago.

Jennifer Emerson, with Sand in tow shaking and silent, followed up by interviewing as many neighbors as she could find that were willing to talk to her about what had just happened. Everyone they talked to had already judged and condemned the deceased man, but none of them had talked to his son. None of them knew where Jamie had gone or why he had been missing. None of them knew why he had come home. Jennifer and Sand went back to the office where Jennifer wrote and filed the story, but all Sand had was a mind full of questions she couldn't seem to form into words.

*

December 1977

Kate was found not guilty by reason of mental defect and sent to Bryce, the state mental institution, down in south Alabama near Tuscaloosa. She was diagnosed as manic-depressive, or bipolar, and paranoid schizophrenic.

When Sand learned the diagnosis, she noted to herself that not all patients with mental illness are a danger to others, and those who pose a threat are rarely cognizant of it.

Mitch told Sand and Steve, "Jamie wants to live with me and Greg, but the court decided to grant custody to Candace. The judge said that he needs a stable family life, and Stacy has a good income. There's no relative on Jamie's father's side who could take him, and Candace was more suitable since Sylvia's on her second husband, and Wendell is unemployed."

"So he's moving in next door to us?" Sand asked. "With Candace and Brenda?"

"And Stacy," Mitch nodded in confirmation.

"I forget about Stacy," Sand said. "He's rarely home."

"I thought Jamie would be better off with Sylvia and Wendell," Mitch added. "Candace is also unemployed, but judges prefer mothers who stay home and raise the children."

"Wendell could at least teach him to play golf," Steve said sarcastically.

*

Brenda:

Children rarely get to make the important decisions in their lives—those are reserved for adults. Jamie would have been better off if he had been allowed to choose for himself, but I was grateful to have him as an adopted brother. The court that decided for him didn't exactly have all the facts about my parents.

As an adult, I believe that I can make reasonable choices, but there's the rub. My choices have consequences, and I don't like to deal with consequences unless they're pleasant ones. Could it be that my circumstances, like my imaginings, are of my own making? And the ultimate choice is, unlike my parents, will I accept responsibility for myself and my thoughts, or will I deny the reality I've created, even though the capability to do so was developed to avoid pain? Are my parents in pain?

Some are so afraid of responsibility, they'd rather let God take over and dictate that they're OK as long as they believe what they're told God said. If I let myself believe that we were handed a divine rule book, I'd expect those that believed it would follow the rules, and that would be unrealistic. To perceive morality as the oversimplified, two-dimensional concept of right and wrong betrays the process of delusion, and I am the daughter of Delusion.

And so humans come together, no matter what the excuse, seeking fellowship in their humanness. That in itself should tell us what we're here to do, but so much for the obvious. Wouldn't it be so much easier to believe it's not our doing? My mother fell into that trap. Everything happened TO her. She never saw herself as a player making conscious choices.

And wouldn't it be so much easier if we only lived one short lifetime and then it was over, and we didn't have to learn from it all and go on to more lifetimes? But to me the idea of just physical life and then physical death is too two-dimensional for the multi-dimensional universe where it all takes place.

I think that when the perception of God is restricted to the male gender of one species, the culture of that perception has closed its eyes to the reality of God's creation. If you want to know the artist, study her art. If you want to know the composer, listen to his music. If you want to know the author, read what she has written. Our Creator is a multi-dimensional lover of diversity, but instead of appreciating diversity, we've managed to develop elaborate social structures aimed at inducing conformity. Our intentions are to promote good by instilling fear of consequences, but quite often the consequence is people devising ways to avoid the social consequences while still doing what they want. My father was a musician. He was very creative both in music and in life. He had a huge sense of white male entitlement and devised his own way of living without conforming to social norms, and there were chaotic consequences for us all.

Chapter 18

Distorted Reflection
(Moon)

Dreams misunderstood are madness
Dreams ignored reflect around us
We create our limitations
And act surprised whey they surround us

Pretending to not be oneself
Distorts the mirror image
Worse is hating one's own self
Denying the inner message

*

Brenda:

When everything around us is in chaos, sometimes the only way we can find our way safely is by our own inner light. But when we cover up that light with desires and schemes, we lose that glimmer of reflection that reveals who we really are. When everything around us is in chaos, it's easy to confuse ourselves with our own precious delusions. That's The Moon card, and it challenges us to maintain our sanity while those around us are losing theirs.

*

Deception Past

September 1984
Gulf Coast

Isabel Akbey drove with her parents, Ibrahim and Maria, on Interstate 10 across the southern tip of Alabama and Mobile Bay, Mississippi, past Biloxi, and into Louisiana and New Orleans. New Orleans was hosting the World's Fair on platforms built out onto the Mississippi River next to the French Quarter. The family had been invited to stay in a house in the French Quarter that belonged to Zia Akbar Ali, an old family friend, almost bald with bifocal eyeglasses, but Sophia and Sonia couldn't join them. By this time, both of Isabel's sisters were married with families of their own and didn't want the children to miss school. Isabel, however, didn't pass up the opportunity to stay in the French Quarter. She had never been to New Orleans before.

Their host, Mr. Ali, had also come to the United States from London years before. He was a mutual friend of Dr. Akbey and Abdel Narim, and he was also hosting Abdel's son, Zakhir Narim. Mr. Ali's home on Ursulines Avenue in the French Quarter was not only an easy walk from the World's Fair, it also had a private courtyard with a lush garden full of subtropical plants and four o'clock flowers in yellows and reds that Isabel loved. Inside the ceilings were high with many bookshelves, Middle Eastern carpets, and the musty, moldy smell of an old house.

Zakhir was younger than Isabel but she found him quite handsome and charming. He wore only white shirts and trousers, which accented his dark complexion, but his appearance was neat and clean. Zakhir was beginning his studies in theology at Duke University in North Carolina, but his father Abdel had agreed that this invitation to the World's Fair should not be missed. Zakhir was as kind and unassuming as he was attractive. He was very much a gentleman.

Isabel began blushing in his presence and having fantasies about being alone with him. On the first of the group's all-day excursions to the Fair, she bought a golden yellow scarf to wear as a veil in an attempt to cover her embarrassment at feeling nervous and giddy around him. She was also consciously trying to exploit his sincere religious leanings. He was most complimentary of her new attire.

The theme of the fair was, appropriately, about water. At the entrance were colorful, bigger than life-sized Mardi Gras figures including Neptune himself. Aside from all the sights of the fair, the endless shops selling mementoes from various countries around the world, the paddle boat ride on the Mississippi River, and the US Space Shuttle Enterprise on display, the most intriguing moment of the vacation for Isabel took place in Zia's kitchen one morning over breakfast.

Maria casually mentioned the time she had visited southern France before the Second World War. "I had suddenly found myself in a village I'd never seen before in this life; yet I knew it as if it was my home. Indeed, I felt as if I had come home. Even though it was my 'first' time there, I remembered where a Roman-built bridge had been and found it exactly where I remembered. I knew I had come home."

Isabel could not believe she was hearing this from her own mother, who had never ever mentioned any such occurrence in Isabel's presence before. She couldn't remember her parents ever discussing reincarnation, even though she had read extensively about it as a young teenager. Isabel noticed how interested, amused, and encouraging Zia, Ibrahim, and even Zakhir were. They were hanging on Maria's every word and then asking questions, begging for more details.

When breakfast was over, the five of them went back to the Fair as if nothing out of the ordinary had transpired. Isabel was quiet most of the rest of the day, lost in thoughts and questions she did not know how to form into words. When the Akbeys parted company with Zia and Zakhir the next day to go home to Warrington, while Zakhir was headed back to Durham, North Carolina, Isabel tried to exchange addresses with him so they might correspond. Zakhir was kind, smiling, and very sweet, but managed to slip away leaving her only his father Abdel's address in upstate New York. Isabel would have to find another way to get his attention.

*

November 1984
Huntsville, Alabama

Sand was at her desk at work. When she unlocked and opened her desk drawer, she noticed that the envelope with Clarabelle's blackmail material was missing. She was startled by its absence, but in all the craziness, she honestly couldn't remember if she had actually shredded it like she had visualized doing so many times. Since no one else at work even knew it existed, and since things at home with Steve, her parents, and Jody

237

had settled down and conversations no longer centered on the murder, she didn't bother to mention it to anyone, not even Steve.

*

January 1986

January 20 was a special day for Sand and Steve Fernandez. It was the celebration of the first ever official Federal holiday honoring Reverend Dr. Martin Luther King Jr. For Sand it was vindication that time could actually bring about change for the better. Of course she was aware there were many in North Alabama who argued that Dr. King shouldn't have his own holiday because he'd never even been President of the United States, but then neither had Robert E. Lee, whose birthday had been honored in white southern states for a hundred years. All Lee had ever done was fight against the Union, which to Sand was treason. She knew from her childhood disagreements with Jonathan that General Lee had simply chosen loyalty to his state over his country, but the resulting bloodshed was enormous. Dr. King, on the other hand, was a man of peace. He was a man who gave his life in support and defense of the Constitution of the United States of America, and because of Dr. King's sacrifice, Sand knew that someday it would actually be possible for someone of African American descent to be President of the United States. Dr. King had made the great American Dream available to Americans who had been previously excluded. That was a far greater accomplishment than some past Presidents.

Then just a week later, the American space program suffered a blow with the deaths of all the astronauts on board the Challenger shuttle when it exploded shortly after lift-off. The country grieved again. Huntsville grieved again. For the first time in US history, the seven fallen astronauts represented both genders and varying ethnicity. One was even a school teacher selected from outside the elite corps of professional astronauts.

The Challenger disaster left some of the employees at Martin Marietta and the Marshall Space Flight Center in Huntsville dealing with varying levels of grief, anger, and guilt over a problem that had not been solved. Some had warned of disaster and others had not perceived the risk. Sand knew it was the nature of risk and human nature trying to balance information overload. Manned space flight had never been 100 percent safe, and all the astronauts knew that when they chose to become astronauts. Recalling the Apollo disaster from her childhood, she knew astronauts' families lived with the risk and worry until the time came that they either had to grieve or their astronaut left the program for some more grounded pursuit.

*

February 1986

One evening at home alone, while Steve was at UAH working on his sculpture, Sand answered the phone. A woman's voice said, "I want to suck your pussy."

Sand was too surprised to respond or hang up. She'd never had an obscene phone call before, but this was a woman. She was so shocked she just listened.

"I want to lick your clit," the voice continued.

"Who is this?" Sand asked, trying to recall where she'd heard the vaguely familiar voice before.

"Steve has a girlfriend," the caller continued. "Why shouldn't you?"

Hearing this, Sand hung up. This was someone who knew her? The caller knew Steve's name. Steve had a girlfriend? This wasn't something Sand could ignore or dismiss. Steve had his own studio behind their home, but he spent a lot of extra hours at the UAH sculpture studio. He said it was because there was equipment there he couldn't afford to buy for his home studio. Sand had believed him until this phone call.

Sand started dropping by the university's sculpture studio unannounced during her lunch break and on her way elsewhere on business. After a couple of months of poking around and talking to others there, she was convinced that the anonymous caller knew what she was talking about. She learned that Steve had been having lunch with one of the art department's nude models on a regular basis, and that same model had been spending considerable time in the sculpture studio, but only when Steve was there. Sand knew the woman wasn't modeling for Steve, because none of his work involved the human figure. She also couldn't place the anonymous caller's voice.

The music secretary confirmed to Sand, "Steve has been spending a lot of time with a coed who makes extra spending money posing as a nude model for the art classes."

Sand felt used and naïve. Steve had often made jokes about her fluctuating estrogen levels,

240

but apparently his testosterone was more of a problem. She also discovered during one of her surprise visits that Patty Compton was still a part-time art student there. The familiarity of the voice came back to her. The mystery caller was no longer a mystery.

*

May 1986

On the night of their eleventh wedding anniversary, as they sat down to dinner, Sand told Steve, "You know you're not fooling anyone."

"What do you mean?" he asked, smiling.

"Really?" Sand continued calmly. "Nude models? You could have had that right here at home. It never occurred to me that the equipment you were using at UAH wasn't made of metal."

Steve was no longer smiling.

She went on, "You must think you're very clever thinking up that line. Well, no matter. MY parents bought this house. YOU are the one guilty of adultery. So I guess you'll just have to move yourself, ONLY your stuff, and your sculpture somewhere else as soon as possible. You can have the bus. I need to buy a new car anyway. AND you'll be sleeping with your equipment from now on instead of in this house."

"Well, that's OK with me," he said, trying to cover his surprise. "Samantha Dickerson has been badgering me for some time to tell you that we want to be together."

"What the hell were you waiting for? More of my income?"

Steve and Sand separated. He moved out of the house and into a studio apartment, as he called it, downtown. He called it that because it had been a shop that he converted to an efficiency apartment with lots of studio space for his sculpture. His girlfriend, Samantha, moved into the apartment with him. Steve wanted a divorce right away so he could marry Samantha.

"Yeah, right," Sand responded, "like I'd agree to that without a fight. Go ahead. Hire a lawyer and take me to court over YOUR adultery." She knew he didn't have the money.

Samantha called Sand one night. "You need to give Steve a divorce."

"You know nothing of my needs," Sand answered.

"I can make your life miserable," she threatened.

"Mission accomplished," Sand responded, "but any discussion of divorce is between me and Steve. You're not in that picture. Besides, I'm doing you a favor." Sand hung up on her. She wondered why it was that women usually seemed to blame each other when they found out the man in the middle had lied to both of them. No two-timer was worth fighting another woman over. Still, she felt betrayed and couldn't help questioning where she had failed, but Jody, Candace, and Sylvia all reassured her it wasn't her fault.

The following week, Samantha's husband, Donald, phoned. After he introduced himself, he told her, "Look, I know all about Steve and my wife. What I don't know is if you or Steve have any children."

"No, neither of us has ever had a child," she told him, surprised to learn that Samantha was also married and wondering where he was going with this.

"Well, Samantha and I have three girls," Donald continued. "None are school age yet. I work full-time and Samantha was supposed to be going to school instead of posing naked and everything else." He paused to contain his anger. "The point is this: the day care personnel, our pediatrician, and our minister all suspect Samantha of abusing our daughters. There have been far too many unexplained bruises and burns, and the girls have been afraid since Samantha moved out that she's coming back. I'm getting a restraining order to keep her from seeing them. I just wanted to warn you in case you have any children, but you don't. Sorry to have bothered you."

"Thank you anyway. I hope your kids are OK." Sand hung up and then immediately called Steve and repeated the conversation.

"No way," Steve argued. "He's just making a case to gain full custody of the children. She'd never do anything to those girls."

"I hope you're right," Sand said, "but where there's smoke, there's fire."

Then one afternoon in October after work, Steve called Sand, who was still at her desk at the *Times*. He sounded frantic. "I just came home and found my furniture, stereo, and television all gone. Samantha is gone too. I don't know what happened."

"Well, I'm sure I don't either," Sand answered. "Guess nudity doesn't reveal the person inside."

*

Franki deMerle

1987

Sand finally agreed to an amicable divorce on grounds of incompatibility, even though they had actually been very compatible. She kept Steve's name and told him, "I changed my name for you once already. If you want a different name from me, change your own damn name." She and Steve remained friends, and her name remained Sand Fernandez. The divorce was final April 23.

Samantha Dickerson was arrested in September for attempting to smuggle illegal drugs and weapons across the Texas-Mexican border. She took a plea agreement. Sand found out Samantha was sentenced to more than a decade in prison.

Sand discovered that she liked being single. She cherished both her freedom and her solitude. She realized that a lot of people never learn to be comfortable alone with themselves and decided that maybe that was why some couples, like her parents, stayed married. Still she never regretted having been married to Steve. He had helped her through some difficult times, but now it was good to be on her own.

She adopted a female kitten from a local, no-kill animal shelter. The kitten, a long haired black and white, was full of life and energy, and loved to climb, run, and dance around the room on her back legs. She loved her toys and she loved Sand. She would climb up on Sand's face at night and suck her nose. Sand vowed to give her new little family member the best life possible. She named the kitten Grasshopper after the Kung Fu television show of the early 1970s that starred David Carradine. Besides, Grasshopper's black and white fur reminded Sand not only of a chocolate sundae, but also her favorite mint chocolate chip ice cream (without the green food coloring), which was also used in another of Sand's favorite desserts, Grasshopper Pie. Sand loved little Grasshopper.

Sand introduced Jody and her parents to the joys of pet ownership. Soon, the Strasbergs in southeast Huntsville welcomed a short-hair, tortoiseshell kitten into their home and named her Dandy Lion.

*

Sand was in a fun house, a place of magic mirrors—not real mirrors with honest reflections, but crazy mirrors with distortions and bizarre tricks of light and illusions. Sand was dreaming.

She came face to face with a woman she'd never seen before. The woman stranger was facing her from the mirror, but she wasn't Sand or anything like Sand. Sand could see into the woman's soul through the mirrors of her eyes—like looking into infinity, only it was illusions instead of true reflection. There were ripples and distortions and magnifications, but there was no presence of Sand's self.

Sand told the woman, "I never forgot. I didn't have to piece together who I was. And I didn't want to go back to it like you've done. I was and am moving on. I've had to deal with the trauma of what happened to me by myself while in a child's body. I'll never understand why you seem to think it's glamorous or special or desirable. What happened to me was the ultimate degradation, and I'm glad to have been liberated from that past.

"As for the family, you're looking for acceptance in all the wrong people. If you really remembered them, you'd see the transitory nature of parents and siblings. We're water, you and I—salt water. And you can never go back. I don't want to, and yet I can't forget.

"Keep your distance, protect yourself, and move on. Trust me when I say you don't know who you are. Find out by living it. Dive deep."

Then the glass crumbled like sand on a beach, only to be deluged, and Sand was drifting and breathing underwater. She had the sense that somewhere this stranger was beached on dry land, cast off by the true feelings of herself that she had not recognized.

*

1992

One morning at work, during spring when the azaleas all over town were in full bloom, Sand was skimming through the Associated Press releases. She spotted a familiar name in an article from Houston, Texas. The story was about a rock group named Double Take landing a contract at the recording studio in Muscle Shoals, Alabama. The band's leader and lead guitarist, Stacy Campbell, was featured in the article because he not only wrote most of the band's material, but he was also a native and resident of Houston with his wife, Coral, and their two daughters. Sand reread the release over and over. Finally, what she was reading started to sink in. Stacy Campbell, her next-door neighbor, was a bigamist.

Candace had become a good friend and neighbor, and Sand was fond of Brenda and Jamie. Jamie and Brenda had grown up and moved out of the house next door to Sand, but Sand still saw them from time to time when they would stop by to visit Candace. They were a nice family. They were good people. They didn't deserve Stacy's duplicity and betrayal. Sand felt she had to expose the truth, tell Candace, and publish the story. Double Take was about to be disbanded. Stacy Campbell would be spending his days in court instead of recording in Muscle Shoals.

*

1994

Candace was never the same after that. Sand tried to be supportive, but Candace couldn't forgive her for shattering her world. After the divorce, bigamy charges, and bankruptcy that followed having her life and what she thought was her identity as his wife stolen by the person she most trusted, Candace started shopping around for someone to replace Stacy. She had never worked to support herself. She had always expected that from her man. She never sought counseling or even browsed a self-help book. She never took time to work on picking up the pieces of her shattered self and putting herself back together. She only groped blindly for a replacement for the missing villain that had hurt her so badly. She latched onto Lindsay Driscoll, short and unshaven, in a bar one night, and they were married a few weeks later on March 15.

What was important to Candace was having a new identity to put the shame of the past betrayal behind her, but she didn't recognize that alcohol was more important to Lindsay than anything else. They'd been married for less than two months when he beat her up. Candace ran to Hope Place, the local shelter for battered women. She didn't stay there long either before she moved in with her sister Sylvia. She didn't have the money to file for divorce, but she did end up filing bankruptcy again.

Meanwhile, her daughter Brenda still adored Stacy, her two-timing dad, probably because she didn't know him. To Brenda he was still the perfect father of her fantasy.

Lindsay, of course, continued to drink. The landlord started eviction proceedings against him because the only lease had been signed by Candace, who no longer lived there, and because no one was paying the rent. By the time the process worked its way through the court system and the sheriff finally went in and removed all of what was left of Candace and Lindsay's possessions, Lindsay had totally trashed the inside of the house and taken off. Walls were bashed in and the place was filthy. No one Sand knew understood why Lindsay was so angry, but then Candace was the only one Sand knew who knew Lindsay.

Then one day late in August, in the company of a drinking buddy, Lindsay Driscoll jumped off the Tennessee River Bridge on a dare. The buddy didn't jump, even though he was also inebriated. The autopsy showed Lindsay died on impact with the water, but he had enough alcohol in his blood to dull the experience for him. It certainly dulled the rest of his senses.

Sand couldn't imagine what Candace must have been going through. First, the love of her life turned out to be a fraud. Then, she had to run for her life to a shelter, and now the man she'd run from had jumped off the Tennessee River Bridge. On top of that, her closest sister had been badly scarred by scalding water.

Sand recalled the first time she'd met Candace when they were teenagers. Candace had been so carefree and happy. It had been a very long time since she had seen Candace happy. Sylvia and Mitch had always seemed to Sand to have a certain inner strength to hold themselves together during a crisis. She'd never seen that in Candace.

Two days after the *Times* reported Lindsay's demise, Sand had a dream about Jonathan Moreau. She hadn't seen Jonathan in years, but after she woke up the next morning, she couldn't shake off the feeling the dream left. It hung over her like a mosquito net. She could see the world around her, but it was somehow unable to touch her through it. She dreamt he was out on the ocean in a little rowboat. She was watching him from down below—deep below the waves and wind and rain that tossed his little boat around. It was so still and comforting where she was. She wondered why he never looked down, only up at the ever-changing rain and sky and into the face of the wind. Sand wondered why he persisted in his little boat that so clearly had such a short life ahead of it. She wondered why he didn't just join her down below where it was quiet, but he never did. He stayed up there where the elements converged and things changed too fast to fathom.

For months after that dream, Sand felt like she was looking at everyone and everything from the peaceful depths. She knew, because she lived and worked in the waking world, that this feeling would eventually give way under the constant bombardment of its reality. But she also knew that when it was gone, she just had to remember to dive deep to find it again. She remembered telling some stranger in another dream to dive deep.

And what was with Jonathan and all that heaven stuff anyway? You couldn't even breathe out there. Drown up, drown down. It was beyond elemental ring toss, and it was quiet. Fire and water, Jonathan and Sand. The difference was he'd struggle all the way, while she would float to the flow of gravity. She had learned to let go, but fire must possess and conquer only to learn that it can't.

*

March 1995

Kate, Sister Kate, Aunt Kate, never found much peace. After she was released from the mental hospital down near Tuscaloosa, she returned to Huntsville and moved into the trailer with Candace and Sylvia's parents. She stayed on her medicines, but eventually the only thing keeping her balanced got out of balance. The medicine that was working so well for her built up in her system until it became toxic. The doctor had to change her prescriptions, and in doing so, she lost her balance again.

Mitch called Sand that night. "Kate shot herself in the head with Dad's .22 caliber pistol. She's still alive. They took her by ambulance to the Huntsville Medical Center, but the police detained all of us for questioning because she was shot in the left side of the head. I told them she was left handed, but they have to verify it. Can you please go to the hospital emergency room to meet her?"

"Of course," she said. "I'm on my way." When she got there, she learned that Kate had been admitted as a Jane Doe, at least until Sand

250

positively identified her. Kate's face was already bruising, and her left eye was pushed outward, protruding from its socket so that the lid couldn't close. Her eye looked dead. Her hands were wearing plastic bags until the police could collect any forensic evidence. The police eventually satisfied themselves that it was indeed a suicide attempt.

At first the Mastersons and Sand were afraid Kate would die, but then as each day passed, they became afraid that she wouldn't. The doctor explained to them, "The bullet ricocheted inside her skull without exiting. It's still in there, but to remove it would only cause more damage. She's permanently blind and unconscious, but I've got her on enough medication to prevent her from feeling pain."

After about a week, Mitch finally convinced Jamie to come to the hospital. The doctors needed his consent as next of kin to disconnect the life support. He gave his consent, and Kate died two days later.

*

April 1995

After the shame of Lindsay's death in the local headlines, and after her Aunt Kate had died, Candace Masterson Campbell Driscoll added Phillips to the end of her name in a surprise civil ceremony at the Madison County Courthouse. Brenda Campbell was her maid of honor, and Wendell Hatfield was the best man since he happened to be in town. Mitch and Jamie chose not to attend or celebrate Candace stealing her brother's boyfriend and intended life partner, Greg. The newlyweds rented a small house in an older neighborhood off Holmes Avenue near the high school Sand, Mitch, Sylvia, and Candace had attended. Greg worked as a car salesman at the Nissan dealership on West University Drive.

Brenda kept Jamie informed of the details of Mr. and Mrs. Phillips's life that she gathered from her occasional visits. Jamie passed the information on to Mitch, who briefed Sand when they would see each other every month or two.

Sand was horrified at the downward spiral sweet Candace's life had taken. She worried about how Brenda could cope with all of it.

Mitch told Sand, "According to Greg, Jesus liberated him from his sin of homosexuality. Cocaine and marijuana have them on a tight budget when it comes to food, clothes, and other luxuries."

"But where are they getting it from?" Sand wanted to know.

"Greg has all the connections," was all Mitch would say.

Sand wasn't sure if Mitch was more bitter or relieved, or whether he was more jealous of his sister, the drugs, or Jesus. Mitch was adamant that the marriage wouldn't last and that Candace was doomed to get hurt again. He and Sand both wondered how much Candace could take and if she was too far beyond damaged to ever learn from her mistakes.

Apparently, according to the third-hand reports Sand received, Jesus, Candace, and blow weren't enough to keep Greg heterosexual. As Mitch phrased it, "It's hard to rewire biology."

Greg would sometimes bring home a boyfriend, and Candace would have to sleep on the couch unless she wanted to take part in a threesome. Since she had no resources of her own, she chose to stay with Greg and to live within the choices he presented her. After two bankruptcies already, no assets of her own, and no sense of her own identity, she was trapped by blind existence.

Jamie told Mitch, "Brenda tried to reason with her. She told her mom that she could come home to any of her family and that she didn't have to put up with this sordid mess, but to no avail."

Candace was suffering from the deadliest illness of all—shame.

Chapter 19

Gravitational Center
(The Sun)

Now has come full circle
Now is all we have
We are but a moment
Culmination of the past

*

Brenda:

The Sun card assures us that no matter how dark or distorted our situation may seem, at the proper time, the Sun will rise again and burn away darkness and the fog of confusion. We can lose ourselves in the past or in worry or anticipation of the future, but sometimes we get so caught up in the present we forget there will always be another day. When lost or confused, all we really have to do is wait it out. Happiness will always return.

*

May 1995

After Candace ran off with Greg Phillips, Mitch's lover, Sand and Mitch began having dinner together every Friday evening. Mitch found himself alone for the first time in his life, and he didn't much care for it, so he moved back to the trailer park in northeast Huntsville that his parents had moved to years ago after the one on Madison Pike had been hit by the tornado.

Mitch informed Sand over pizza one Friday evening, "Jamie admitted to me it wasn't his father who had abused him when he was little. He ran away from home because he was afraid his dad would be angry about a failing grade on a school paper."

"Really?" Sand mumbled, remembering that day when she witnessed Jamie's mother, Kate, murder his father. Jamie had grown up to be a levelheaded, heterosexual male, who was proud of his job with the city's sanitation department. Sand knew that Mitch and Jamie had become close. Sand thought of the contrast between plain-looking, sensible Jamie, and his beautiful but sensitive and extremely emotional cousin, Brenda.

"Yeah, he was supposed to bring the paper back to his teacher with his father's signature on it, and he didn't want to face his dad with it. He didn't want his dad to be disappointed in him because he was already hiding the secret of his mother touching him in ways she shouldn't have. Personally, I think his father already suspected something was amiss, which is why he got sole custody. But I didn't tell Jamie that. Jamie always believed Kate had murdered his dad because he had taken Jamie from her. Jamie never believed that her behavior that day had anything to do with her mental illness, and he never believed her sexually abusive behavior with him had anything to do with illness either."

"Really?" Sand mumbled again, not bothering with any more pizza.

Mitch continued, "She took too much from him. He can't empathize with her in any way."

"He's not alone there," Sand said, thinking of all the people she'd known who'd found fault with others in their lives for much pettier reasons and had trouble forgiving them.

Mitch added, "I told him, 'Not forgiving is far worse than any crime or illness.'"

Sand understood Jamie's reasoning. It made sense in its own way. Lots of perfectly sane and normal people abused children and committed murders, and lots of manic-depressives and paranoid schizophrenics didn't. Family members always had a hard time accepting mental illness in one of their own. It hit too close to home and exposed too much about their gene pool to outsiders.

It was Kate's own family that had pushed her into the convent to start with, because they didn't know what was wrong with her or how to deal with her. The convent, Kate's adopted family, had encouraged her to leave in favor of her relationship with Jamie's father because they didn't know how to deal with her either.

Sand's own family had as much difficulty dealing with an incestuous rape. She wondered if her grandfather had ever forgiven his brother. She wondered if Clarabelle had been able to. Probably not. She'd not only had to cope with the trauma, but also the guilt trip her own relatives put on her.

"I'm glad Jamie never had to deal with the draft," Sand commented. The United States had since replaced the draft with a volunteer army.

"Military service is a great thing for those who are willing and able and choose it," Mitch observed, "but that kind of forced conformity isn't healthy for everyone."

"No kidding," she agreed. "Look at the impact it had on Jody's fragile emotional state, and he never saw combat."

"Being part of a very controlling institution is not the best course in life for some," Mitch restated. "Fortunately, Jamie hasn't shown any signs of manic-depression or schizophrenia, but he understands the hereditary risk and says he'll never have children."

"How's your mom?" Sand asked. Mitch gave her a look that showed he understood what she was implying, but he didn't answer.

"Jody's been doing volunteer work at the Humane Society," Sand offered.

"I know," Mitch said curtly. "My mother's fine. She doesn't have Kate's illness."

"He used his volunteer experience to finally get a paying job at a pet store," Sand continued. "It's just behind Parkway City Mall. In the process of assisting a customer, he told me he befriended a lady somewhat older than himself. She never had children and wanted a pet to nurture. The problem was that her husband wouldn't tolerate an animal in the house, and she was afraid if she brought one home, her husband would abuse or hurt it."

"So he's seeing a married woman?"

"Married to my boss," Sand explained. "Danielle James herself. The two of them have decided to make a break from their habits and start a new life together."

"Really?" Mitch said, sitting back in surprise.

"Really," Sand confirmed, "but they're just in the planning stage. I don't think Thomas has a clue."

*

December 1995

Thomas and Danielle James divorced shortly before Christmas. Jody and Dandy Lion moved in with Danielle not far from his parents' home in southeast Huntsville. Thomas moved into an apartment.

Sand sold the house on North Rose Drive in January and bought a two-story back in Sherwood Park. She and Grasshopper enjoyed playing ball on the stairs. They were very happy together.

Sand noted that Thomas tried to put on a front to keep anyone at work from seeing how hurt, lonely, and bitter he was. He avoided talking to Sand as much as possible. She understood, but she didn't understand why he often took out his anger on Sylvia. He and Sylvia engaged in shouting matches over the pettiest trivia and usually, but not always, Sylvia would burst into tears. Sand figured they'd been working together for so long that it was just normal family behavior.

Sylvia frequently worked only a few hours a day or just didn't bother to come to work. She always called. According to her many reasons for not working, she had to attend funerals for endless relatives and in-laws, and there were endless medical appointments for complications from her burns. There really were complications from the burns. She had scar tissue in her esophagus, stomach, and lungs from the scalding water she had swallowed and inhaled, and Sand knew Sylvia had more to deal with emotionally than anyone Sand knew except for Candace. The one question Sand couldn't find an answer to was, "How were Sylvia and Wendell Hatfield able to support their lavish lifestyle with so little income?" It was a question Sand had asked herself before, only about someone else.

*

February 1996

It wasn't unusual to see police officers, detectives, and sheriff's deputies coming and going at the *Huntsville Times*. What was unusual was the day the Huntsville police arrived with a search warrant for Thomas James's desk, files, and work area. A search warrant was also served for his home. Even his sports car was searched. Sand saw the documents taken from his filing cabinet right before Thomas was arrested for blackmail. She recognized those papers even though she wasn't close enough to read them. She remembered the package that had gone missing from her locked desk drawer so long ago that she had convinced herself she had destroyed it.

Thomas was taken away in handcuffs in front of his entire staff. Sand cringed at how humiliated he must have felt. It all happened too fast for her to make any sense of how the detectives had come to find that dreadful package in Thomas's filing cabinet.

Not long after that, a former sheriff committed "suicide" by parking his car in a vacant parking lot late one night, leaving the engine running, using his unusually short arms to shoot himself in the chest and abdomen with his own shotgun pointing upwards, smearing his blood all over the front seat and dashboard, getting out and crawling to the back of the car, and inhaling the exhaust fumes from the tailpipe. Suspiciously, there was no murder investigation. Sand couldn't help but wonder if it was somehow tied to Clarabelle's blackmail package, but she clearly understood the matter was too dangerous to look into. Meanwhile a former city councilman, one mentioned in the blackmail package, fled the country.

Thomas James was convicted of blackmail and sent to the state prison in neighboring Limestone County. Sylvia Hatfield was promoted to replace Thomas James. Sand wanted to remain friends with Sylvia, but she didn't think she could manage that with Sylvia as her boss, so she applied for jobs with the *Huntsville News*, the *Times*' only rival. She took the first job she was offered and was grateful she didn't have to take a cut in salary.

Sylvia accepted Sand's congratulations on her own promotion. "I hate to see you go, but I understand," she told Sand. "You can always come back to work here. I'd be glad to have you."

*

January 1997
Warrington, Florida

Dr. Ibrahim Akbey retired from his private practice. He sold the two-story house on Second Street in Warrington and bought a beautiful condominium for himself, his wife Maria, and their youngest daughter, Isabel. It was in a beachfront

high-rise called Eden on Perdido Key. All they had
to do to smell the fresh, salt breeze from the Gulf of
Mexico was step out onto their private deck facing
the water. For Ibrahim and Maria, it was the
culmination of the American dream. They could
spend retirement in peace while living the good life.

After living most of her life in the two-story
house on Second Street, Isabel felt she had no
personal space. She had her own bedroom, but it
was smaller than her previous one. Compared to the
house, the entire living space was small.

One night shortly after they'd moved in,
Isabel dreamed she was in the new condo with her
parents. She felt exposed and trapped. She also felt
invisible at the same time. She had no privacy, but
still no one seemed to notice she was there. It was
maddening. Ibrahim and Maria yelled at her and
criticized everything she did or didn't do. She felt
no one could see her for who she was.

Isabel was stuck in the wrong place and
didn't know how to get herself free. She wanted to
get back to her life, but she couldn't find it. Then
her mother told her she had to go back to high
school because she had never finished. Isabel knew
she had to finish high school before she could get
her job back at the hospital, but she just couldn't
face going through all of that again. So every
morning, she stayed in bed while her mother yelled
at her to get up and go to school. After several days,
her mother gave up and didn't bother anymore.

One day when Isabel was tired of hiding in
bed and her body was stiff and sore and she hurt all
over, she got up. She could hear her mother in the
kitchen, so she moved as quietly as she could. She
didn't want the yelling to start again, but it was
difficult because she was clumsy from being so

stiff. And she had no energy. She hadn't eaten for days, and her head felt fuzzy. She made it into the living room where her limbs gave out, and she simply collapsed on the floor. She heard her mother come into the room. Isabel heard her pause for a moment and then walk over to where Isabel was lying on the floor. Maria paused again. Then she stepped over Isabel's body and left the condo. Isabel continued to lie there alone in the condo on the living room floor until she woke up.

*

June 2001
Huntsville, Alabama

"By the way, I've been meaning to give you this," Mitch said to Sand one night when they met in a restaurant on University Drive for dinner. He handed her an old but familiar manila envelope.

Sand was shocked. She ran her hands over it several times and then looked up at Mitch. "But where—"

"Jamie asked me to return it to you," he continued. "He said he took it from Sylvia's safe at home after he found the combination written down in the desk drawer in her den. He knew from listening in on some of her phone calls at night, while he was visiting over the past several years, that she was blackmailing a couple of people. When he found this in her safe, he figured out this was what that was all about. Since it seemed to be connected to your aunt who was murdered, he thought you should have it instead of Sylvia. Besides, she shouldn't have it to begin with."

Sand opened the envelope and looked inside. It was the original set of ledgers and photographs that Jody had found in Clarabelle's laundry room. Sylvia had used it to get her promotion and get groping Thomas off her backside at the same time. Sand shook her head. "Thomas never had a clue it even existed. I should have destroyed this thing years ago," she told Mitch.

He nodded in agreement.

*

September 2001

By the time religious extremists hijacked commercial airliners and used them as bombs to destroy New York City's Twin Towers of the World Trade Center on September 11, the right-wing religious extremists in the United States had renamed themselves conservatives and elected George W. Bush as president. The hijackers, mostly Saudi Arabians, didn't represent any country or government, except they were allied with the Taliban which had taken control of Afghanistan, reduced women to the status of slaves just like in Saudi Arabia, and, like Saudi Arabia, were totally against the democratic principles on which the United States was founded. So the United States attacked Afghanistan, but it wasn't enough for the conservative extremists.

Back at the end of Jimmy Carter's one and only term as president, there had been an uprising in Iran led by a Moslem cleric. A ruthless dictator had been overthrown. The Shah of Iran had maintained his position with the support of the United States. The new rulers viewed the United States as satanic because it had supported the Shah—guilt by association. The US embassy in Tehran was overrun and hostages taken. Americans were very vocal in their cries for blood and vengeance. The radios played the very popular song *Bomb Iran*, a takeoff of the old Beach Boys song *Barbara Ann*.

In spite of the uproar, not unlike the vocal uproar of the Moslem militants on the other side of the world, President Carter chose not to bomb and kill the hostages. For this he was voted out of office. That was twenty years before.

Now, all around Sand in the Bible Belt of the Deep South, people were angry and bloodthirsty for vengeance, even though the Bible said that was God's purview. Sand had learned long ago by vainly trying to have sensible conversations with some of them that most conservative extremists had never even read the Bible. They weren't supposed to question what the ministers and the president said, unless the president was a liberal. They had turned the word liberal into a derogatory term, because in their narrow little world, being open-minded was a sin. They had a lot in common with their opposition, the Islamic extremists that blamed the United States for being prosperous.

The actor Richard Gere was booed off a stage in New York City for suggesting that compassion, the common ground of Islam and Christianity, and calm were called for. Families of the victims of 9/11 were pushed into the background in favor of war. Back when Timothy McVeigh had attacked the Murrah Federal Building in Oklahoma City, no one called for vengeance against disgruntled American extremists, and in hindsight, Sand was extremely grateful for that. But now the conservative extremists used their power to start another crusade in the Middle East while they chipped away at the US Constitution at home with the Patriot Act. While trying to make sense of all of it, Sand recalled the words of founding father Benjamin Franklin, "They who would give up an essential liberty for temporary security deserve neither liberty nor security."

*

2002

Sand was dismayed when, once again, the US space program suffered another disaster. Another shuttle, the Columbia, disintegrated on reentry. Again employees had raised questions about safety issues, but the risk was balanced against the need to keep the shuttles flying. In a business built on risk, and while the astronauts who died understood and chose to take those risks, there were more grieving families, friends, and public left behind to reevaluate the risk against the loss. The images of all the scattered pieces collected across east Texas were gruesome. It was darkly ironic to Sand and Mitch that most of the families lived in Houston but had been at the Cape in Florida expecting to greet their loved ones there after the shuttle landed. Instead their loved ones' remains had landed in pieces back in east Texas.

Sand and Mitch talked about how most of the 9/11 terrorist hijackers were Saudi Arabians. Saudi Arabia treated women like slaves, had a tiny aristocracy ruling its desperately poor population, and stood firmly in the way of democracy in the Middle East. The ringleader of the terrorists, Osama bin Laden, had been born and raised in the Saudi

Arabian aristocracy. Sand and Mitch wondered if the United States would finally stand up to the Saudi oil business.

Iraq, Saudi Arabia's northern neighbor, was a dictatorship, but at least women were free in Iraq to go to school, work, and have lives of their own. Unlike in Saudi Arabia, Iraqi women weren't required by law to cover their heads and faces in public like they were somehow diseased and contagious. So the United States invaded Iraq.

Sand and Mitch were totally perplexed how it had come to this.

Iraq???

Iraq was run by yet another ruthless dictator who had been backed by the United States. Thus began another lengthy, unwinnable war for the US. Law-abiding citizens who chose to exercise their constitutional rights to assembly and free speech were viewed as threats by the US government and labeled "un-American" by the conservative extremists that didn't much care for the Bill of Rights.

Sand came to understand that history did indeed repeat itself until people learned from previous mistakes, but first they had to be willing to remember what happened before and what the consequences were. She and Mitch learned to keep their voices almost to a whisper when they discussed politics over dinner in any restaurant.

"Americans don't like to think about consequences," Sand commented to Mitch one evening in a hushed voice.

"A lot of Americans don't even like to think," he responded. "They just want action now, and consequences be damned. It's all a circle. Once light hits that mirror, it's going to come back at us," he prophesized and then changed the subject. "By the way, Sand, why don't you publish your poetry? I know you've had individual poems published here and there, but you've got enough for a book."

"What would be the point?" she answered. "I'm an unknown. Poetry is rarely a big seller. Who'd be interested?"

"I wasn't thinking about you making money on it. There are lots of worthwhile charity groups that could use the proceeds. If it was a good cause, people might buy it for the cause."

"I'll give that some thought," she promised.

Chapter 20

Letting Go of the Past
(Judgment)

Frightening to feel betrayed
But we are no different
Hating someone's such a waste
When we all seek forgiveness

*

2003

Sand unloaded her newly purchased computer from her compact car with difficulty and managed to get all the boxes safely into her home office. After unpacking, carefully following the directions that were simplistic enough even for her, connecting all the cables, and letting all the software wizards complete their wizardry, she clicked her Internet icon. Wanting to just play around a little, she typed "dreams" into her search engine. The search results were exactly what she'd asked for, but not at all what she wanted.

She thought a moment. "Symbolism," "spiritualism," "occult," and "New Age" were equally just as vague, so she thought some more. She thought of Mitch and how he loved to talk about the symbolism in the cards he read. She also remembered that his niece, Brenda Campbell, played with Tarot cards. Mitch had given Brenda her deck as a gift one Christmas a few years ago.

Mitch had told Sand recently, "Brenda's pretty good at the cards."

"Exactly what does that mean?" she asked him.

Mitch explained, "The art of 'divination' is nothing more than seeing oneself in a mirror or holding up a mirror so that someone else can see themselves and where the path they have chosen to follow leads.

"People who consult the Tarot just want to see themselves more clearly. They're looking for answers that can only be found in themselves, but because they don't see themselves for whom or what they are, they look for the answers outside of themselves. That's why I gave Brenda her own deck. I thought it might help her. Of course I explained it to her too—about the cards just being a reflection of whomever looks into them using archetypal symbols common to us all, like dreams. She's bright. She picked it up quickly.

"The card reader isn't a psychic or fortune teller," Mitch had continued. Mitch loved to talk when the subject was something he knew about. "The card reader is just the person holding the mirror. There's nothing evil or scary about it, and anybody that says that is just superstitious out of ignorance of archetypal symbolism and probably has never even heard of Joseph Campbell or Carl Jung, but I digress."

Sand understood that Mitch had inadvertently pushed one of his own buttons but caught himself. She smiled and nodded.

He went on, "The person having the reading only sees himself or herself as honestly as he or she is able. That's the only catch. But even people with both eyes closed can dream, and dreams are the same as the cards in that they use symbols to show the dreamer his or her real self and where the path he or she is on is going.

"When we deny parts of ourselves, and as humans we so often do, we're not whole. What I don't like about most religions is that they encourage the believer to give away part of their ability to perceive themselves on their own terms, and as a result, the believer is giving away part of their own identity. Of course not all religions do that, just the more fundamentalist versions, and even then it's up to the individual to choose how much of their free will and identity to give away. I know some people wouldn't have any kind of moral compass at all without a religion, but again I digress. I just get very annoyed when people that won't even look at themselves in a mirror condemn something they don't bother to understand." Mitch took a breath and exhaled slowly.

Sand waited patiently for him to continue, as she knew he would.

"Where was I before I got off on the religion thing?" he asked.

"Self-denial means you're not whole," Sand prompted.

"Oh, yeah," he went on, catching his own thread of thought. "It's just that opening one's eyes to oneself, seeing the parts one has denied or simply ignored, is how we become whole. It's how we heal our wounded or injured parts. Poor kid's been hurt enough already. I thought learning the Tarot might help Brenda find herself and heal."

"So that's also your interest in the Hindu religion?" Sand asked. "Everything being part of the One—it's about healing yourself."

"That's the reason anyone is interested in any religion," he confirmed, "unless somebody just scares you into believing you're going to burn in hell unless you join up. As far as I'm concerned, that's no different than sorcery or organized crime demanding protection money."

Sand sat at her new computer and thought about that conversation a few minutes more, and then she searched for "Tarot meanings." She found an interesting website with an article on the historical origins of the Tarot Card deck. The article described the twenty-two Major Arcana cards, the ones that didn't get converted into the current, standard fifty-two card playing deck. There was an exception. The Fool had become the modern Joker. These cards were all numbered, but The Fool's number was zero.

The cards' meanings were not given as fortune-telling devices, but rather as an allegory for human personal, spiritual development or evolution. The position of Justice and Strength, numbers eight and eleven respectively, were often exchanged in modern Tarot decks. Sand remembered Mitch having said the very same things years ago before anyone had personal computers.

Sand thought it was interesting that in the context of this allegory, number thirteen, Death, was more in the middle than at the end. She found it odd that this story told by the historical cards put The Fool, or Joker, next to the last of the twenty-two cards, because it symbolized a choice at the time of physical death. The Fool, number zero, was after number twenty, Judgment, and before number twenty-one, The Universe.

Judgment was really about letting go of one's own judgments. It was necessary just to see things as they were. We had to let go of our judgments to see ourselves as we really were. Judging distorted the mirror.

The Fool was said to represent Divine Light in human form. The other Major Arcana symbolized the progression of the individual seeker's life through the linear world of time and space. They signified the events and experiences through which we realized, defined, and identified our lives and selves. The Fool also represented true enlightenment, which was always considered truly foolish by those completely mesmerized by the seeming permanence and reality of the physical world. According to the article, anyone who was truly enlightened would be considered a fool by the unenlightened, who considered themselves practical and down to earth. Those allegedly normal, worldly people were unable to distinguish between the enlightened and the truly foolish, but since they were the truly foolish for thinking the enlightened foolish, true enlightenment was all a game of mirrors.

The Fool, or Joker, saw the humor, absurdity, and futility of all the things people believed in and trusted would endow their lives with permanence and stability. The Fool understood that Nature danced ceaselessly. In time, nothing stood still. Nothing was permanent.

There was also apparently a special relationship between triads of the Major Cards, excluding The Fool, if laid out in rows of seven. Again the article Sand was reading stressed that this relationship was for spiritual contemplation rather than fortune-telling games. The presence of only The Fool, the card of choice, in the modern playing deck seemed to underscore the author's point that attempting to foretell the future was a waste of time. Sand found that was interesting. She recalled the old adage that "life makes fools of us all."

Sand typed "reincarnation" on the keyboard and hit the enter key. The fourth website she tried turned out to be autobiographical testimonials by people she'd never heard of describing their reasons for believing they were reincarnations of other people, mostly historical figures, but some claimed less than celebrated past lives. Some were stories of coming to their realizations by way of dreams, memories, déjà vu experiences, and synchronous events.

After reading a few testimonials, Sand skimmed through the index. The only order she could find to it was by date of publication. The testimonials came from all over the world. Then Sand spotted a familiar byline from Pensacola, Florida. Isabel Akbey had announced on this website that she believed herself to be the reincarnation of Nadia Narim, a British spy and heroine from World War II. Sand had never heard of Nadia Narim. Her first thought was of the time in high school just before school started when she had shared with Isabel her dreams of dying in the oven. If Isabel had been there in that life or time, why had she not shared her own memories with Sand? Sand remembered Isabel telling her about reincarnation, but she never once mentioned having memories of her own. Had Isabel been patronizing her?

Sand had truly believed Isabel was her friend. After all, it was Isabel she had chosen to confide in about something so personal as her memory of death. If Isabel had only talked to her about her own memories, Sand wouldn't have felt so alone. Sand also recalled Chrissie Jackson telling her about meeting Isabel when she had come to town and never bothered to contact Sand. Maybe Isabel hadn't been the friend Sand had mistaken her for. Sand was disappointed that the friendship had really been one-sided.

She continued to peruse Isabel's entry. Nadia Narim had been decorated posthumously for valor and for giving her life to fight Nazi Germany. After the family fled France to England just ahead of the invading troops, Nadia had joined the British military forces and gone back into occupied France undercover as a radio operator. Isabel had included a picture of Nadia with her testimonial. At first Sand was struck by the total lack of resemblance to Isabel, but then she realized there was something vaguely and eerily familiar hiding behind those dark eyes. Nadia's coloring was different from her own, but there was a tangible resemblance to the face Sand saw in the mirror. Nadia's was a haunting expression—haunting but familiar, giving away only the slightest hint of fear but nothing else—a soul submerged behind an expression intended to give nothing away. There was something eerie about the image. Sand involuntarily shuddered.

She looked again at the picture of Nadia Narim, so hauntingly familiar. This was definitely not Isabel. Could Sand have actually known Nadia? Sand still had a vivid memory of having been stripped naked by the soldiers in black uniforms, beaten, dragged to the crematorium, shot in the upper back, and shoved into the oven. Her last thought was "liberté." She had shared all of this with Isabel. Why had Isabel said nothing about Nadia or past life memories of her own and yet published this on the Internet? What was going on here?

Sand read further. The Narim family was influential, well-connected, and family friends of Isabel's parents. The wealthy and influential were considered successful and were admired by others living their normally stressful lives. To have known such a family that included a bona fide war hero was good conversation. Sand's cheeks had turned red and were beginning to burn as she realized Isabel had not been forthcoming with her. And now, in this testimonial, was she being any more forthcoming?

Nadia had been raised by a religious Moslem family in a time and place where women weren't trusted with their own lives, but instead treated like perennial children. Sand realized Isabel would identify with this, where Sand would rebel against it. Nadia had grown up in a family of influence with a sense of service to others in the community, but her unrealistic expectation of influence over the war from inside occupied France resulted in her being caught, imprisoned, and executed. Maybe her decision to leave home and risk death was more desirable than staying home and giving up the freedom to make her own decisions. Sand could identify with that, but Isabel had never displayed any independence. The Isabel that Sand remembered was always in Patty's shadow, taking her cues from Patty or from someone else when Patty wasn't around.

Sand read that Isabel was still living with her parents. Isabel had announced to her family that she was Nadia. Both the Akbey and Narim families seemed to have accepted it amicably enough at first. After all, there was a family photograph of Isabel on a horse and a family photograph of Nadia on a horse in similar poses and outfits. The pictures of the two women on horses were simply added to the testimonial for … well, Sand wasn't sure why the pictures were there since the two women didn't bear the slightest resemblance. She was finding the story incredulous as it related to Isabel.

Sand liked to ride horses, but without the fancy uniform, helmet, or other trappings. She just liked to get out on the mountain trails and in the woods away from the city and just feel free, especially to feel the breeze in her hair on a hot, humid day. She even loved the smell of a horse and a leather saddle. She'd never owned a horse, just rented at stables outside town or up on the mountain. To some people, horses were utilitarian beasts; to others they were sport, and to some they were symbols of aristocracy, but to Sand they were wonderful, wild animals and companions who symbolized the joy of unbridled freedom. She could understand young Nadia in the early twentieth century doing what was expected or demanded of her, but not the Isabel she remembered. But which Isabel? Isabel had posed for the picture, but she was very good at posing as different characters or roles.

Sand found Isabel's tale disturbing. Isabel could write well, but she had failed to connect the dots. She hadn't managed to go beneath the surface and find the real Nadia. Sand wanted to know more about her. She sat back in her chair and closed her eyes trying to remember everything she could about Isabel. She wanted to know how Nadia's personality related to Isabel's. She tried to pin down Isabel's personality in her memory, but what she remembered was that Isabel had always been all about not being Isabel.

Isabel's family presented itself as mild-mannered and charming enough, but she had spent her consciousness disowning them in her mild-mannered, charming sort of way. Sand remembered Isabel not wanting to go back to Florida to live with them. She remembered her always being in Patty Compton's shadow. Even when Sand and Isabel were alone, Isabel usually let Sand do most of the talking. When Patty wasn't around, Isabel let Sand take the lead. Isabel was a follower.

"So who was Isabel really?" Sand asked herself. "How could she go from being a war hero to being the Isabel I knew?"

Isabel had talked of being from another dysfunctional family. She even joked about it. Now it seemed to Sand that Isabel was trying to please her family through her past life claim. Sand knew she would have remembered if Isabel had ever mentioned Nadia or a past life memory. She opened her eyes, leaned forward toward the computer screen, and continued to read.

Isabel had grown up hearing the stories of her father's friends, the Narim family, and how talented, influential, and well-connected they were before World War II uprooted them from their home and power base on the outskirts of Paris, France. Again Sand paused. Sand remembered being with the French Resistance. Isabel had grown up hearing stories about Nadia's family long before she met Sand, yet she never once mentioned it to Sand when Sand told her about her own memories. There was something very wrong with this picture Isabel had painted.

Sand had confided in Isabel how she remembered smuggling radio parts in stuffed animals past the occupying Germans. Nadia was a radio operator, yet Isabel had said nothing about it to Sand. Sand was beginning to feel anger toward

Isabel for withholding this information from her all those years ago while appearing to be the expert in explaining the concept of reincarnation. Isabel was no dummy. The connection between Nadia's life and Sand's memories would have been obvious to her. Sand may have even known or worked with Nadia in France.

She continued reading. Together Isabel and Maria Akbey had pieced together the comparisons that Isabel came to believe were evidence proving that she had lived as Nadia in her most recent past life. She even contacted Abdel Narim's family and informed them of her return to the flesh as Isabel. Abdel had responded favorably, but then Maria would have known Abdel would not have been threatened by Nadia's return as Isabel. Maybe Maria knew the response might be different with Abdel's brother, Salim.

"Aha," Sand exclaimed as she realized Isabel had never had any past life memories to begin with. Grasshopper jumped up and ran to Sand's chair. Sand instinctively reached down and rubbed the cat's chin.

There was a lot to be said for sibling rivalry, but Sand couldn't imagine that Nadia's escape from her family into what was perceived as heroism was easy for the two brothers, both of whom were raised in a time and place that favored sons over daughters, and neither of which ever did anything comparable to Nadia. Nadia didn't exactly ask her family's permission to serve undercover in an occupied country, probably because they wouldn't have allowed it. Nadia had never told them about her assignment—she couldn't because it was a military secret. If it had been Sand, she wouldn't have wanted to tell them. She would have even sought out such an assignment for just that reason.

Then Isabel had published her testimonial on the Internet declaring herself to have been Nadia. Isabel wrote that she'd remembered hundreds of past lives by reading and traveling as a child.

"Ha! She never mentioned any of this to me," Sand told Grasshopper.

Isabel didn't talk about how her family reacted to the mention of such things. She never talked about her family when Sand knew her, except to say they didn't want her. Isabel said online she had recognized lots of people she read about in history, so many that she was sure she had lived as part of all of their lives—hundreds of lives. She had found a book written about Nadia's life in the Akbey family library that had been sent to her father by Abdel on Ibrahim's request. It was an obscure book about a person, who not only wasn't famous, but who was just one of millions who were put to death by people whose business was killing other people. The author of Nadia's story had been a friend of Nadia. In her testimonial, Isabel told of knowing before she read the book that it was going to be an important memory. Well, that just didn't make any sense to Sand, who remembered her death before she ever learned to read.

Isabel said she was upset when she read about Nadia's betrayal. Sand was upset reading Isabel's betrayal. After having confided in her all those years ago, she felt Isabel was making a mockery of Sand's memories. Sand wondered that Isabel had not been having disturbing dreams about this all along. Sand knew from her own experience that recurrent nightmares would be an expected phenomenon having been reborn after such a short time and having been executed. Yet Isabel had never described any specific memories from early childhood, nor had she given any details. She never mentioned dreaming about any of it, neither when they had talked in high school nor in this online testimonial, which Sand found very odd. But maybe, in all fairness, Isabel had felt it was too personal to post on the Internet. The time to share would have been when Sand had opened up to her, and that was very personal. Isabel had never mentioned any memories or dreams that might have been related when she and Sand had talked about her own dreams that time in high school before the school day started.

Sand wondered how Isabel's birthmark reconciled with Nadia's death, but Isabel didn't say exactly how Nadia had died. She only said she'd been executed. Isabel never mentioned her birthmark either, but that was personal too. Still Sand knew from personal experience the manner of death would be the climax of the story that would bridge the two lives.

"Just how did Nadia die?" she asked herself. She remembered her own birthmarks. There was the tumor removed with dry ice from her finger right after birth, the round blue-black mark her parents had described to her on her upper back that had faded in childhood, and the brown teardrop on her right forearm, which was only now starting to fade. She had always felt the finger had been broken while being beaten by the men in black uniforms, the mark on her back was where the bullet entered, and the teardrop on her arm was where the concentration camp tattoo had been. She wanted to know exactly how Nadia died and if it could explain her own birthmarks.

280

Isabel wanted to be involved in Nadia's family and their religion, even though Nadia had chosen to leave their religion behind before going back to France by converting to the Anglican faith. To Sand the very notion of Nadia reborn wanting to return to Islam was absurd. Why go backward when she'd risked and forfeited her own life to get away from her family? It made no sense to Sand that Isabel wanted to be part of all that repressive, sexist, old-world lifestyle after having had a taste of independence as Nadia or while living in the present in a country where women were free. Isabel insisted she was drawn to the older, more conservative manner of dress. Sand remembered that Isabel had liked costumes that allowed her to not be herself. Isabel also related how she was taken by surprise when Nadia's brothers had yet another disagreement, as brothers would. Isabel had sisters; she should have expected that.

"None of this is real," Sand told Grasshopper, who was now lying on the desk in front of the computer screen. In continuing to read, Sand found what she felt was the most profound comment in Isabel's online statement. Isabel said she wasn't really interested in Nadia's death. Sand was amazed. She had to stand up and walk around to let that one sink in.

Birth and death, however unpleasant, were the biggest transformations in the cycle of reincarnation. People didn't normally remember being born; most just hit the ground running and moved on accepting their new situation and possibilities. If they did remember dying, maybe they learned to keep it to themselves. But to say the transition between one's own lives wasn't of interest to oneself? Sand was perplexed.

281

People didn't often admit openly to thinking of how death offered them a new situation and new possibilities. Sand's recurring nightmare about that singular death in a Nazi crematorium was her earliest memory. It never changed or evolved, just repeated over and over, and was impossible to ignore. Maybe that's why she found death so interesting. Or maybe she'd just seen a lot of it this time around while living in an environment that was considered relatively safe compared to other parts of the world. Maybe death was just naturally interesting to mortal beings.

After a lifetime of pain and pleasure, friendships, family, relationships, attachment, ideals, and identity, Sand would have thought that how a person died was not only as important as how a person lived, but a sudden and violent death, a sudden and unforeseen ending to attachments and identity, would tend to stand out as a milestone. Of course, Sand realized that her personal opinion was shaped by her own experiences. The thought which one carried through the door of death would surely be the true Ariadne's thread back through the centuries of oneself.

She sat back down in front of the computer. However Nadia had died, any execution was sudden and violent. Sand thought again about her own birthmarks and how they related to her death memory. She wondered in what manner Isabel's former self might have been killed to have left that birthmark across her abdomen—or maybe it was from some strange injury in close proximity to Isabel's former death. It just didn't fit with any standard form of execution Sand had ever heard or read about.

Deception Past

After a lot of online searching, Sand found the book Isabel had read. It was no longer in print in the United States, so she ordered it from the United Kingdom. It arrived a few weeks later. Sand devoured the book. The pictures of Nadia, the description and pictures of her family all sent chills up and down her spine. The pictures of Salim and Abdel were hauntingly familiar. She shuddered when she read about how Nadia's feet had been bound by an Asian nurse in infancy to keep them small. She remembered all the teasing she'd endured about walking like a penguin and the braces and arches she'd had to wear in her shoes as a child.

Nadia's story was eerily familiar, not because of Isabel's testimonial, but because Sand recognized herself. There were little details that gave away the direction Nadia was going in her life. For example, even in those times, she had preferred trousers to dresses any day. Personally, Sand only wore a dress every several years if a good enough occasion presented itself, but mostly it was jeans, blazers, and sneakers in her wardrobe these days.

The last year of Nadia's life had been spent imprisoned in southern Germany in solitary confinement, where she had been given knitting to do by her guards. Sand still enjoyed the quiet accomplishment of knitting. And Nadia had liked to write. She wrote poetry and had short stories published. Sand had been hoping when she started reading the book for a clue, a partisan or friend mentioned, that might lead her to discover her own past life identity. She was shocked to learn it was Nadia Narim herself.

Kindness was often extended to strangers and friends, but rarely to family. The book written by Nadia's friend was a kindness to the Narim family. In the book, it was Nadia's lifeless earthly remains that were shoved into the oven and cremated with countless others, but Sand knew better. She had been conscious when they put her in the oven. The book failed to mention her last thought, "liberté," but then how could the author have known that?

Sand thought about contacting the author, but decided enough time had passed that maybe it was best not to open old wounds. Maybe Isabel's lack of interest in her death was also a kindness to Nadia's family. She was, after all, trying to give them back an attachment that had been broken by it. Maybe that's why it was such a weak attachment between Isabel and Nadia's brothers that only one of the brothers communicated with her from a distance and for such a short time, but not the one Nadia was close to.

By that time, Salim was old and surely stubborn. After reading Nadia's biography, Sand couldn't imagine Salim would have had any reason to want Nadia back to compete with or question him when Isabel contacted him. Unless he had changed dramatically, she fancied he would have welcomed neither the intrusion nor the attention he would have been expected to give her. Sand certainly would never have been willing to submit to his decisions for her. His older sister had always been the leader of the two, but now he was in charge of things and had been for decades.

Or maybe he just knew better. Isabel was looking to embrace the old ways, not discard them and move on like Nadia. Sand had always sought independence. Sand simply wasn't interested in the power and influence Salim had built his life's work on. Their father had been the same way in Salim's eyes, but Salim was not his father. His father had been a progressive man of his times. Salim was stuck in his father's time. Abdel had also capitalized on his father's reputation and set himself up as a guru to his followers. Isabel wanted to go back to that time and be submissive. She was willing to surrender her passive personality to being taken care of by men or parents or authority figures. Sand couldn't imagine why. Then she realized it was to Abdel Narim's commune that her old friend Rick McDevitt had taken his bride for their honeymoon. Valerie hadn't bought into it either.

Sand read Nadia's biography very carefully, every word. It seemed to describe a very honest depiction of Nadia from the author's perspective, but there also seemed to be quite a lot missing from Sand's point of view. There was nothing in it about smuggling radio parts in stuffed animals from the coast of Normandy to Paris. There was nothing in it about rescuing downed Allied pilots and getting them back to the safety of England. If Sand's dreams and memories were actually Nadia's, the description of Nadia's death was kindness rather than fact.

It had been a long road for Sand, learning to balance the passive with the long repressed aggressive inside herself. She had learned over the years that what she didn't acknowledge came out as her demons, and if she didn't learn to direct it outwardly at those who triggered it, it attacked her inside with depression and despair. All this goody-goody talk of turning the other cheek, being meek, and rolling over and playing dead in life just wasn't real or healthy in her opinion; it always resulted in the reality of the demons making their presence known in the worst possible way. She had learned she simply had to set her boundaries where she could cope with them, and enforce those boundaries to maintain any semblance of a comfort zone. Life was just too short to play dead. The trick was knowing when to let go, to laugh, and to forgive.

Sand reasoned that it was easy to want to identify with someone else. Everyone did it at times and often many times in one lifetime. People needed each other; they found comfort in common ground. Sand would have picked someone with happier circumstances if she'd been free of memories and birthmarks to choose who she might have been in a past life, but then maybe Isabel identified with Nadia because she wasn't happy. There was no way for Sand to understand Isabel claiming to be Nadia. She was determined to try.

In what she read online, Isabel seemed to overlook Nadia's many obvious faults, much the way one does when first in love. Isabel also referred to Nadia only in the third person. One who remembered usually did so in the first person, and it could be very confusing, but then Sand had never had another name for her past life before she read Isabel's testimonial.

Sand considered that dying for a cause that happened to succeed didn't automatically mean that the deceased was successful. She needed to know and understand the motives behind the actions that led down that path, but Isabel didn't question any of that. Sand had always found Isabel's idealism impressive, but now she found Isabel's choice of identities a bit odd, and she had to admit to herself that she felt like Isabel had stolen her dreams and memories. Sand felt invalidated. She felt like she was being denied existence. She felt she'd been erased. She felt betrayed and violated. She was glad she had lost touch with Isabel and that Isabel was no longer part of her life.

No, she wasn't. It had been her choice to tell Isabel about her dreams. She was confused. She honestly didn't know why Isabel had done this. Maybe Isabel had somehow conned her into giving her another identity to hide behind. Maybe Isabel truly didn't remember where the memory of Sand's dreams had come from and honestly thought now that they were her own. It had been many years ago that Sand had told her. And Sand had never heard of the story of Nadia Narim's life until she read what Isabel had posted on line. If she hadn't read what Isabel wrote, she might never have found out that there was a record of the past life and death she remembered.

Sand recognized Isabel's focus was more on the philosophy and lifestyle of the Narim family in accordance with her present life heritage. She had struggled all of her life to come to terms with that heritage and the times she lived in. If she couldn't reconcile the two, maybe she let go of the present and future in favor of the past.

After Sand had finished reading the book about Nadia, she understood the past was not what Nadia's life was about to Isabel. Isabel had said online that Nadia was half dead after her father died, but Sand clearly saw his death was how Nadia had found her sense of duty.

She paced around the house for some time pondering everything she'd learned. "So this is what it's like to have an epiphany," she told Grasshopper, who couldn't seem to figure out if they were playing a game going back and forth. Then Sand's eyes focused on the stack of poetry she had gathered together with the intention of following up on Mitch's suggestion to publish the collection as a charitable fundraiser.

As she picked up the manuscript and glanced through it with a sense of accomplishment, she remembered Chrissie Jackson and her dreams that were reminiscent of Emily Dickinson. Something there didn't make any sense either. To her knowledge, though limited, Chrissie hadn't published. She did an Internet search for Chrissie's name and found nothing. She was a recluse, so that wasn't unexpected. Maybe Chrissie published under an alias? It hardly seemed likely that Chrissie would even deal with an agent or publisher. And yet, during her lifetime, Emily Dickinson had worked at getting published under her own name.

Sand sat back and looked across the room. There was the book about Nadia Narim. Isabel read the book before claiming the identity. Chrissie had read Emily Dickinson's biographies and poetry before she started writing in her sleep. She knew all about Emily before she started having the dreams. That certainly offered a more rational explanation in Sand's mind. What she couldn't figure out was how she had such vivid dreams and memories of her own before she was old enough to read or even know what radio tubes, Nazi concentration camps, and crematoriums were—unless her memories were real.

Chapter 21

Freedom to Choose
(The Fool)

Guilt haunts those with conscience
Fear of being wrong
Everyone craves innocence
The river rolls along

Until it empties into the ocean
No longer forced to bend
By boundaries and limitations
Life begins again

*

Brenda:

The Fool is human nature. The Fool must make a choice. It's a hard one. It's one we all face. The only choice in life that really matters is whether to forgive.

*

June 2005
Perdido Key, Florida

Isabel dreamed she was walking on the beach with the actor Brad Pitt. They made small talk about the weather and the relaxing sound of the surf as they walked. They came upon some friends

who happened to be Moslem, but more
fundamentalist and less educated than Isabel's
parents. These people were telling Isabel that, as a
true believer, she was obligated to take a stand
against the United States. Isabel objected meekly
that the United States had been good to her family.

They went into one of the condominium
complexes that lined the beach of Perdido Key and
up the elevator to an upper floor. Pitt led the way
into a condo, and they all followed him. Once inside
the condo, Pitt disappeared, and the others started
dragging boxes out of the coat closet. The boxes
were packed with bricks of C-4 explosives,
detonators, and timers. Isabel watched in
amazement as the people she was with started
assembling time bombs. They ignored her while
they worked.

She absentmindedly started fidgeting with
one of their finished products. None of the timers
had been set. To Isabel's unpleasant surprise, as she
toyed with the homemade device, the timer
suddenly sprang to life. The digital display lit up
showing one second, and then there was an ear-
shattering, deafening silence. Everything went
black.

When Isabel awoke, she was lying on the
beach amid a pile of burnt rubble. There were
uniformed people moving toward her with chains.
Their mouths were open and moving, and their
faces seemed both angry and distressed, but she
couldn't hear what they were saying. She couldn't
hear anything at all. They cuffed her hands behind
her back, shackled her ankles, and dragged her
away. Then she understood. She had set off the
bomb she'd been fiddling with, and everyone else in
the condo complex was now dead. She was deaf

from the explosion. She was a mass murderer. She was going to prison for the rest of her life, however long that was.

When Isabel woke up from her dream, she tried to make sense of it.

???

Brad Pitt???

???

Drab tip (+T). No it wasn't an unconscious anagram.

???

What did she know about the actor Brad Pitt??? Well, recently she had seen him in a movie with Anthony Hopkins where Pitt played the character of Death.

???

Death was leading her into a trap where she would be betrayed and made the scapegoat. Death had a nasty surprise in store for her. There was a time bomb waiting for her somewhere in her future. Somehow the very religion she relied on for identity had assembled it and placed it in her hands.

*

July 2005

Isabel had staked a claim to her past, but the only future she could foresee for herself was living with her parents and living their lifestyle. She had nothing of her own. Her only identity was one in the past. She had not received the attention she had hoped for from the Narim family, especially Zakhir. She felt trapped in the beliefs she had chosen. She felt trapped in her gender and trapped in the past. Her unconscious was trying to warn her about whatever future lay in store for her. She felt

oppressed by the low pressure of the atmosphere
weighing down on her. There was a hurricane in the
Gulf of Mexico heading straight for the western part
of the Florida panhandle.

It was Isabel's day off from work. While
Marie was frantically packing a suitcase, Ibrahim
told Isabel, "Hurry up, Isabel. Pack a bag quickly.
We need to leave the coast before the roads become
too crowded."

"I'd rather just stay here and ride it out,"
Isabel argued. "You and Mom go on."

"No," He said emphatically. "You know
how Hurricane Ivan demolished Pensacola Beach
last year. We're not taking foolish chances with our
lives. We're on an island for heaven's sake."

Isabel nodded her assent and packed her
bag. As she did so, she thought of the people in the
dream assembling their explosive devices. They
drove inland in separate cars across the state line
into Alabama. Isabel waited until her parents had
fallen asleep in their motel room where the three of
them had sought shelter from the inevitable storm
surge. Then she quietly left the room, got into her
car, and drove back down to Perdido Key and their
condo.

The condo complex was dark and deserted.
Isabel turned on the lights in the condo, got a bowl
out of the kitchen cabinet, and went into her
parents' bathroom. She emptied the contents of their
medicine cabinet into the bowl. Then she sat down
at the dining table with her bowl of pills and a bottle
of Jack Daniels and began to consume her last meal.
The electricity went out, but it didn't matter. She
could hear the wind howling outside and the
crashing of the surf.

After she'd finished, Isabel kicked off her
shoes and walked barefoot outside onto the beach.
Fighting against the powerful winds, it seemed to
take forever to reach the edge of the water. She
realized her body offered less resistance to the wind
if she dropped to her hands and knees and crawled.
Sand stung her face and eyes. At last she felt the
cold, saltwater swirl around her legs washing the
sand through her toes. She smiled to herself. This
was the most exciting night of her life. Now she
was part of the big, violent force of Nature that
required neither social status nor gender identity nor
artificial prestige. This was the honest expression of
the inner turmoil and personal chaos she had been
feeling but unable to externalize for so many years.
Now she would finally become part of something
important, something impossible to ignore. She
would assume the name of the hurricane. Her new
identity was Dennis. All she had to do was be there
to become part of it. Never once did the thought of
how her parents might feel when they learned what
had happened cross her mind. It was not her habit to
consider them. She was thinking only of herself.
Darkness enveloped her. Sleep overcame her. She
evaporated into the storm.

*

Brenda:

The last thought of one's life is inevitably
the most habitual, the most practiced, and the most
indicative of one's true self. It is the first step into
the next world and the direction one will face and
seek in the next life, because it is what you are truly
about. You don't take the body with you; you don't

take the name or the myriad of things we use as identity; you take your thoughts. You take the pattern of thoughts that are your essence.

Freedom. What is it? Ideally it is freedom from fear, stress, chaos, and self-destructive excess. It is freedom to be oneself. How is it achieved? How is it possible? One can act on one's environment and influence others in ways that only they may choose. One can influence one's body, but one may actually only change one's mind. Be careful here. You can only influence your habits and choices. Self-deception is so easy. Change must be practiced to take effect.

Can the fight or flight response be overruled by forgiveness? Tolerance and adaptation must replace fear of violation and differences. Security is maintenance of protective, personal boundaries that allow constructive, nontoxic exchange and communication. This means elimination of use of poisonous substances as defensive weapons. The body must accept the risk of external contamination of ideas that may appear to conflict with its own opinions without anxiety or retaliation. The question is how to maintain protective, personal barriers that are enforced without toxicity; how to live peacefully without being a doormat; how to be open without losing yourself in the exchange; how to be diplomatically assertive without being passive-aggressive. An answer might be insight meditation as a way of life, or practicing active listening skills, or developing nonconfrontational communication skills combined with a sense of humor. Whatever the choice, the goal is to maintain function, integrity, security, and peace simultaneously. Surely it's possible with practice—lots and lots of practice.

Deception Past

First we have to get out of our own way. Nature is constantly balancing itself naturally. Our conscious desires and deceptions only act against that natural balance. Our thoughts direct those desires and deceptions. It's like a dream in which we see ourselves as one of the characters—then perception shifts, and we realize we are everyone in the dream.

Isabel was looking for pieces to pick up and put back together. Most people are doing the same on some level. Feeling rejected is like pain—once you've been sensitized to it, it amplifies itself until it suddenly shatters your whole existence. And you never see it coming, at least not consciously. You get so desperate for acceptance you imagine it in the least little polite formality, and then just when you've convinced yourself it's real, you're brushed aside, and what you thought was reality shatters like thin glass.

Rejection is pain. Separation is pain. Not being included is one of the most intense pains in the human experience. It's caused by selfishness, it's caused by intolerance, and it's caused by judging, but those causes are created by the rejected. It can be caused by insensitivity of others or just apathy or lack of awareness. It's caused by fear and by ignorance. But mostly it's caused by lack of forgiveness on the part of the rejected. It's so common, it almost seems like the whole purpose of life as a human being is to face and deal with being cast aside. It's why we're afraid of change when we're in a comfortable place. And when we're already uncomfortable, we're afraid change will make an already bad situation worse. But changing one's mind is the most powerful weapon of self-defense anyone has.

History and religions are passed down to us at the mercy of peoples' fears. There, but for the fear of pain, we believe. And the ones who suffer the most are the true believers, the truly afraid, and the it-must-all-be-literally-true types. I wish they could understand that no matter what, it's all OK. I wish everyone could understand that no matter who they are, they've suffered enough. I wish I could understand that when I'm afraid. Fear is a habit that's hard to let go of—after all, it's hard wired into our brains. It's easier to change our minds than our brains. Reality can dissolve fear without effort. The problem is our perception, but even when our perception gets in the way, with great effort we can still learn tolerance. We can educate our brains because the ability to learn is also hardwired into us. Just as fear dissolves tolerance, love can dissolve intolerance without effort. We just have to choose how we perceive.

If we've lived before and had other roles and identities, I suspect there's a clear message in the deaths of those roles and identities. We have to take on a new role and a new identity each time we step through the door of birth. It doesn't seem like a wise investment of time to try to claim credit for the deeds and accomplishments that death has denied us. It's just a thought, but maybe we should be focusing on what we're doing in the present.

Peace comes from the balance between remembering and letting go. Peace is acceptance of the present.

Just as light dissolves darkness and love dissolves fear, beauty overwhelms and dissolves anger, frustration, bitterness, and depression. It's no small thing to do or create something beautiful, but true beauty is given freely. Multilayered beauty is kindness, and kindness and beauty are the real reasons we exist. It's that simple, overwhelming experience of kindness and beauty that has the hold on life. Some don't see it. Maybe they're blinded by their own tears, but it's always there where and when we least expect it. Our only job is to perceive and appreciate it. Appreciation of simple kindness is the path to joy.

With births and deaths now in the billions, it's no wonder people are being born without time to prepare for their next life's role. In an information age deluge of biographies, faces, and stories, it's easy to lose oneself in every other perspective. It's also easier now to find a record of our most recent past life. The real art is defining and accepting oneself from all those defining moments presented to us by the moment. There's no need to be concerned with attachment if each moment is let go of as each moment is accepted.

I've heard that when the moment presents a situation traumatic enough, an individual identity can split like sands being pounded by the surf, ground down into ever more infinitesimally smaller parts. Some may argue that this constant splitting into ever smaller parts is a bad thing, and that we should be striving to go in the opposite direction. Then I look up at light splitting into a rainbow, glimmering across the gray clouds, and I know better.

*

July 2005
Huntsville, Alabama

Candace Phillips came home from the grocery store during a heavy downpour of rain to find a note in Greg's handwriting tacked to the outside of the door to the laundry room, which opened onto the carport next to the back door of the kitchen. She was standing there holding her bag of groceries when she read the note. It was addressed to her, and it warned her not to enter the laundry room, but instead it instructed her to just call the police. Greg said in the note that he couldn't live anymore with what he had done thirty years ago to his boyfriend and his boyfriend's business partner. Greg needed to know, once and for all, if Jesus would really forgive him.

Greg explained his version of what had happened in mostly misspelled words. He had met Dennis at a bar. He had never even known Dennis's last name until he read it in the newspaper afterward. In the bar, Dennis had bragged about selling weed, and he told Greg he had a big deal going down that night. He offered to cut Greg in on a share of the profit if Greg would just come along and keep him company. Greg couldn't remember how much Dennis had promised him. Both he and Dennis had been drinking a lot.

Dennis took Greg home with him to the house of his partner, Clarabelle. It was a ranch style house with the kitchen at one end and the bedrooms at the other. Greg did not remember anything about Dennis living there. He just remembered that Dennis had a key and knew his way around the house. Clarabelle was apparently in her bedroom with the door shut. Greg never actually met her.

After a few more drinks, Dennis revealed his big deal was to murder Clarabelle because she'd been blackmailing his supplier. After that, Dennis planned to burn the house down with Clarabelle's body in it to destroy the evidence. He promised Greg that no one would ever know Greg had been there. Greg was too drunk to understand Dennis was serious.

They drank and schemed through the night. Then early the next morning, Clarabelle came out of her room and was angry that Dennis had brought another stranger home and that they were so drunk. She ordered Greg out of her house and told Dennis to clean up the bottles and dirty glasses. Then she stormed back into her bedroom and slammed the door behind her.

Dennis was livid at being humiliated in front of Greg. He opened the kitchen door and left it open, and then went into the office where he took the phone receiver off its cradle. Then he went to the back of the house.

Greg was sitting at the table in a stupor when he heard sounds from the bedroom end of the house, but just sat there until the commotion started. Then he got up and went into the hallway to see what was going on.

Clarabelle was on the floor on her back, and her red pajamas appeared to be wet. As he knelt over Clarabelle, Dennis had his back to Greg and probably didn't even know Greg was there. Greg heard the sounds, "click, click … … click," and then smelled the sickening burning smell and realized Dennis had decided to combine the original two steps of his plan by killing her and burning the evidence at the same time. Greg groaned. Still crouching down, Dennis turned around at the sound.

Greg pushed Dennis back in disgust and Dennis dropped the cigarette lighter. Dennis's clothes caught fire. Greg grabbed the gold lighter and, when Dennis began screaming, Greg ran out of the house and kept running until he could no longer catch his breath. He vomited in the street a few blocks from the house, and then walked home.

Candace slowly set the bag of groceries down on the floor of the carport. Greg wanted to know if Jesus could forgive him. Candace paused. Then, contrary to the admonition not to enter the laundry room, Candace opened the door. Greg had wrapped his head in a blanket before putting his loaded gun to his mouth and pulling the trigger. In his own way he had tried to keep her from seeing him like that. He even chose to do it in the laundry room since there would be a mess to clean up. Of course the next thing Candace did was lift the blanket.

After calling 911, Candace fled the house on foot in the pouring rain. Everyone was looking for her. The police were looking for her, knowing she was a victim in shock. The rain was pounding down in torrents, but no one knew what had happened to Candace Phillips.

Chapter 22

Liberation
(The Universe)

Break it down to atoms
Down to quantum bits
All of it's connected
Every molecule fits

All is interconnected
In a gravitational dance
None singled out or selected
An equal game of chance

All seen in varying perspective
We choose which view to take
A species so selective
The choice is ours to make

Forgiveness frees the fetters
Dreams display the dawn
Compassion brings connections
Time travels on as one

*

July 2005

    Sand dreamed she was standing on the
beach at night watching the dark clouds swirl into a
spiral. The wind moving the clouds picked her up,
and she flew up into the night over the dark ocean.
She didn't fly of her own volition, and she had no

control over her flight path or destination. The wind carried her out over the sea, and she simply enjoyed the ride while understanding there was to be no return.

The dream was disturbing when she awoke, but she chalked it up to the previous evening's weather forecast of a hurricane in the Gulf of Mexico that was expected to make landfall at Pensacola. North Alabama was already experiencing heavy rains from the storm, with winds predicted to increase dramatically. No doubt there would be tornadoes afterward. The overall feeling between the low pressure system and the high humidity was oppressive.

The next night, Sand dreamed she had abandoned her car by the side of the road and was walking away. She had no direction in particular except just away.

She walked along the deserted road for a while until her car was long out of sight. She still had her car keys in her hand, playing with them as she walked. Then she saw a field alongside the road and decided to cross it.

She came across three men and a woman playing Frisbee. They asked her to join them. Sand smiled and thanked them as she declined their kind offer. She crossed through a small wooded area and came out on the other side. A highway cut across her path. As she was trying to decide which way to go from there, a beat-up silver sports car came by, slowing down as it passed her. She watched as it stopped, backed up, and then stopped alongside her. She recognized the driver as the actor Brad Pitt. He flashed his dazzling smile at Sand and asked if she wanted a lift. Sand smiled back and climbed into the passenger seat.

Sand and Brad made small talk as they drove down the road until they came to a city. They drove around for a while until they caught sight of the three men and a woman that Sand had seen earlier playing Frisbee in the field. The four were walking along a sidewalk, but they saw Brad and waved. Brad parked the car, and he and Sand joined the four.

The six of them walked a couple of blocks to a high-rise apartment building. They took the elevator up to the twenty-seventh floor and then walked down the hall. Brad Pitt produced an electronic key card from his pocket and inserted it into the lock on one of the doors. They went inside.

The apartment was sparsely furnished. In the living area were two sofas and numerous cardboard boxes. Brad and the other four set about unpacking the boxes while Sand watched. It all seemed curiously pre-orchestrated. She was surprised when the boxes turned out to have been packed with automatic weapons parts, ammunition, C-4 explosives, and detonators. She asked them what all this stuff was for. They told her it was their job and hers to defend the liberties of others, and that she should make herself useful instead of just standing around.

Sand slowly started to unpack a box of explosives. Noticing her hesitation, Brad came over to her with a weapon, knelt down, and began to show her how it worked. She told him that she doubted she could aim straight, and that if she tried to fire a gun she was sure her hands would shake too much to be able to point the thing. She thanked him, but said she'd stick to handling the explosives.

Brad put the weapon down and reached across to another box. He pulled out a detonator and explained to her how to attach it to the C-4. Sand repeated the instructions back to him, and he seemed satisfied that she understood. She sat there on the floor while the others busied themselves with loading the guns.

Sand asked, "Exactly what do you intend to blow up?"

The other woman replied, "We'll be told the target when the time comes."

"Just who's making these decisions?" Sand wanted to know.

Just then there was a knock at the door. Sand was left with unanswered questions as a male voice identified itself as being from the Department of Homeland Security and ordered them to open the door.

The others, Brad Pitt included, picked up guns as the door was kicked in. Sand didn't have time to think, but it was obvious her new friends were intent on shooting it out. She didn't want to be left unarmed in a firefight, so she reached for a weapon as she dove behind the sofa. She didn't know who started shooting first, but she remembered the explosives were right out in the middle of the floor directly in front of the front door of the apartment. She knew the sofa provided no protection except from sight.

Bullets were flying through the apartment, and the din was deafening. Sand stood up, pointing her gun at the door and squeezing the trigger. By the time she'd emptied the weapon, there were bodies piled in the doorway and out in the hall. The silence was more deafening than the noise had been.

Brad stood up and looked at her in disbelief. "What did you do that for?" he asked her.

Puzzled, she didn't respond. Instead she stepped over the bodies and into the hallway. There were more law enforcement personnel waiting there to greet her. She put her gun down on the floor of the hall and raised her hands in surrender. She was quickly tackled, knocked to the floor, and her hands were cuffed behind her back.

Sand was taken down twenty-seven flights of stairs and outside to a waiting police van. Once she was booked, she found herself in a solitary cell with only a bed, toilet, and surveillance camera. Her hands had been recuffed in front of her right before she was put in the cell. There was no space to spare in the cell, and no place to go to evade the camera's watchful eye. Worst of all, there was nothing to do. She couldn't even exercise in her limited space with the handcuffs on. She was totally alone and soon very bored.

Time passed. Meals were slid into the cell through a slot in the bottom of the door. More time passed. Sand had plenty of time to think. She began to realize that she would be standing trial for shooting the Homeland Security agents. She wondered what had happened to the other woman and the three men she had first seen innocently enough playing Frisbee in a field. She wondered what had happened to Brad Pitt. None of them had been in the police van with her. She hadn't seen any of them while she was being processed into the jail.

She remembered the last thing Brad had said to her, "What did you do that for?"

Sand began to wonder what had really happened and what this whole bizarre situation had really been about. More time passed. The woman had told Sand that they were employed to defend liberty, but that's exactly what they had caused

Sand to lose. As more time passed, Sand began to think there was something very wrong with this picture, and that maybe she should figure a way to opt out. She lay down on the bed and pulled the one blanket up over her shoulders with her back to the camera. She brought her hands up to her face and used her teeth to bite through the skin of her wrists.

The sound of the alarm was a great relief to Sand. She was glad to be jolted awake by it. She laid there and considered the dream. Homeland Security was obviously symbolic, and in the dream she had unintentionally found herself at odds with it. Was she somehow shooting herself in the foot in life? Killing her future sense of security? Attacking her own defenses? Being her own worst enemy?

Were the Frisbee players leading her in circles? Was she more interested in making a lot of noise than aiming at a target, or did she just not have the confidence to even get the goal in her sights?

And Brad Pitt???

???

Brad Pitt was famous and successful. He was married to another famous and successful actor. On screen, Brad Pitt was just another actor. Off screen, Brad Pitt didn't discriminate by ethnicity or nationality. He didn't determine human value by economic status. He advocated for the less fortunate of the world. He didn't distinguish between us. He didn't judge others to be them. There was no them. Just us.

Sand realized she could either be a prisoner of her own choices, or she could be free from self-determined limitations and boundaries by perceiving all existence as us and them. She smiled to herself as she went about experiencing this new light on this new day, and made up her mind to stop procrastinating about publishing her poetry for charity.

When she went into work at the *News* that morning, she heard all about Greg Phillips's suicide and the note he'd left. She wondered what he had done with Dennis's gold cigarette lighter.

Weeks later, Candace was sighted by a friend of Brenda's in Tent City, the local homeless camp in the woods on the north side of town. Brenda and her friends were still searching for Candace, even though everyone else had given up. The rest of the family never saw her again.

Sand went looking for her former neighbor and friend. She also wrote a series of stories for the *News* about the people of Tent City, how they lived, and how they'd ended up there. There were a few makeshift tents composed of old blankets, but mostly it was a lot of cardboard boxes and lean-tos made from a creative assortment of natural and man-made items. The stories of how the residents came to be living there were all individual. The overall feeling of the itinerant community seemed to be that society had no place for them. They were free of things, expectations, and relationships that had tied them down before, and now they were free to live for the moment, because they'd been rejected by the rest of the world and had no other choice. They were refugees from the lives they had allowed others to take from them.

The people of Tent City that talked to Sand told her they were glad to be alive and glad to wake up in the morning. There were many winter nights that someone among them didn't wake up the next morning. There were many summer days that some didn't survive the heat. But most were there rather than in homeless shelters because they were free to not be conned by the Jesus salesmen who ran the shelters, or because they were tired of begging for space.

Life was hard for them, they had no physical comforts, and illness came to individuals with a vengeance, but most of them weren't able to afford health care in their former lives anyway. Many were there either because not being able to afford health care had left them unable to work and pay for housing, or because trying to pay for their health care had taken everything they'd owned, including their homes.

Once Sand found a woman who might have been Candace, but life had taken a harsh toll, and Sand just wasn't sure if it was Candace or not. Either way, the woman had nothing to say to Sand or anyone.

Sand was proud of what she had written. She felt it was more important than who had murdered which victim or what ceremony was planned by city hall. *The Huntsville News* ran the stories, and they generated a lot of reader interest by way of letters to the editor. Most of the letters were negative from "conservative" extremists and judgmental types, but some expressed compassion and offered alternative solutions. Sand felt she'd made a small contribution and maybe a little bit of difference in her community and in the lives of people she didn't know. Sand had in common with those modern day nomads the belief that her life and theirs were all worth living. Now she felt she had proven it to herself.

But, in fact, Sand's words didn't change anything at all. She never found Candace. She never changed the lives of the homeless. People who read her articles mostly did so with preconceived views. Some felt pity. Some wanted to help the homeless by eliminating their makeshift camp and either running them out of town or arresting them. Imprisoning people for being homeless didn't make any sense to Sand. Others wanted to bring them back into the society the indigents had become outcasts from, but that proved to be easier intended than accomplished. Still some at least tried, and Sand was grateful for that. There was limited public housing that some of the homeless found their way into. It was a start. Still others were awakened to the fear that they too could end up homeless, and they were right—they could.

Sand's point was that the homeless were individuals who needed help but didn't know how or want to ask for it, or didn't know anyone to ask. Most readers were disgusted that some of the homeless had found hope or contentment in a feeling of liberation, however delusional by society's material standards, and interpreted that to mean the homeless preferred to be homeless. Most were repulsed by the knowledge that other people were living this way within "their" community. Most chose to be judgmental so they could reassure themselves that they would never be like those unfortunates.

Sand wondered who was really more unfortunate. She understood many people felt safer denying that it could ever happen to them.

One weekend, Mitch Masterson stopped by Sand's house in Sherwood Park for a visit.

While putting Grasshopper on his lap he commented, "Life is transient at best. It's made up of moments, and it's far better to try to give happy moments to others than to try to prolong life without happiness. There's so much unhappiness in this world already.

"Maybe if churches and schools taught the art of forgiving, we could break through this vicious cycle of unhappiness. They talk about it, but people need a 'How To' guide to forgiveness.

"Greg should have been able to forgive himself for being drunk and stupid, but he didn't know how. I mean, who did he think he was anyway? None of us are perfect. Well, most wouldn't have entertained ideas of drug deals and murder and burning a house down, but other than that, he was just drunk and stupid.

"People don't know how to forgive themselves or others for whatever mistakes could have opened the door to the depths of the universe if fear hadn't closed their eyes and hearts to the opportunities. But since everyone always makes mistakes, and since everyone comes back again to make more mistakes and opportunities, no one is unforgivable or unlovable."

"No one is unforgivable, and no one is unlovable," Sand repeated out loud and then continued to repeat over and over silently to herself. She decided it would be her mantra.

Mitch didn't have any more to say, so they sat there comfortably together in silence with Grasshopper for a long time. Eventually Grasshopper broke the silence with a very long and loud purr.

No one was unforgivable. No one was unlovable. Everyone returned and got another chance. Finally Sand spoke. "I can forgive instead of fight. Maybe I can avoid repeating the horrors of the past by learning to love and forgive. I have nothing to prove. I'm forgivable. I'm loveable."

Grasshopper continued to purr loudly.

*

2007
Brenda:

So why have I told you all of this? Why have I shared this painfully personal story? Because I am the mirror. I am the one they see when they look in the mirror. I am the one Sand sees when she goes looking for my lost mother. Sand isn't really searching for my mother—she's searching for herself. And my mother is lost even to herself. I doubt she even remembers what a mirror is at this point, since hers shattered, but if she ever does piece it back together, I will be who she sees when she finds the courage to look there. But if Sand's search for my mother has helped even one lost soul, and it has, then it's been worth it.

In my more peaceful moments, I like to imagine that my mother shattered her own delusions in that horrific moment of finding Greg's note and then his body. I like to believe she was freed from her self-destructive patterns of behavior and ran off to a new life. Deep down inside, I know she did.

My cousin Jamie shares my belief that she's passed on to a new life. We don't know why her body wasn't found, unless it was but was just never identified. It probably happened that same day. We couldn't judge her for it. She couldn't possibly have been rational after what she had learned and found.

311

She had known for years about the ghastly murder of Sand's Aunt Clarabelle. And she knew when she married Greg that there was so much just not right with his picture, but there was no way she could have suspected the truth. He was like an uncle to both Jamie and me, and we never suspected. If Uncle Mitch ever suspected, he certainly never let on. I think he was as shocked as everyone else.

I never met Isabel. She never knew me. I doubt she ever knew I existed, but we could have been sisters. Her mother never really knew her either.

Chrissie met Isabel, but not long enough to understand how very much alike they were. Isabel thought she wasn't loveable, so she tried to be someone she believed was.

Wounded people don't see themselves for who they are, and to find out they're damaged and have to heal themselves is a hard lesson. It's tricky, like trying to cut your own hair while looking in a mirror. It's like having a concussion or brain injury. You know you're injured if someone tells you. Then you know you're not the way you should be, but you don't know what's wrong or what's missing, because the injured part of your brain can't function to tell you. It's like there's a curtain or wall separating you from part of yourself, but you can't see what it is, because you can't get behind the barrier to find out.

The biggest danger with being emotionally wounded or shattered is that you can try to replace what's missing with someone else. If you do that, then you're not only wounded, you're not even yourself. You can't heal that way, because there's no longer a place for the wounded part of you. Even worse, you've convinced yourself you're whole again. But you're not even yourself.

My mother's delusional thoughts in her last moments were that she was unlovable by the monsters she had married. Like Isabel, Greg, and Kate, she didn't know that no one was unlovable or unforgiveable or that everyone would come back and get another chance.

Emotional predators go after wounded people like sharks after the scent of blood. They're not really monsters, just animals. Predators seeking prey is just natural to them. It's a dangerous world. The weak, the vulnerable, and the injured are the most susceptible to becoming prey and losing themselves to someone else. Some are so damaged they allow themselves to be taken over by other people's ideas of who they are and should be, and sometimes the contradiction is just too painful to live with. I imagine it must feel like having your limbs simultaneously pulled in different directions until you break.

I have a vivid imagination. All damaged people also do, even if they don't realize it. It's perfectly natural when you can't remember an event, or don't want to, or it's too painful to remember what actually happened, to unconsciously substitute a more palatable memory or a reasonable facsimile just to fill in the gap. No one wants to see themselves as anything but whole, so the mind automatically compensates. Imagination is only a problem when you don't know it's not real.

I lost both of my parents because they each lost themselves to their own delusions. I lost a good part of my life because I bought into their delusions. Isn't one's identity too precious to give away like that? Did my father think so highly of himself that he believed he could lead two lives at once? Was he so desperate for success that he decided to double his chance of winning by losing everything, or did he not remember or not know he was already someone's husband and someone's father when he married the other woman and fathered her children? I never felt I knew him, so I created a fantasy I could adore and look up to. For part of my life, I wouldn't listen to anyone who spoke badly or truthfully about him, and during the rare times I had with him, I had convinced myself that I was his only daughter and his pride and joy. I gave away my real self to try to please the man who shattered my life, but I chose to give myself another chance in this life. If I couldn't get it right this time, I would eventually.

I've always been a lot like my mother. She never saw herself in the mirror. She never saw her kindness, her sensitivity, her ability to make others feel at ease or comforted or secure. She only saw herself as how valued or not she was by a damaged man, and as a result, she never comprehended her own worth. It didn't seem to matter to her that I told her how important she was to me, because I wasn't the one she wanted to see her as important.

I understood this well. I wanted to be important to my antisocial, narcissistic father, but in his mind everything was only about him.

When my mother's life was shattered by his duplicity, she was desperate to prove to herself that she could be important to a man. She was trying to complete herself by absorbing a male identity instead of finding the parts of herself she had denied or repressed so she could heal. She was desperate to prove that she was loveable, but her desperation made her vulnerable. Instead, she became the prey of more predatory animals like my father, men who were only interested in their own selves, which they had lost and were replacing with their prey.

I've always been a lot like my mother. It's not easy to admit to myself that the man I'd put on a pedestal and looked up to all those years was the jerk others saw him as. He just never reached true manhood. He didn't function by the same rules as civilized people, because he'd never quite evolved into a mature, socialized adult. I finally realized that.

Now when I look in the mirror, I see a human being with scars and delusions, but a worthwhile, loveable human being. I know that someday Dad will get another chance to grow out of himself, and I forgive him.

I'm older, but I'm alive, learning and enjoying myself. Now I can love other people and respect their separate identities without trying to appropriate them as my own. I've forgiven myself for what I've come to think of as my lost years. I hope I'm a lot like my mother. I hope that somewhere, somehow, some kind, nonpredatory soul has offered her a mirror, and that she has the courage to look with open eyes that cried way too much in this lifetime.

I'm not the smartest person in my life, but I know now that waiting for someone else to fulfill my expectations is wasting time better spent living the life I choose to live. If I can figure that out, it's possible for every victim and every self-absorbed predator to realize that relying on others to fulfill their lives is just delusional. Expecting some supernatural being on the level of God to come down from an imaginary heaven and intervene in an individual human being's life is no different than

315

waiting for the world to end—and that's just plain suicidal. Suicide is the ultimate denial of self-forgiveness. All it gets you is another life to try to work it out. I believe that if there is a God, he or she is beyond the pettiness of human lives and expects us to work it all out for ourselves. It's called free will. I've learned that it all comes down to choices we make. We choose. I believe we're happiest when we choose to do what comes most natural to us.

The most important choice we can make is to forgive. Even former Governor George Wallace, before his death, asked forgiveness from the people of color he had fought so hard to repress.

I'm happiest when I follow my own path, even if no one else at the moment shares that path, because eventually I meet others on that path. I don't give my free will away to some organized religion, because as I see it, religions are no different from my father. Predators need prey to buy into what they're selling in order to fulfill their own fantasy. That may not be true for others, but that's how I see it.

Forgiveness is the key to being at one with the Universe, my last major Tarot card. People who are hurting want someone else to make them better, but if they're just waiting for that to happen, they're choosing to suffer even though it hurts. I'm only speaking from personal experience. Delusions are addictive and painful. I found out the only way to make it all OK is to just see what is as it is.

First I had to see myself as I really am. Then I had to accept that it was OK to live my life as myself. After that, forgiveness came naturally.

Now that I've confronted my fear of seeing my mother's face in the mirror, I can begin to discover my own identity. I'm OK, and I wish everyone freedom from suffering, the ability to forgive, and the compassion to love themselves for who they really are. Everyone is forgivable. Everyone is loveable.

Epilogue

August 2006
Monte Sano Mountain, Alabama

Chrissie Jackson opened her eyes to darkness. Had she been dreaming? But it was so real. She could still smell the fresh summer evening air.

Wait. She had been sitting up at the desk where she usually wrote. She was now lying down in bed. She could clearly hear the sound of the air conditioner running. She sniffed the air, but it didn't have that same fresh smell. It was the same dream she'd been having all these years.

She closed her eyes and lay very still, trying to hold onto the memory of it just as Sand had taught her all those years ago. She could see the papers on the desk before her clearly this time. She had a pen in her hand. The skin of her pale white hand was showing signs of age. What was the poem? She focused on the scrap of paper in front of her:

> "The sky knows not what it is
> To tread the world with impassioned feet"

She felt an overwhelming sense of loss and sadness. She saw her own hand put the scrap of paper aside. Then she saw the other pages she had copied neatly in her own penmanship. The two lines were written in a handwriting not her own.

What was this loneliness that had overcome her? Why was such heavy grief engulfing her? Her face was wet with tears. Whose hand had written

318

these lies? What were these poems she had been copying?

They weren't hers. She set the two lines aside because they were an incomplete poem. Her work wasn't to write the poetry. Her work was to preserve her sister's writing. Her sister was gone now, called home, back from whence they all came. Her sister was gone.

The understanding hit her like something heavy slammed into her chest. If she wasn't Emily, who was she? Chrissie felt the wetness of tears on her own face. Her entire adult life she had believed herself to have been Emily Dickinson—all because of one recurring dream. Now thirty-five years later … now what?

She felt like she was floating. She couldn't determine which way was up, down, or sideways. She had no sense of gravity or direction. She felt lost and alone. All she had was a question shouting in her mind, "Who am I?" over and over and over. She had lost all sense of place and identity.

Chrissie woke with a start. She was sitting straight up in her bed. A hint of daylight peeked through the dark green curtains covering her bedroom window. The voice was still ringing in her ears. Someone had called to her. She listened to hear it again, but there was only silence. No one else was there, but she was sure someone had called her by name. She'd heard it clear as a bell, "Vinnie!"

Chrissie sat there, awake in her bed, with the realization that she had not lived before as Emily Dickinson. She had been Emily's sister, Lavinia.

Acknowledgements

Special thanks to Charles Bishop who taught English Literature at Louisiana State University in New Orleans in 1972; to Dr. Adrian Finkelstein, Kevin Ryerson, and Elizabeth Frakes for their help and validation; to Dr. Tom Dooley for helping me deal with PTSD from growing up in a very racist and violent environment; and to Marta Moran Bishop for making this second edition possible.

Author's Note

All the events in this book came from my memory, mixed with my imagination, and were altered to fit the story. Each character was based on my perception of two or more individuals mixed with myself—also to fit the story. As each real person has their own point of view, I did my best to be true to my characters.

The symbolism from the Tarot is real. I used to collect Tarot decks for the artwork and differences in interpretation of the symbols. I didn't imagine any particular deck as Brenda's; I just tried to sum up my understanding of the collective interpretations.

The title, **Deception Past,** came from a very scenic place in the state of Washington, Deception Pass. It too was altered to fit the story.

As with life, please take from this story what has meaning for you and leave the rest. Best wishes and thank you.

Reviews of Other Novels by the Author

A Tale to Last the Ages 5***** Review by Marta Moran Bishop

Five Flowers by Franki deMerle is a beautifully written tale of five women who reincarnate through several lifetimes. From living life as five of King Henry the VIII wives, through Whitechapel England during the days of Jack the Ripper to America's 1960's.

So well research is the history, that I was able to imagine life in the eras in which she placed her characters. Traveling back in time, learning what life was like as both a queen to a hippie, I was given a glimpse of what it was like to be a woman then.

Lifetime after lifetime these women fight to learn to find independence and are swept up in intrigue, murder, betrayal and the ultimate sacrifice. Will any of these women break free from this man they find themselves drawn to like a moth to a flame? The same man who eventually betrays them each lifetime? Will any of them find enough strength in themselves to do this and what will the cost to them be?

I loved this book, finding myself unable to put it down. Kudos to Ms. deMerle for taking on such a fabulous and interesting subject and making it into a story to last through the ages.

Highly recommended.

Dragonfly Dreams – Review by Martha A. Cheves
'Shortly before 2:30 AM, Daphne awoke from a
vivid dream. She dreamt she was in Scotland and
had just been widowed. Her husband had been
murdered. It was some distant time in the past, and
she was dressed in a long black gown with a stiff
white headdress She could feel the tightness of her
corset contrast the softness of her gown's material
on her skin. Richard was there, but other people in
the dream were saying he was responsible for her
late husband's murder. She was confused and didn't
know what to believe. She had thought she could
trust Richard, but a voice in the dream announced,
"During the Protestant Reformation, these sides
were divided." As she wondered what that meant,
Richard captured her and took her against her will
to a castle, where he raped her. Then, when he left
her alone with a woman companion to look after
her, the two women escaped. They disguised
themselves as men and used bed linens to climb
through a window and down the castle wall. She
was terrified…At first, when they told their story of
what had happened, they were given sanctuary by
kind people. But after about a week or so, word
came to the household from the authorities that she
was to be held as a prisoner again. She did not
understand why. Then she was told that Richard had
also fled Scotland and was also imprisoned, but in
another country.'
	Daphne Robin and her sister Deandra were
both accustomed to strange dreams. Deandra has
dreamed, since childhood, that she was a soldier
with lots of brothers. In her dream she was a man
and someone was beating her face in. Daphne's
dream about Scotland came shortly after her
marriage to Richard Gatorman, owner of a

construction company as well as Daphne's boss. Scotland was a place Daphne had always wanted to go to so when the dream coincided with Richard announcing that they would be honeymooning in Scotland, she let her excitement override the possibility of a warning. But, Richard had always been the perfect mate. He was loving, caring and offered her everything she could ever want…so she thought. The honeymoon would turn out to be the beginning of her seeing the true Richard she had married. A marriage that she soon realized had been a big mistake. The only out for Daphne becomes sleep in which her dreams have her flying the skies with a handsome man. If it weren't for her dream time she would probably give up on life itself.

Deandra, being an officer in the Army, enlists the help of her friend Major Ursa-Barrios to help Daphne escape the abuse being inflicted by Richard. Major, as he likes to be called, has had his own dreams over the years. In his dreams he helps a young lady and falls in love with her. Could Daphne possibly be the woman in his dream? Could Major possibly be the man in Daphne's dreams?

As Deandra, Daphne and Major come together, they start searching for the answers to their dreams. Deandra wanting to know who the person getting their face bashed in is and who are the brothers. Daphne wants to know who the woman in Scotland could be as well as who she soars the skies with. And Major wants to meet the lady from his dreams.

Franki deMerle has done it again with a book of mystery, love and a certain air of suspense. The more I read, the more I wanted answers to the character's dreams but I wasn't really expecting what the dreams actually turned out to be.